Never Full and Never E

Author: Andy I Williams
Cover image of landscape: Estelle Marais
Cover design: Michael Guilfoyle and Gemma Guilfoyle at Guilfoyle Design Ltd
Proofreading: Michael Guilfoyle and Rhys Williams

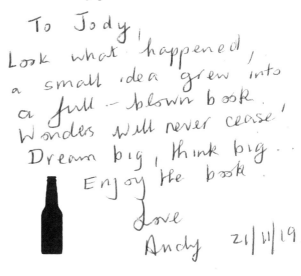

To Jody,
Look what happened,
a small idea grew into
a full-blown book.
Wonders will never cease!
Dream big, think big..
Enjoy the book.
Love
Andy 21/11/19

Acknowledgements

*Thanks to Rhys Williams and Michael Guilfoyle for being the first readers and
providing technical help. Thanks also to my wife and family for their love, support
and encouragement during the creative process. A big thank you to Peter and Paddy for
their kindness in showing me around the streets of Prince Albert and the neighbouring
countryside.*

This book is dedicated to Barbara Ann

Contents

Never Full and Never Empty

Chapter 1

The End

Lips pursed as if paused mid-sentence. Eyelids closed, probably by the steady fingers of a nurse. Tom Morgan's mother was dead. He gazed at the opened bible lying on the bedside table and imagined the priest administering the last rites before retiring to his quiet room, between worlds.

As soon as he was ushered into a dimly lit side room, he knew. Sat there, the truth was unavoidable. No more oxygen bottles, no more face masks, no more draining of the lungs, no more faint hope. She was gone.

"I'm afraid your mother passed away an hour ago," the nurse had said as she sat him down in the office, imparting the news in a practiced yet sensitive way. "I'm so sorry you didn't make it in time." She'd placed a comforting hand on his shoulder but he'd lost the power of speech. You think you can prepare yourself for the death of a loved one, but you can't rehearse the moment when it becomes reality.

"She's still in the ward love, if you'd like to see her. Take your time." He watched her silent shoes shuffle away.

***

Tom stood in silence, listening to the unsteady breathing of the other patients, clinging on to life beyond the curtains, with their eyes wide open in the middle of the night. His mum's life shrunk from wide angle to the confines of this ward, her last breath taken in the company of strangers. He took a mental photograph of this shuttered world: embroidered purse, half-drunk Lucozade, a tissue protruding from the box like a crinkled leaf, a blue comb laced with grey hair. Death invariably dredged up the past but gave it a revisionist taint. He just remembered the good times, the laughter, the unconditional love. He edged closer to the bed and stood over her, touched the cold skin and gently ruffled her hair.

It was over twenty years since his father had died and he'd made the conscious decision not to view his body. He'd regretted it ever since. At a younger age, the thought of retaining an image of a corpse had unnerved him. Maybe now, reconnected with death, this was some form of atonement. Cloistered by the curtains, he felt strangely calm, as if all the clocks in the world stopped ticking at the same time, and he said his last goodbye.

***

He slipped out of the ward, avoiding the frightened gazes of the sleepless and looked out of the sixth-floor window for the last time. The grey dullness of the skyline dominated by the transporter bridge across the river conjured thoughts of a Lowry painting. He imagined the streets full of sleepwalkers in hospital robes, pacing through the night; passengers in a wordless world. Tom walked to the end of the corridor, past a room full of purple plastic bags stuffed with the clothes of the deceased. He pressed the anti-bacterial hand wash for the last time. Skirting the empty trolley, he headed towards the lift, turned right at the Urology department, with its puddle outside, and escaped the hospital that never sleeps. He'd seen enough of nurses collecting phlegm for analysis.

Outside, the cold air brought the truth. He slumped on a bench, feet surrounded by cigarette ends wobbling in the wind. To the left was a funeral parlour, eerily close, waiting for the next person to slide downhill through its doors. The men with white gloves and hushed tones are never far away. Death comes to us all, a racing certainty but we marginalize it for our own sanity. It happens to other people, strangles them with its icy fingers but leaves us alone. Head in hands, he felt the warmth of tears in his palms.

The sound of the automatic doors woke him up.

"Got a light love?"

With the first sense of waking, it seemed to be some mad woman walking around with a coat stand but he soon recognized the patient with a drip; saline tube framed by the glass panelled door. She had been in the next bed to his mum a few wards ago. "She's got a cerebral cough," his mum had said as he combed her hair in the style of Adolf Hitler, causing the nurses to laugh.

"Sorry love, I gave up a few months back."

"How's your mum?"

"Worse than unwell," Tom said, jumping up and heading for his car, wherever the fuck he'd parked it.

He found it in a side street next to a discarded mattress and shards of broken glass. Welcome to Newport, with its boarded-up shop fronts and air of yesterday. He plugged in the iPod and dialled up *Pink Moon* by Nick Drake and hunkered down in its melancholic refrains. The weeks of visiting had taken their toll, aimlessly wandering the streets between the allotted times, buying clothes he didn't want in Marks and Spencer's. He reached into the glove compartment for the miniature bottle of wine, cracked it open and gulped it down, throwing the empty to join its brothers near the mattress.

***

Tom threw the keys on the sofa and sniffed the stale emptiness of the air. He looked around his mum's deserted house, now rendered lifeless. The cigarette burns on the carpet near her chair seemed bigger and more pronounced. Slippers lay neatly at the side, never to be worn again; underneath the sofa, the sight of a well-thumbed Mills and Boon and the crumbs of a ginger biscuit or two. The world's largest magnifying glass, capable of burning a colony of ants, next to a leather-bound copy of an old Radio Times. These were now relics in a terraced mausoleum. He had often thought of this house as a living entity; a sanctuary in which to hide away from the harsh realities of life. Now it was as dead as she was. Its days would be numbered. The past would have to be boxed up and the empty shell put on the market.

He looked at the clock. 3.30 am. Sleep should beckon but the prospect of fitful nightmares scared him. Too late to ring the ex-wife and she would only feign interest and stifle a yawn. The kids would be upset; nobody else to ring at this hour. Anyway, he didn't really do talking, not important talk anyway. Lacked that ability to open up and express any genuine feelings unless he had had a barrel load to drink;

that liberated the tongue but unfiltered talk always got him into trouble, made him clam up the next day and worry about every syllable he'd uttered. Mornings sifting through hazy recollections left him carrying the rucksack of regret.

Tom eased the cork from the bottle with a practised hand and poured a large glass of Crozes Hermitage. He wanted to feel numb, erase the day from his memory. Drink was a crutch he couldn't walk without. It ruled his life.

On the small table, next to her favourite chair was a pad of paper and a pen. He looked at her last list, scrawled messily, far from the perfect italics of her youth. Flicking the page, he summoned his thoughts and began to write. When he committed to the page, he took some solace in the fact that he could express his feelings freely in his own private auditorium. Poetry was a safe haven for someone of a shy disposition, an emotional laboratory in which he could pursue his research by candlelight. Looking back over time, these poems were a diary, charting the highs and lows, the down and outs of days.

***

A few hours later he woke, head thumping, face down with a mouthful of hair, on the moulting white rug in front of the fire, legs stiff as snooker cues and a searing pain in the groin for company. A Waterford crystal glass lay smashed on the fireplace, spilt wine oozing like a pool of blood. Three empty bottles stood to attention. He vaguely remembered stumbling to the garage in search of more alcohol. Gingerly exploring the pocket of his jeans, testing for dampness, he pulled out his mobile phone, checking to see if he had any messages. He noticed an outgoing call- 4.35 am. Some long, weird number he didn't recognize. Curious but in dire need of a strong coffee, Tom decided to check it out later. Knowing the state of play, it would probably cost a fortune.

In the Sole Company of a Bible Opened

Chepstow 01963 488172 is deleted.
Erased from the airwaves
But   I   am   between   calls.

Fingers poised to dial,
ready to listen to tales of leaky washing machines
and bar snacks on cold afternoons;
to tell you how my kids are doing
and that we will be down for your birthday.

The last car journey down the M4 put an end
to all of that.
Driving rain left a braille transcript of your life
splashed across the windscreen.
Endless paragraphs wiped with each sweep of the blades.

Swept in a side room;
I knew.
Walked into the ward of frightened old ladies
with wild eyes raging, hands gripping NHS sheets,
You, the other side of the curtain
In the sole company of a bible opened.

Mum you are as cold as the ice cubes you loved to chew,
Lips pursed peaceful, sentence draped incomplete,
blankets tucked taut as bandages.

And I kissed my Celtic cross, gazed skywards,

told you what a good job you did,

how much I loved you and I walked away into my own dark night.

Chapter 2

1975

Tom folded his poem and slid it into the back of his English exercise book. He looked out of his bedroom window at the slagheap, perched precariously on the hillside; the patchwork quilt of fields, a verdant green below. He felt empowered; something inside him had been released. He walked downstairs, put on his coat and weaved his way through the estate, took the top road past the foster home, into the small woods. At the base of the tallest tree he paused, looked up at the one, lonely branch at the very top. He remembered them throwing a rope over it. They'd been obsessed. It was the only tree in the whole wood they hadn't climbed. Three of them it took, to haul the dullest of them skywards. The make shift seat, a thin stick, creaking with every tug. He smiled as he recalled their victory dance. The yowls had echoed through the trees.

The whole gang were at the bus stop, laughing and jostling. The old folks, with their sad eyes, could hardly contain their annoyance. They lumbered on first, followed by the bubbling posse of kids flashing the thin bus passes in their new plastic sleeves. He sat at the back, in the corner and looked at the new red-bricked library with the sliding doors. Proper posh it was, smelt like a brand-new book hot off the press. He wondered if there were poetry anthologies waiting on the shelves for him. He'd sneak in on the weekend to check it out, on his own of course. This was a private thing. He watched his friends wolf whistle the girls in their blue uniforms heading to school, wicker baskets primed for home economics. In half an hour he'd be making a non-descript screwdriver, turning the old lathe, with one eye on the rugby goal posts out the window. He caught the eye of a girl. She smiled. He quickly turned away.

***

Tom checked his diary- English room 4L. He made his way across the courtyard of the 'all boys' Comprehensive (a contradiction in terms he would only recognize in later life) and trudged up the grey, concave steps. The sound of feet echoed down the corridors as they filed into the room with high windows and wooden desks, indelibly etched by generations of hands. Most headed for the anonymity of the back of the classroom until the unfortunate few were ushered forward by Mr Jones, owner of the sharpest nose; he who could part curtains when his hands were still in his pockets.

"Ok boys, it's poetry today. Toads Revisited by Philip Larkin. Turn to page 18. Off you go Evans, big loud voice."

Amidst the disgruntled mutterings, Tom felt a warm wave of exhilaration. It was as if the high windows had opened and countless images had stormed in, circling above.

"Focus, Morgan, we've lost you. Read the last stanza."

During the discussion Tom was careful not to volunteer too many answers. He felt he instinctively understood the nuances of the poem, but he didn't want to raise his head above the desk lid, risk the wrath of his classmates. Everything was about maintaining relative anonymity within the group.

The bell rang and there was a mad scramble to leave. Tom held back and waited until the last child had left to gulp in the freedom of the playground.

"Tom, is there a problem?" Mr Jones looked at him with concern. He collected the textbooks from the desks and stacked them on the shelf.

"No."

It seemed a stupid idea now, he was only a kid and writing was for grown-ups, university types with posh voices. He blurted it out.

"I've uh, written a poem. Will you read it?"

"Of course I will lad." He smiled.

"I can see you've been enjoying the poetry sessions. Leave it with me. See you next week."

Somehow Tom had expected more but Mr Jones was in a rush. He tucked the poem in amongst his papers and was off to the next lesson, striding purposefully down the stairs, leather soles clicking on the worn-out steps.

Tom sauntered out, wondering how he'd summoned up enough courage to hand over the poem. He remembered a similar feeling when he had bought some perfume in the south of France for a girl he liked in junior school (yellow dress and ringlets, teeth white as ice cream). Looking back, years later, he would recognize it as the first, tentative signs of sexual awakening. He had clasped the phial for days, waiting for the moment to impart the gift, searching for the right thing to say. Eventually he thrust it into her hands outside the sweet shop on Lewis

Street after school and speedily departed without saying anything. No word of a thank you ever passed her lips and it was never mentioned again. He rode his bike to where she lived, hoping to catch a glimpse of her, that same day, but never did.

***

The rain rattled the windows as Mr Jones launched into his introduction.

"Right lads, it's Larkin again, Mr Bleaney, page 10."

Tom closed his eyes and took the words in, lost in the sadness of it all. There was something about these poems that sucked him in. It meant something on a deeper level that he didn't yet comprehend. Looking up at the high ceiling, he wondered if the Victorians had deliberately designed these rooms to create space for the syllables to slosh into each other, fizz like fireworks.

As the lesson ended Tom turned towards the door and laughed at the Dylan Thomas poster with the added Mexican moustache, probably Potter who had done that, but next to it was something new. There was his poem – Him 39- with his name in big bold letters beneath it. Shit. He hoped nobody had noticed but at lunchtime it started. "Tommy Wordsworth are you? Fucking nonce."

He tried to laugh it off, saying at least it was better than Gwyn James' attempts at porn, but he knew he was sunk.

"You big gay bastard, people like us don't write that crap."

He walked away, sat under a tree overlooking the main road and watched the cars dribble by. He pulled his Parka coat tight around him, obscuring his face. How could he have been so bloody stupid, giving them ammunition to shoot him down? He'd seen kids destroyed for being different and he'd set himself up to join them; idiot, bloody idiot.

At lunch time, he hoped they'd forgotten about him, tried to join in his usual game of touch rugby but when one of the gang shouted "Fuck off Larkin, this is a man's game", that was enough. In those tender years feelings are amplified and the world is a painful, small place. You sit inside a bubble that can be pricked at any moment.

Tom slunk away and found a temporary sanctuary behind the swimming pool with its broken window panes, the smell of chlorine belching out. He sat in silence mulling over the abuse and thinking how it was probably going to get a whole lot worse before the end of the day. He contemplated hopping over the wall and making a run for it, absconding from the chain gang, maybe catch the train home, take his blazer off and pretend he'd been to a funeral if a guard questioned him. But in his heart, he knew that tomorrow he would have to face the same old music, and the day after that. He took solace in the rhythmic clanking of stones as he arched his arm up high and aimed at the boiler house door. Maybe there was a way out. He quietly made his way to the English room, rehearsing his speech under his breath.

***

"Mr Jones, can you give me my poem back?"

"Why, what's the problem?"

"I'm taking dogs abuse. I've had a guts full." He was close to tears.

Mr Jones ushered him forward and they sat on opposite sides of the desk.

13

"I had a feeling you'd be back when you saw it on the wall, giving you some stick are they?"

Tom nodded. Mr Jones frowned, shook his head.

"Why did you have to put it up there, sir?"

"I'm not going to take that poem down, Tom, you should be proud of it. It's your words, your creativity on display."

"But I just wanted you to read it, quiet like, and talk to me on my own about it."

Mr Jones stood up and walked towards the poem, turning back just before Tom thought he was going to tear it down.

"There's a lesson in this lad, if I take it down, they win. In a couple of days they'll move on, pick on some other unfortunate child, you'll be yesterday's news soon enough." Tom didn't believe him, he couldn't see past the next few minutes, let alone hours.

"When you get to my age, you'll remember this day and thank me. You can't see it now but trust me. Now go on, scram, hang in there, and keep writing, I really like the poem, you've got a talent, use it."

Tom looked at Mr Jones with his grammar school gown and crisply ironed shirt. He liked and respected him, indeed found him inspirational, but was all this crap really worth it? He half wanted to tear down the poem himself and be done with it, but something within stopped him. Those words up on the wall were his, even if he didn't really understand what his own poem was about, they came from his head, his heart and they were coming thick and fast. No kids, even if they all sat on him, could stop him. He had to write, it took him to places that lit up his life. He walked out of that room with a newfound determination. He'd ride out the storm.

Him 39

Pray at the altar,
Walter.
Tell God about your aversion to people;
Your ignorance, idleness and vices.
Tell him that your head
Is full of cups and Chaucers,
High healed ideals
And nothing that is concrete or real
Tell him your life is a monotonous
Windscreen wiper –
Every time you get up you fall down.
HEY IS HE LISTENING?
TURN YOUR HEARING AID ON.
For God's sake,
Pray at the altar,
Walter

Chapter 3

How can the son of an alcoholic become one himself? How can someone who has witnessed his mum crap herself in bed, hide vodka bottles in toilet cisterns, see imaginary men dancing on top of the television, hurl vile abuse at all and sundry, become one himself? Answer me that. Is it some genetic propensity that propels you down the chute, a self-fulfilling prophecy? Does some deep-seated weakness rule you with every frosty, firm pull of the pump? Answering that question brings the counsellors, the drinking diaries (multiply written intake by ten for a true figure) and the 'tell me about your childhood' cross-examination.

***

Walthamstow, London, the sky a pavement grey. Tom opened the door of his flat, stepped over the letters and headed for the fridge. Opening a can, the reassuring sight of bubbles and froth tempered the jittery hands. On the table was an unfinished Stella abandoned when the phone call from the hospital had unexpectedly summoned him to Wales. The remnants of a ready meal lay scattered on the counter, cold and coagulated. He gazed at the ceiling, mouth dry, skin moist with drinker's sweat, and guzzled the beer.

Opening his laptop, he checked his emails; nothing of note, just the usual Amazon offers and a travel update from TfL. His phone buzzed - a message from Steve about a surprise 50th party for a mutual friend. He didn't feel like going and fending questions. People always felt they had a social obligation to acknowledge bereavement but could never get beyond stumbling banalities. Glancing through his call list, he saw the long number again. The one he'd somehow dialled in the middle of the night. Probably some call centre in the sub-continent. He googled the dialling code; South Africa? How the fuck had he rung there? The wonders of the not-so-smartphone. He searched the number. The results came up: The Showroom Cinema, Prince Albert. The photo of the art deco cinema reminded him of the cover of Styx's album Paradise Theatre, the inner furnishings a relic from a glamorous bygone age, the neon lights alluring. Clicking a link, he saw a sleepy looking town nestled beneath a mountain. He read the accompanying blurb.

"The nothingness (die niks), the wide-open spaces and the deafening stillness…. balm for the soul at sunset, this is the magic of Prince Albert at the gateway to the Great Karoo."

Hell, it looked inviting.

He stood up, restless, and walked around the room, stopping by the window. A couple were arguing, caught in a silent movie, faces framed by split- screen aluminium. He picked up his keys and wallet and left.

The urge to drink was beginning to throttle him. He had always thought he could control the mighty beast, use it to his advantage but lately he'd become a luckless passenger, lurching from one stop to the next. He passed the drunks with their bleary red eyes, huddled under the clock on the corner of Wood Street and recognized himself within them; a step above maybe but just a small step.

***

"The usual, darling?" said the barmaid.

"Yeah, pint of Bass please."

Tom settled in a corner and downed his first, the thirst of many. Drinker's time weaved its web. The minutes clinked glasses. He gazed around the bar stools and tables, saw the pasty faces of the regulars and drifted into the sunken world of no hopers; the seedy underbelly of society. Rolly walked past, in his one set of clothes for all seasons, jabbering away. He smelt like a cat had pissed in all his pockets and doused his betting slip. Lonely fronds of hair, occasionally combed in a sober moment, stuck to his forehead.

"Yeah, yeah, gotta tenner on the favourite. It's baawnd to come in, c'mon my son!"

Tony sat by the jukebox in between lessons. He was a driving instructor who slept in the back of his car; topped up more on the beer than the petrol. Everywhere Tom looked people had had the colour drained out of them. It was a sepia world close to the optics. They'd all seen better days but few of them could remember much more than their last drink. He'd never classed himself as one of them, more a frequent visitor to their world, but fucking life was heading that way.

He ordered a Guinness with a whiskey chaser.

"You're pushing the pace today, love." said the barmaid.

"You drinking to remember or forget?"

"Both." He replied.

Sat in the corner he felt the alcohol kick in, dulling the pain, bringing with it a familiar fuggy warmth. Life's rough edges smoothed out. This was his life now, a life of little prospect, swaying from one drink to the next. The wheels of the cart had rolled loose and now he didn't care who saw him or what they thought. Fuck the whole lot of them.

In the toilets, the pungent smell of bleach jolted him. He propped himself up by the wall and looked at the cracked mirror. Salt and pepper stubble, an eye here an eye there, like a Picasso painting. It was late in the evening when he staggered to the bar to buy a fresh one.

"One for the road," he slurred, gripping the bar to steady himself.

"You've had enough, darling. Go home, sleep it off." She turned to serve another customer and he saw the word 'delicious' embossed on the back of her jeans in shiny silver sequins.

"You could fit a fucking short story on there, love." He laughed, couldn't stop himself.

"Get out and don't bother showing your face round here again." Her raised voice caused a temporary lull in drinkers chatter. All eyes were on him, not that he noticed. A few of the regulars, the pub police, stood up and walked towards him. He tried to focus but his vision was blurry.

"I'm going, I'm going." The last thing he needed was a good kicking. He struggled to get his jacket on; it was as if he was trying to fight it. The loose change in his pocket rattled like a box of false teeth. Notes, a wad full, always ended up as coins by the end of the night. A few customers laughed and held onto their drinks as he lurched towards the doors. Outside, under the street lamps, he walked with the legs of another man, mind and body dislocated. Oblivious to the sounds of the streets; the screech of an ambulance, rap music pumping from the tower blocks high above, he swayed from kerb to shop front in search of a straight line and the way home. The roads became quieter, houses blending in endless repetition. He was swallowed by the anonymity of the city, sunk without trace in the suburban streets.

***

Tom slumped on a sofa abandoned by the roadside, next to it an up ended fridge, copper wires ripped out for money. There he sat, like some contemporary art installation. He was lost; the wires in his head were disconnected too. The gassy confidence had given way to self-loathing. He stumbled on in the vague hope of sighting his red door and white, wooden fence with its missing planks. In the early hours, exhausted, he sheltered from the rain in an underpass. Lay near the deserted bicycle lanes, in amongst the crisp packets and empty cans. Life litter, lit up by the streetlights. The last thing he remembered was an image of the cinema in Prince Albert, back lit by a setting sun.

Straight Lines

He said he had turned a corner,
neglecting to mention
his propensity to turn left four times.
Routinely returning to square 1
with its straight lines
and bullish 90-degree angles.

Locked on a pavement slab
he witnesses the pylons
march by
and the bus stops
congregate in the park.

Chapter 4

She felt the sweat on her brow, armpits damp beneath the blouse. She'd forgotten what she was going to say next, forgotten the open-ended questions, the content, everything. She glanced down to look at the bullet points on the cards she'd prepared the night before, but they were jumbled up. One of the kids in the front row had got hold of them, chucked a few under her chair. The man in the suit and tie, clipboard and pen at the ready, sat there expectantly. A hush came over the class. They were waiting too. She looked at the clock: it was 11.23. It would be forever 11.23, the moment when it ended. The sleepless nights, the worry, had led to this. She caught her reflection in the classroom window. She was pale and drawn.

"Miss Thompson, the children are waiting."

She looked at him blankly, unable to say a word, let alone string a sentence together. It was as if she was an imposter who'd wandered in from the street.

"Miss Thompson, please continue with the lesson, this is affecting the children's learning."

He was increasingly agitated now, standing up and walking towards her, face red, eyes angry. With her brain in lock down, it was fight or flight, back to the primeval senses that drive us in the moment of panic. She deftly sidestepped him, walked out the door, down the long corridor and out of the school (failing to register the shock on the secretary's face). She stumbled on like the walking dead, blindly stepping across the road, oblivious to the sound of a car slamming on the brakes to avoid her. Into the park she went and slumped down on a bench. The tears came; a trickle at first, then the flood.

The truth was she felt trapped. It was if she was following a pre-ordained path towards retirement. She had seen older teachers clinging onto their careers, burnt out and bitter, once gifted people worn down by the daily grind of paperwork or the endless stream of aggressive parents baring their teeth at the door. But it was more than that. Lately, she'd been living under the cloud of yet another Ofsted inspection-FUCKOFFSTED. When news of their imminent arrival circulated she'd gone into meltdown. In preparation for the visit there'd been an endless round of lesson observations; people sat in the corner of the room with clipboards grading her performance. Stress levels were high and there was constant pressure. You had to improve and keep on improving and the goal posts were always being moved further away. Above all, she feared failure. It towered above her night after night, looked her in the eye and laughed. The thought of the dreaded 'satisfactory' grade falling like an axe, dispensed by the men in suits; it was the stuff of nightmares.

***

Sat there on the park bench, her whole life passed her by; a long train that never stopped at a station, the scenery a blur. She was hit by the realization that life's greatest failure was not being true to oneself. Maybe there was another life waiting for her. She wiped away the tears and thought about the future. The park was empty save for a diminutive figure entering through a distant gate. An old man slowly came into focus, walking down the path, his long black cane tapping between footsteps. He was wrapped up like a mummy but, as he got closer, she recognized him. It was an elderly neighbour and she'd taken him a Harvest donation of food from the school. He'd laughed at the combination of tins, baked beans and figs, and asked if there were any toilet rolls buried at the bottom of the box. They'd got talking after that and struck up an unlikely friendship.

"Carla? School closed today?"

"Nope, it's open."

"You sick or something?" He moved further away from her on the bench. She laughed.

"No, sick in the head maybe. I walked out, mid lesson."

His eyes narrowed.

"That's a bit drastic innit?"

"I can't stand it anymore Frank, it's too much pressure, I think I'm going under."

She shivered. Her coat was on a hanger in the staffroom.

"How long's this been goin' on?"

"Feels like a lifetime."

"You talked to anybody about it?"

"Just you."

He rubbed his chin, scratching the week old bristles.

"Sounds like burn out to me, go and see the doc, tablets'll sort you out."

He was taken out by a fit of coughing, face puce.

"I'll see you in the waiting room." She smiled and gave him a tap on the back to pull him round. He wiped his mouth with an ancient handkerchief. She saw his monogrammed initials on a faded corner.

"I'm not long for this world, girl."

"It's just a cough Frank, you'll live to see another day."

"This is serious, Carla, you can't just walk out of work. They'll sack you."

"Sounds crazy but I don't care; I want out." It was strange to admit it but that's how she felt.

"Fair enough but there's ways of doing it, you know, proper."

"It's a bit late for that now Frank." She was briefly possessed by a gassy feeling of confidence.

He gave her the old timers look.

"Thought this through have you?"

"Yeah, I have." It was a lie, but she knew in her heart what she wanted to do.

"I'm going to travel the world Frank, step out from the shadows. What do you reckon to that?"

She was expecting a lecture - you have responsibilities - but his reply surprised her.

"You only live once, girl, and you've got a lot more time left than me, bloody go for it."

She hugged him.

"I'm scared Frank."

"We're all scared deep down Carla, but we try not to show it. You'll be fine, if I was forty years younger, I'd come with you."

He looked at the worn-out ring on his finger and wondered what her upstairs would think. She'd been dead these past ten years and the old house was an empty place without her.

"Fancy a cuppa?" she said. The autumn leaves were swirling round their feet and it was getting cold.

"A cup of Rosie Lee with a beautiful woman." Who could turn that down?

"I'll have a bit of that darling." He rubbed his hands together and dropped the cane. She picked it up for him. They walked slowly to the gate, linking arms. She lent her head on his shoulder. They took the long way home, avoiding the school gates.

Late that night, lying in the bath, ambient music in the background, she wondered whether she'd been impetuous. The earlier Demob elation had given way to self-doubt. School was the only world she knew. The prospect of life out of the comfort zone was daunting. There was to be no more 7.30-6.00 following the same timetable, now each day would be different, new situations to be encountered, new people to meet. For the first time in years, the future would be unpredictable.

***

Carla looked out of the window as the train slowed. She smiled; twelve weeks away from the British winter had been a liberating experience. This was her stop. She stepped out onto the empty platform; saw the lonely petrol station and the run-down motel. The hustle and bustle of Cape Town seemed a lifetime away. The place was empty apart from a scruffy dog sniffing around a bin. There were some old, rusty wagons dumped in a siding, wheels entangled with weeds.

The heat was stifling, and she pulled her hat down to protect herself from the midday sun. She sat on a bench and checked her phone. Greg had said he'd be there to collect her but there was no sign of him. She heard the sound of a car in the distance; watched it come into focus as it neared the station. A tall black guy got out and walked towards her.

"Hello, are you Miss Carla?"

"Yes?"

"Mr Joseph is busy miss, he asked me to collect you." He shook her hand firmly and picked up her bag.

"Just the one?"

"Yea, I've been back packing round Africa for three months, travelling light."

She sat in the car, calm enough about the change in plan. Weeks coping alone had hardened her, made her more adaptable.

"Do you work for Mr Joseph?"

"Ya, in the coffee shop."

"I worked in one when I was a student. That was a few years back." She smiled at him.

"How far is it to Prince Albert?"

"About forty kilometres miss."

She looked out at the barren desert. It conjured up an image of cowboys roaming the vast open spaces of New Mexico; the flat-topped hills and mountains in the distance.

***

They drove down the main street. She took in the cafes, gallery and opulent cinema. Charles parked on the main street and carried her bags

27

inside. Greg was standing, hands in pockets, on the veranda. He'd aged; skin like old leather, face drawn, worry lines etched on hollowed cheeks.

"Well hello Carla, long-time no see." He smiled at her but it looked like an effort.

"Hi Greg, great to see you." He pecked her on the cheek and she could smell the booze on him.

"The feeling's mutual, life's full of surprises."

"Thanks for putting me up. Bet my email was a bit of a shock after all of this time?"

"It was a bolt from the blue but it's a pleasure. Come in, I'll show you your room."

She followed him upstairs.

"Listen, I'm really busy, make yourself at home. I'll catch you later."

He closed the door and she sat on the bed, pensive. It wasn't the welcome she'd expected, not that she'd anticipated a red carpet, but to be met with indifference was disconcerting. Maybe the idea of chilling out in a quiet town for a few weeks wasn't such a good one after all. She hung her two dresses in the empty wardrobe and sat in the chair by the window. A cooling shower beckoned. Before she undressed, she sent a text to Frank. He liked to know she was safe.

Chapter 5

I knew Kincaid wanted to kill me. I saw it in the coldness of his eyes. Saw it in the way his hand squeezed the life out of the bottle. Maybe I could make a break for it before McCabe and the rest of his gang showed up, give myself an even chance. I sipped my bourbon, sat at a corner table beside the piano and took it all in. This day had been coming for a long time; Texas wasn't big enough for the both of us. I stood up, headed for the swing doors, and felt his gaze burn the back of my neck. Slowly I walked the street, not looking back, heard the clatter of doors behind me, the faint sound of feet above the howling wind. Still I didn't turn, pacing steady, slow'n easy.

I stopped, turned, watched Kincaid, waited for the first hint of movement, trigger finger at the ready…BANG

Tom awoke with a start, the blaze of light on his retina frightening him. He tried to lift his head but the searing pain in his neck made him cry out. A man in a white coat slowly came into focus.

"Steady, keep still," said the doctor, "you've had a nasty blow to the head."

Tom heard the metronomic beat of the bedside monitor pulsing nearby and saw the drip wire hanging from the bag. The scent of the hospital took him back to his mum's ward. He shivered.

"What's going on?" he asked the doctor, trying to piece together the fragments of his memory.

"You've been mugged, taken a blow to the head, do you remember anything?"

"Uh? I know I was drunk, been in the pub for hours but then it went blank."

"A cleaner on an early shift found you this morning. You were lying on the pavement in an underpass by the North Circular. Jog a memory?"

What do you think bloody taxis are for, the doctor thought to himself, sick of the endless run of patients arriving with alcohol related injuries; two in the morgue in the last twenty-four hours and more on the way no doubt.

"I've seen too many people waste their lives binge drinking; you don't want to be one of them." Tom saw the dismissive look on his face. He was battle worn.

The doctor wiped his bleary eyes, tired of witnessing man's infinite capacity to destroy himself from the inside out. His pager buzzed, and he left at pace. The much-needed coffee would have to wait. He turned back at the swing doors.

"We'll monitor you for a few hours then you should be able to go home. You're a lucky man."

The blinding headache didn't feel like luck, but the doc was right.

"Oh, there's someone outside to see you, I'll tell the nurses to send her in a bit later. I am sure the police will want to talk to you too."

Tom looked inwards, saw the metal box with its heavy padlock but couldn't bear to open it or even look for the key. The more his problems mounted, the more he hid away. He closed his eyes and blanked his mind.

The nurse brought him a cup of tea and biscuits and he eased himself up.

"I'll send your visitor in, ok, she's been here a couple of hours and she said she has to go to work soon."

He saw the doors flap as she approached at pace, all lipstick and leather trousers. Clare was not a happy woman.

"For Christ's sake Tom, you had me worried. Look at the bloody state of you." She said angrily.

"It's about time you sorted yourself out, you've got responsibilities. Think of the kids. I can't tell them about this."

"Hold on, what about are you ok?" he said. He wondered where the new man was, probably sat on the leather seat in his BMW polishing his designer sunglasses and looking at himself in the mirror.

"The doctor said you'll be fine, you've got to pull yourself together and stop bloody drinking, get some fucking help."

She managed to say it with quiet venom, a tone he had become accustomed to in the dying days of their relationship. How the mighty have fallen he thought as he remembered their first flush of romance, how everything felt right and natural all those years back. They had had some good times together but that was long gone, a former life. Another chapter confined to the waste bin.

"Look, this is a wakeup call, I'll change, get some counselling." He knew he was on dodgy ground.

"Don't mention that word change to me, how many times have you said that? It's bloody meaningless unless you do it, look, I've gotta go to work, I'm late as it is, I'll ring you later."

The sound of her heels echoed down the corridor. It was strange to see her wearing a different woman's wardrobe; she had reinvented herself since the break-up. He was still busy dis-inventing himself, if there was such a word. He couldn't think straight. Tom glanced at the bedside table glad to notice the absence of a bible opened. He closed his eyes and tried to get some sleep.

The nurse woke him, checked his pupils and switched of the monitor. "You're free to go, we need the bed. Take it easy for a couple of days, if you get any prolonged headaches come back to us straight away."

She handed him a bundle of clothes and pulled the curtains around him. The trousers were stained with nothing but an empty wallet in the pocket. The jacket was torn, blood on the collar, but it was all he had until he got home. He slipped down the corridors, hoping not to bump into anybody he knew and thinking he was giving tramps a bad name. He didn't have the energy to concoct a story. He just wanted the comfort of his own bed.

The trees at Hollow Ponds waved goodbye as he set off for Wood Street, pulling his jacket tight to keep out the wind. He passed the numerous fast food outlets and the drunks with red faces counting their coppers near the off licence, crossed the road to avoid the curtained windows of the funeral directors and the wicker-basket coffin.

***

Lying in a hot bath, clothes binned, he soothed his aching limbs. He tried, as a counsellor had once told him, to take a helicopter view of his life. Piece the fractured parts together to form a sense of the whole. It didn't look good. Everything seemed to be flowing in a powerful downward spiral. He was tired of looking back and locked in an unpleasant here and now. He thought of his life as an endless row of dominoes. One flick and the whole lot would come crashing down. What he had to do was somehow break the chain, remove some dominoes to limit the damage. But damage limitation was just the first step, the road to recovery would require more resilience than he felt he possessed. What was clear, however, was something had to change otherwise the alternative didn't bear thinking about.

Tom dressed and made himself a strong coffee with hot milk. He ordered a new bank card online and checked his balance. There was enough money to survive for six months; the redundancy pay out had been big. The trick was not to squander it on booze as he had been doing. The daily trawl around the pubs had to stop. He checked the fridge for food. It was empty, apart from a few cans of lager and some bottles of beer. His hands shook as he closed the door, resisting the urge to crack one open and take the edge off the day. The prospect of his mum's funeral loomed large. It was strange how someone in their early fifties still needed the comfort of a parent. Despite the fact that she was old and infirm she had always been a passive sounding board and backed him, even when he had dug himself another deep hole to lie in. He wanted to call her for his daily chat and realized how reliant he had become on the parental umbrella that shielded him. Now he was alone, next in line for the trip upstairs. Later, in bed he drifted in and out of sleep, feeling the night sweat take hold and the dreams bite in.

Kincaid lay dead, blood masking his face. The town shrunk behind me as I headed for the distant hills; the rhythm of hooves, the sound of angry voices closing in.

The Last Cowboy

As the wind cuts the dust with its blades of scorn,
I touch my gun on which vengeance was sworn.

As the heat of the day burns deep in my dreams,
My life's torn apart, ripped at the seams.

As the gunshot shatters the bar room mirror,
A blood splattered face, a deathly shiver.

As I run through the streets pursued by the gang
The gallows beckon, where bad men hang.

As the director shouts 'cut' and the scene is complete,
There's a plastic cactus and tumbleweed neat.

Chapter 6

The bricks of Glyntaff crematorium were as grey as the sky on that Friday morning. Two groups of funeral goers viewed each other uneasily, waiting for their appointed time. Life recycled in twenty-minute slots. Last season's wedding outfits altered by a black tie, the odd, faded rugby club blazer dry-cleaned for the occasion. Hushed small talk lost on the wind. Feuding family members briefly reunited in a moment of grief. The most callous amongst them already thinking of making a tentative bid for the old girl's furniture before the final curtains closed behind her. These details were oblivious to Tom; faces were blurred, conversations forgotten. Later he would remember very little of the day apart from the sight of the coffin bedecked with flowers that probably weighed more than her, slowly passing him by.

He made his way to the front row and sat between his children, holding their hands tightly. He felt sorry for them. How do such young minds process the levels of grief, how can they come to terms with the fact that their grandmother is in that box over there balanced on a steel trolley, ten minutes from the flames? Tom remembered seeing his grandfather's coffin march wearily by and being unable to suppress his laughter, sat in the back row with his cousin. The stern rebuke from dad had missed the point. As a child it is impossible to summon up the accepted social response. The emotional capabilities haven't had time to develop and sometimes never do. Laughter often stems from embarrassment and an inability to cope with the pressures of such surreal moments. There are no twilight courses in grief management. No ten easy steps to keeping a straight face.

Tom looked at Lizzie's big brown eyes and saw the tears welling up. He put his arm around her shoulder and hugged her gently. Jeff stared at the priest who was mumbling something about taking your last journey on your own and how she was going to a better place. Clare had been unable to get time off work so there sat the three; all lost in their private thoughts.

The lectern was a lonely place. Tom stood there, raised above the expectant faces. He wondered why he had been so insistent on delivering the eulogy. He unrolled his crumpled speech and somehow stumbled through it, knuckles whitening as he gripped the stand. He told of her fight against adversity and her worth as a mother but said nothing about her battle with her demons over the years. Some things are best left unsaid. With a few cursory goodbyes they were in the back of the limousine, bound for the hotel, with the sombre white gloved men who only laugh at weekends.

***

Tom had over catered. The advice had been - think how many people you expect to come and then divide it by half. He hadn't listened. After everyone had left, he undid his tie and sat in the corner overlooking the river, staring at the army of sandwiches; enough troops to take on the world.

"Dad, we can't just throw them away. It's such a waste." said Lizzie.

She was right, a youthful beacon of correctness in a busted world. She fiddled with her phone and came up with the idea of donating them to a good cause. A few calls later and they were heading to Cardiff to a centre for the homeless. Driving down the terraced streets Tom realized this was the end of an era. Soon he would have no base in his homeland, the strong ties would be severed forever and he was to be let loose, a floating ex-pat. Despite living in London for twenty-six years he still regarded this as home, an indelible part of his identity and it was with a sense of loss that he entered the outskirts of the city.

***

Tom stepped over the empty beer cans, carrying the trays of sandwiches towards the homeless refuge. He told the kids to wait in the car. As he turned a corner near the entrance, a group of down and outs circled him, one of them shouting- "What've you got there then?" Their faces scared him, with their eyes empty as the factory units that surrounded them. He entered the building feeling as if he could be lynched at any moment for wearing a suit and tie. The manager was thankful and told him the food would be gone in five minutes. There but for the grace of God he thought.

They drove in silence, joined the M4 eastbound towards London. It wasn't until they crossed the Severn Bridge that anyone felt like talking.

"Dad?" said Jeff. "What did that old man mean when he was talking about ants in London?" Tom laughed. An elderly relative from North Wales had found out that they lived in London and recounted his only visit to the city in the 1950's.

"It was like lifting up a stone with a load of ants underneath, I bloody hated it, I even saw a woman drinking," he had said. "He's not a fan of big cities Jeff. He's spent all his life in a small village."

"Dad?" Tom looked at Jeff in the mirror and could feel the weight of a big question coming. "Why don't you just say sorry to Mum and we can be a family again?"

"It's not as simple as that Jeff."

"But in school we just say sorry and we get a fresh start, get back to normal."

"It's difficult to explain, Jeff. You might understand when you are older but me and your mum don't get on anymore. It's best if we don't live together. Just remember, we both love you and will always be there for you."

Lizzie sat expectantly, waiting for Tom to elaborate but he was done with talking. He sat in guilt-ridden silence. Dealing with the death of his mum, despite the undoubted emotional strain, was easier because it was beyond his control. It was unavoidable. The collapse of a family, on the other hand, came as a direct consequence of behaviours and actions. They had been like two alligators fighting in a fish bowl, oblivious to the outside world.

In the early evening they reached the edge of London; the land of road rage and screeching horns. They entered the anthill, negotiated the lanes of the North Circular and took a right at the Crooked Billet roundabout. Tom parked up, a safe distance from Clare's house, his old house, still with the blue Victorian door he had found in a skip and renovated. He hugged his children, told them how proud he was of them and watched as they walked to the door, waving at him. The upstairs curtain twitched and Tom saw the outline of Clare framed by the window. He felt a pang of ill-judged jealousy at the prospect of the boyfriend loafing round his old bedroom and sat there like a low life private detective on a stakeout. He opened the glove compartment and grabbed a miniature bottle of wine, downing it in one.

It would be a few days later when he'd collect his mum's ashes and drive to the wilds of west Wales. Alone, on the mountaintop overlooking the sea, with the estuary curling like pensioners' fingers, he stood. The solitude suited him, gave him time to collect his thoughts. With the wind cheering, he released those ashes, turned to the rolling hills and vowed to change his life.

Sweet Jar

Dust in a sweet jar
that's what you are,
in a brown hessian bag
heading uphill
and it's me who is puffing now.

I circle the peak.
Settle in my private
amphitheatre,
hidden beneath the rocks,
sheltered from the wind.

I release you
with sporadic shakes.
You coat the heather
like a cloud canopy
arching over
a tropical rainforest.

Chapter 7

It was the silence that derailed him, made his eyes flicker from phone to window, door to phone. Holed up in his room, the rising damp of paranoia climbing the walls, Greg Joseph was in fear of his life. Radebe hadn't been in touch for a few days, something was wrong, seriously wrong. How could they have rumbled him? He'd covered every track in a safety blanket yet somehow, somewhere along the line, he had made a mistake. Radio silence meant just one thing, they were onto him and wouldn't stop until they'd hunted him down and disposed of him; dumped him in the vast emptiness of the Karoo, probably with a bullet between his eyebrows.

He cracked in the clutches of the early hours, woke Carla, rapped the spare room door hard until she opened it, bleary eyed. He concocted some cock and bull story about a family emergency back in England and how he had to leave for Cape Town immediately to catch a plane. She stared at him blankly, trying to take it all in. Half-heartedly, she mumbled something about running the coffee shop for a couple of weeks if that would help and at that moment he would have said yes to anything. His brain was scrambled and he was incapable of any cogent thought.

Carla turning up out the blue was a mixed blessing. He had read her email with vague disinterest and never thought she would actually turn up on his doorstep. Africa was a big place and Prince Albert certainly wasn't its epicentre. He had been surprised how attractive she had become, far from the gangly student of yester year. He remembered filling those empty student days debating idealistic dreams. In those sunlit evenings the future lay before them, shimmering and inviting. Now time and events had worn him down, he was a husk of his former self. He had little time for small talk and, frankly, could have done without the distraction of her visit. Ok, she had helped out in the coffee shop, laughed when she remembered being the world's most incompetent barista at Starbucks when she was a student, but he'd been counting the hours until she left.

***

Within five minutes he was gone, leaving to the sound of the bats murmuring in the eaves, foot pressed to the floor, eyes, big as bush babies, scanning the rear-view mirror as Prince Albert shrunk to a dot in the distance. He watched a white Mercedes closing in at speed, braced himself for the crunch of a bullet, the sound of shattered glass but it shot past, racing into the darkness. He sped on in grim silence, hands gripping the wheel, knuckles white, palms sweaty. At this time of night, the traffic was minimal. The sullen hours were punctuated by the odd long-haul juggernaut but with time he began to relax, safe in the growing belief that he wasn't being pursued. As he slowly calmed, he began to think of the contingency plan he had put in place in the event of the world coming crashing down. He had never thought he would have to implement it but needs must. Prince Albert was history; he would never set foot there again.

***

He arrived in Stellenbosch at 8.30, battling the commuter traffic, parked up near the Spar and picked up a few provisions for the next few days. He scanned the car park but it was virtually empty apart from the odd mother in a gleaming 4x4 and a couple of disgruntled car guards. He felt sufficiently confident to head to the Mugg and Bean for a strong coffee and a croissant before driving to his safe house. A few years ago, when he'd gotten himself in a mess, he had rented a flat in a block near the University. Most of the flats were rented by the transient student community and Greg had chosen the flat because of the hustle and bustle of the area. The endless throng of people provided the ideal social backdrop; wear student garb and a beanie and you became just another member of the faceless thousands. He parked his car behind the buildings, away from the main street and climbed the stairs, the sound of loud music reverberating down the corridors. Inside, he looked at the basic furniture, the bland decor; this would be his temporary home. A bolt hole where he could plan his next move and try and make sense of the predicament he found himself in. He had to get out of South Africa as quickly as possible but not by an obvious route. The main airports weren't an option. They would be staked out. Radebe's tangled web of connections were too widely spread, from townships to upmarket shopping malls, they walked the streets. This would need careful planning and clinical execution, something he prided himself in. He scanned the street. A few tourists, with cameras waiting to be stolen, ambled towards the curio shops and the market, wallets bulging, happy to spend and keep on spending. Greg envied their laughter, their freedom to roam. He unpacked the few essentials he'd hastily thrown in a bag and thought of Carla, blind to all this madness.

***

Johnson sat outside the Java café, glass of beer in his hand. He called Radebe.

"Hey baas, Joseph is holed up in his flat in Stellenbosch. He bought some food in the Spar and headed straight there, not moved since. Malherbe is keeping an eye on him."

"Good, tell me if he makes a move," said Radebe, making a church spire with his fingers, slowly exhaling air between them. Nobody got to double cross Mr Radebe and live a long and fruitful life.

Chapter 8

Heathrow, terminal 5 had the air of a glorified greenhouse, exotic plants substituted by a multicultural melee of people briefly intertwined; the rush of comings and goings, hellos and goodbyes, a transient runway that never sleeps. Tom checked in. The bag was well under the weight limit, not surprising considering it only contained a few shorts and t shirts and an empty book he hoped to fill with new poems. He looked at his passport photo and thought he resembled an angry Italian pizza salesman who had witnessed some catastrophic event, or, at the very least, someone who was constipated. The moustache, worn like a Welsh badge of honour, clung to his lip for dear life.

He answered the standard questions; yes, he had packed the bag himself. No, there was nothing sharp in the toiletry bag, no bomb making liquids. Soon he was through security having survived a near miss. His trousers had tried to head south as his belt and wallet lay in the tray, waiting to be scrutinized by the machine that sees everything and the man who looks bored.

Four hours to departure, four hours to fill. He struggled to find a seat. Families split into insurgent groups. Someone supervised base camp, sat on sentry duty, bags occupying the seats of invisible others, off sniffing the scent of a bargain, roles to be reversed ad infinitum. Tom amused himself by trying to spot the large groups that lovingly frequent these social spaces. There is always a religious choir, seconds from bursting into song, off to faraway places, fuelled by a missionary zeal, or a sports team, replete with team tracksuits, days away from the glorious dignity of defeat on foreign soil. He dodged the darting children, parents trying in vain to tire them out before the twelve hours of the seat belt. He swerved around the tiny tots propelling themselves helter-skelter on mobile cases; lions, tigers, zebras but no porcupines or hedgehogs? He scanned the bookshop shelves and wondered why airport books are so bloody big? It's as if they have been given steroids to bloat the print billboard size. Do they imagine we are all partially sighted in the land between countries? The people working in the shops had the look of a long walk to the gallows.

Tom ordered a coffee and looked out of the glass box, watched the wheels drop and the landing crews scamper. This was his base camp, one step away from the unknown. The thought of it was exhilarating yet tinged with an element of fear. As much as he wanted to escape the clutches of his former life, the drifting from pub to pub culture that consumed him, he sensed that the experience about to unfurl before him would be raw and elemental. He had to drop the greyness, the familiarity, the unhinged reality of his current path and find some answers to questions he was frightened to ask himself. Above all, he knew he had to look inwards without the aid of a counsellor or a self-help book. He knew there was pain there, festering. He believed, to some extent, in the redemptive power of the sun but a glowing tan wouldn't solve his problems. He had to take a good, hard look at himself, peel away the layers that protected the very core of his being. The very thought of it made him uneasy, made him want a drink, to feel that reassuring numbness.

He watched the couples drinking in the bar opposite with certain envy. That was him once, laughing and joking, the life and soul of the party. Drink as a dependable friend, lubricating the lips, massaging the ego, conquering the shyness, pulling the girls. But he couldn't stop; no on / off switch, always wanting one more for the road. Never full and never empty. Friends would have enough or fall asleep but not him. He would rejoice in the dark majesty of his art, wallow in the revelry, drink till the lights went out and carry on when they came on again. Subtly, over time, he ceased to care how he was perceived by anyone, wife, women, work, friends, strangers, none of them mattered anymore. He did not give a flying fuck and still he drunk like the thirstiest fish in the deepest sea. A world governed by wine and the whoosh of a widget. Yeah, he had fun in the early days, there were stories to tell, he'd dined out on them for years but the lure of the glove compartment mini bar had got him in the end. How many times could you sit in a quiet corner of a Sainsbury's car park and glug one down, bent double, hiding from yourself? All of these thoughts flooded his brain as he sat there, impassive, Americano in hand. Six days sober was not much to write home about but at least it was a start.

***

It was while hunched over his laptop a few days ago that he had made his decision. He'd found himself going back to the images of Prince Albert; the art deco cinema, the serenity of the mountains, the town basking in the sun. Something locked him in, drove him towards there. That inadvertent, random phone call had led him here, to this cut off point. He would remove the clothes of his past, hanging on him like a heavy coat and embrace the future. What was there to lose? Most things had already been lost. He thought of his kids safely tucked up in bed in his old house, and his mum scattered on the hillside He'd be back, a better man.

The boarding call came. Tom checked for his ticket and passport and joined the queue. He plugged in his iPod and dialled up *I.G.Y.* off Donald Fagen's *Nightfly* album. Lush.

Tin Geese

The tin geese have come home to roost,
ready to gorge on the latest batch of fattened grubs.
Trapped in a consumer capsule,
they buy books to drop in hotel pools,
sunglasses to sit on.

Watch the dance of hand luggage
pirouetting across the patterned floors.

Listen to the phrase books flap
and languages collide;
Conversations peppered with the sound
of the universal sneeze.
"flight 883 is now boarding at gate 42 "
airports - portals to the world.

Chapter 9

He looked at the photo on his bedside table and wanted to climb in it, rekindle the moment, and start his life again, in that field with the sun setting, the red glow embracing them. There was dad, long hair floating in the breeze, head tilted back, laughing. Mum with her arms round him, his sister peeping out from under a blanket, smiling at the camera. Jeff turned, looked at the alarm clock. 7.45 am. He dressed, did his school tie up the way dad taught him. From his bedroom window he watched the planes scribing the sky, wisps of white trailing behind. In a few hours dad would be up there with them. He said he would only be gone for a couple of months, but Jeff didn't believe him. He didn't believe in anything anymore.

Chapter 10

Carla opened the shutters of Celestino's coffee shop and felt the heat of the morning sun. She looked out at the main street of Prince Albert, wider than a Parisian boulevard but quiet at this time of the morning. Soon it would come to life as the workers trudged up the gentle hill to start their days in gardens and restaurants or on one of the local farms. Some rode bikes slowly; others listened to music, moving and talking animatedly. She checked the tablecloths were clean and arranged the furniture neatly on the veranda. Lately the place had been busy with tourists passing through on the way to Cape Town or Joburg. A steady flow of locals called in too, so she welcomed this early morning solitude. The staff would arrive in ten minutes and the first customers soon after. She smiled to herself. It was a strange world. A couple of weeks ago she was just a guest visiting an old university friend but now she was running the coffee shop in his absence. He'd had to return to England; some form of family emergency. Perhaps it helped explain his peculiar behaviour. He'd hardly talked to her during the previous few days. His eyes had been oddly lifeless. Maybe one of his parents had died. He'd been too distraught to string a proper sentence together. She'd seen the anguish in his eyes, poor soul. He must have been close to them.

Charles and Sheila arrived for work at the coffee shop just as an old couple sat at a table on the veranda. They were in their eighties. The old man dutifully moved a chair for his wife and ordered two cappuccinos with scones and jam. They talked in quiet tones and held hands under the table. Carla liked observing the customers and trying to work out their background by looking at their clothes and noticing their mannerisms. The man had an air of authority and carried himself well, maybe an old school policeman. His wife was stylishly dressed, with a bohemian scarf and understated jewellery. They were probably up for a weekend break from the suburbs of Cape Town, attracted by the quietness of the Karoo. A couple of locals called in and asked if she had heard from Greg, but he hadn't been in touch since arriving back in England and she didn't want to contact him unless it was absolutely necessary. She was enjoying the experience of running the business and, so far everything was going well. She looked at the clock and smiled; 11.23, but a different 11.23 now. Her former life, the endless hours of stress and the sleepless nights, was becoming a distant memory.

Carla had settled into a relaxed routine. The mornings were spent overseeing the coffee shop. Charles and Sheila did the majority of the work. She just handled the financial side of it and made sure it was fully stocked. In the afternoons she had gotten into the habit of exploring the wide-open spaces surrounding the town. Greg must have been a keen cyclist at some point, though she had never seen him go for a ride, and he had let her borrow one of his bikes stored on the back terrace. There were endless loops stemming from the hub of the town and she had quickly become addicted to these solo ventures, basking in the solitude they provided. She had always enjoyed exercise but, with the pressure of work, visits to the gym had become onerous and, at best, sporadic. The evenings were spent reading or eating out at one of the restaurants on the main street. She took in the odd film at the sumptuous cinema that seemed so out of place, dropped in from a different age. There was an upcoming Hitchcock season. She loved those old films.

***

The afternoon sun beat down like hammer on steel. Carla clipped her feet into the pedals and made her way towards the graveyard and the dirt track. As she increased the pace, she felt the breeze streak through her hair. She passed the kilometre signs, stocky concrete posts or metal signs hanging on the fence, as she rode on towards Weltevreede, the fig farm nestled beneath the Swartberg Mountains. The dirt track was deserted, the landscape emptied of sound. She passed through a small settlement; small kids dressed in rags waved at her, a pack of dogs sprang from beyond the shacks and nipped at her ankles. She saw the severity of the hill in front and gritted her teeth, settled into a firm rhythm. No matter how slow the progress, she was determined to get to the top. She thought of the thrill of descent from the peak, it spurred her on. At the summit, she gulped in the air and hurtled down the valley, screaming round the bends, inches from the precipice, body hunched low over the frame. The road flattened and straightened like a string pulled tight and she began to slowly ease up. She gently rolled into the farm courtyard and rested up in the shade of an out building. The place was quiet. The shutters of the farmhouse were closed to block out the afternoon sun. There were no cars in sight, probably gone to George to get some provisions. She shared a few crumbs of her sandwich with a bird that had been watching her from the branch of a nearby tree. The cool drink eased her parched throat. She soaked up the silence.

Being alone gave you time for reflection. Now she realized that stepping off the treadmill had been the right decision. You didn't have to be a clinical psychologist to recognize that she'd been on the brink of a nervous breakdown. All the signs had been there, but she'd buried her head in work, hoping it would all go away. In the end, you have to look after yourself, face your problems head on. That was clear now. Under the cloudless sky, far from the tensions of her former life, she could view her past with some detachment. There was more to life that grinding yourself into the ground. She knew that others felt that life had passed her by. Friends judged her, were married with kids, but she had never really found a soul mate. She'd been in a number of relationships, two or three long term, but had never felt strongly enough to fully commit to any of them. In the end she always walked away. It wasn't failure, just the way her life had panned out and she wasn't going to beat herself up over it. She was happy enough in her own skin. Life in the slow lane had confirmed that.

She took in the view: the sharply defined mountains bordered by the bluest of skies, the sun parched terrain stretching into the distance, burnt brown, harsh yet beautiful. There was something about the serenity of her surroundings that sucked her in. It soothed the soul. She was surprised that she found herself imagining living here. The slow and steady beat of life seemed idyllic, far from the frenetic madness of the city and the machinations of a stressful job. She thought of Frank, holed up in the British winter. She was worried about him. As her world expanded his had shrunk to the confines of a few small rooms. She had the feeling he was close to giving up on life, rattling about in that old, empty house with just the TV for company. He didn't talk much about his wife, but she knew he missed her. The house was full of photographs of them in happier, younger days. Fleeting moments preserved in rectangular frames, smiling memories caught in time.

She packed up her things and set off for home. The heat was stifling, and she took it easy. The gentle slopes she'd cycled down near the town were deceptive; the return journey was more taxing than she'd anticipated. She rounded a bend and slammed on the brakes, some animal, it was unrecognizable, had been smashed to a pulp. There were skid marks on the track, where the car had tried to avoid the collision. The stench of the warm blood made her gag. The vultures, hunched over the carcass, were seemingly oblivious of her presence; their beaks gorging on the road kill. Unable to move, she watched the brutality of life play out.

With the benefit of hindsight, she would have seen it as a sign of things to come but she moved on, unnerved by the experience, unaware what lay ahead for her, around the sharp bends of life.

Chapter 11

The book dropped to the floor, slipping through his fingers as he fell asleep in an armchair near the window. The sound of it hitting the tiles jolted him. He sprang to life and scanned the street for the hundredth time that day. A deep-rooted fear had set in. The reading matter hadn't helped. Greg had found *Brighton Rock* by Graham Greene at the back of a cupboard and had begun to read it in the early hours of the morning to relieve the boredom. The parallels with his own situation were not lost on him. Just as *Pinkie* felt like a big player, so did he but they were both small frys, caught in a net of their own making, both delusional. He cursed himself forever getting involved in the sordid business, but the lure of easy money had reeled him in. The more he got the more he wanted, any moral scruples were forgotten when the cash rolled in. There was some serious money to be made, enough to set himself up for life, if he was careful, if the plan was watertight. Now cabin fever had set in. Three days staring at the blank walls and the non-descript furniture, endless hours of tedium played on the mind. He made himself a black coffee. The milk had run out, and provisions were getting low. Half a bag of pasta and that was it. The sink was full of dirty dishes he had no desire to wash.

Outside, at the end of the street, sat in the cab of a white Toyota Hilux, Malherbe yawned and took a sip of his coffee. He picked up his binoculars and scanned the windows of the flats. He briefly lingered on a girl undressing, smiled to himself and panned across to Joseph's flat. There he was again, looking up and down the street like a frightened pensioner. The nerves had set in. Malherbe had seen it all before. It wouldn't be long before the claustrophobia took hold and he made a run for it, probably under the cover of darkness. He rang Radebe.

"Hey baas, Joseph's stir crazy, he's gonna crack."

Radebe interlocked his fingers and squeezed his hands.

"You watch him, if he makes a move follow him."

"What then baas?" Malherbe knew the answer before Radebe replied.

"Get him somewhere quiet and kill the bastard."

Malherbe sighed. There was a gun, a machete and rope in the boot, tools of the trade. He would take great delight in disposing of Mr Joseph. The thrill of the kill never left him. It was better than sex; adrenaline pumping the veins, a pulse at the temple. Orgasmic.

***

Greg watched the sunset; the street had finally quietened down. He'd lost count of the number of cyclists who'd whizzed past during the day dressed like Chris Froome, all latex and granite thighs. The runners were just as bad, with their heart monitors and water bottles wobbling in their hands. The whole town seemed to be sponsored by exercise. Sitting here like a terminally ill patient waiting to die, how much longer could he stare at the door, wait for the footsteps nearing it? Nobody had been loitering in the streets looking up at his flat. Maybe he had gotten away with it. He couldn't stay here any longer. He would go insane. The bag was packed, late into the night he would slip down the corridor, drop down the back-fire stairs and drive away a free man. Maybe head up the west coast, over the Orange River into Namibia. An image of the wide-open roads through the Namib Desert brought a smile to his tired face.

Chapter 12

Tom wondered how the heap of metal managed to stay airborne for so long. He wasn't a man of science and had never understood the mechanics of flying. A short trip to watch a rugby match in Dublin or Edinburgh was fine. By the time you mounted the steps and wandered to your seat you barely had time to sit down before disembarking. He usually had some drink on board to ease the tension and the camaraderie of his friends to rely on. A long-haul flight was a different proposition. Twelve hours in a tin pipe sat next to a stranger with a lisp and expanding waistline was not his idea of fun. The fact that his neighbour fell asleep as soon as he clunked his seat belt and snored like a contented hippo added to his discomfort. After a few hours he wanted to get off, open the door and step out onto a cloud. There was turbulence around the Equator, the plane lurched and leapt as if steered by a drunken reveller. Tom thought of Alliot Verdon Roe, the first man to fly an all-British plane back in 1909. He'd briefly left the ground on the Walthamstow marshes. The man's handlebar moustache was stronger than the wings, stacked like wafers and paper thin. The propeller, two canoe paddles tied with string. Or that's what it looked like in the old photo, the railway arches in the background.

The trolleys bisected the seats, aiming for the errant elbows and stray toes, the uniforms dispensing wine and gin and tonics to all and sundry. Tom resisted the urge and opted for an apple juice, unleaded cider as he referred to it. He couldn't sleep or get comfortable and began to question his decision to make the journey. It was a bloody long way to go for an interior monologue. He stood up and joined the queue of tracksuits at the toilets, silent faces in need of a sleep. He hated being locked up with a bunch of strangers and was glad of the privacy of the small room. The mirror never lied; his features were pale and drawn, hair flecked with the hint of grey. The decades seemed to be speeding up, but old hazel eyes were still there. Misplaced vanity led him to believe he could still turn a woman's head. Or he liked to think so, not that he had had any takers lately. Shaky hands and drinker's stubble weren't exactly alluring. He needed time to sort himself out before anyone from the opposite sex would find him attractive. Falling in love with himself again was the first step. Understanding what was behind that face in the mirror would help. Someone knocked the door, he had been in there ages. He pressed the flush, it sounded powerful enough to suck out your entrails.

The screens flickered in the darkness, heads tilted, mouths agape, inviting the germs to sail in on a sea of stale air. He slid into his seat, plugged in his iPod and dialled up *Freddie Freeloader* by Miles Davis because he was feeling kind of blue and fell asleep to the swish of the cymbals, the honk of the horn.

***

Passport stamped, sitting in the hired car, Tom activated the satnav and typed in Prince Albert. The intense heat had been a shock to the system, after the fridge that was London. The sky seemed bigger, a cloudless blue, stretching into the distance. The sun was on steroids, flexing its muscles. He felt overdressed in his jeans and quickly jumped in the back seat, changing into shorts and t shirt. He joined the N2 with a vague sense of unease. Stories of carjacking and crime statistics filled the column inches of the British press and, much as he tried to ignore them, they were still at the back of his mind. He weaved the lanes nervously, getting his bearings and passed the vast expanse of Khayelitsha, the sun reflecting off the mass of tin roofs. The wide green verge was a whole new world. A group of men pushed a trolley full of firewood towards the ramshackle buildings. A lipstick of prostitutes lurked by the roadside, one squatted, lifted her short skirt and urinated. A couple of cows chewed the grass lazily. The police cars sat pointing towards the township waiting for the walls to break. Most striking was the sheer volume of people walking roadside. Their faces blurred into one disgruntled pedestrian. A group of bare footed children kicked a football towards a tin can goal.

The diversity in traffic was an eye opener. There were sleek white Mercedes with hot leather seats and beat up wrecks belching smoke, combi taxis bursting with people and 4 x4's with lone blondes at the wheel, heading to the shopping mall. Tom eventually mastered the yellow line system where you eased over to let the speedsters fly by. He was overtaken by a man with a gleeful smile minus a steering wheel, just a monkey wrench to dodge the lanes with. It seemed to be a land of contrasts; the haves and have nots uneasily co-existing.

He drove through Stellenbosch – it reeked of money – and headed towards Paarl. The hillsides were scattered with wine farms, the lines of vines attached to the earth like hair on a scalp. The prospect of a cool Chardonnay underneath a sunshade had him drooling but one glass wouldn't be enough. He'd want a barrel full.

When he joined the N1 the traffic thinned, he drove through beautiful valleys and began to relax. He stopped at an Engen service station and ordered a salad and an Americano with hot milk on the side. His new signature drink, he thought ruefully. Two empty months lay ahead of him. Two months to unlock himself, something no counsellor had ever been able to do. They had burned a few layers but whenever they got close, he clammed up. He was fine when talking about his family, in fact he waxed lyrical but when the spotlight fell on him, he disappeared into the shadows and cancelled subsequent appointments. He was an expert at hiding from himself. Sat there, coffee in hand, he knew deep in his heart, the root of the problem. He'd thought about it every single day of his life since it had happened but never uttered a word about it to another single soul in all these years. It was like a cancerous growth slowly devouring him from the inside out. He winced, the mere thought of it made him sweat from every pore. The face, the blood, it came flooding back.

Back in the car he calmed down. A couple of weeks rest and recuperation were what the doctor ordered; some gentle observational poetry writing would dampen the nerves. It was early afternoon by the time he turned right onto Prince Albert road and drove the last few kilometres into town, the Swartberg Mountains looming in the distance. He turned into Mark Straat and located the property he had rented. The owner was already there, waiting for him, keys in hand and a welcoming smile to boot. She had seemed impressed when he said he was a writer. It was a wise decision not to introduce himself as an alcoholic with mental health issues. She left in a trail of dust, wishing him a pleasant stay. Tom unpacked and helped himself to a complimentary Rooibos tea and a rusk. He stretched out on the bed, grateful for the air conditioning's gentle whirr. A quick nap and then he would explore the town. The cinema had been even more impressive than in the photograph, not in keeping with its laid-back surroundings and built on a rich man's whim no doubt. He had seen the notice of the upcoming Hitchcock season. If *North by Northwest* was on, he would definitely go. It was one of his favourite films. He had once called himself Gary Crant when he was drunk, much to the amusement of his friends. The coffee shop on the corner looked inviting too; he needed a base now that propping up the bar wasn't the order of the day.

Chapter 13

Radebe had a heart of mould, incapable of any sympathy, especially for anyone who broke the silent code of honour. Born on the wrong side of the tracks, he had dragged himself up from the gutter and escaped poverty through a life of crime; profited from the misfortune of others. Before the age of ten he was a drug runner, or, strictly speaking, a drug cyclist delivering packages through the suburbs of Cape Town after the sun went down, his trainers twinkling in a twilight world. His reliability brought promotion. By the age of fifteen he was pushing six foot and a fine physical specimen. He became an enforcer, armed with a knife and a gun. He carried out the orders of the gang boss with ruthless efficiency, got the nickname of "no sweat" because of the chilling calmness with which he dispensed with undesirables.

Radebe lost his father when he was three, mown down in a hit and run in Khayelitsha. Mum was hooked on drugs, an absentee parent. He had nothing better to do than trail the street gangs in his beaten-up shoes, watching them laugh when they counted their money, deep within the shacks. Would he have turned out ok with the right guidance, with a positive role model to aspire to? Nobody could answer that question, least of all himself, sat in his tailored suit overlooking Cape Town harbour from his penthouse window, Robben Island in the distance. His 'long walk to freedom' had left many casualties in his wake. He wanted the white man's money; retribution. He saw the disparity of wealth through his sunken eyes every day of his fucking life. The private schools, the swimming pools, the manicured lawns with their sprinklers and garden boys sat uneasily in his mind, in stark contrast to the seething mass of the township with its faded tin walls and flickering street lights, sewage in the gutter, stray dogs fighting over scraps.

Radebe turned the gold ring on his finger. It was a habit he had developed whenever there was a pressing problem. He was so close to being the main man. There was only Gleason in Joburg above him. He pulled the biggest strings but if he trod carefully, played his cards right, it could be him at the top, master of his own universe. But nobody trusted anybody; it was a murky world where you had to have eyes in the back of your head because someone somewhere was watching. You couldn't afford to make any mistakes.

The problem was that bloody idiot Joseph. In retrospect he should never have got him involved but now it was too late. He had met him a few years back on the campus of UCT when he was delivering drugs there on a regular basis. They had struck up a small friendship that led to Joseph taking the consignment of drugs off him and distributing them to the students, collecting the money for him into the bargain. This arrangement freed him up to increase his drops in the surrounding suburbs and lessen his presence around the University. Joseph had tried to tell him about his post graduate studies, but he had feigned interest and made small talk until the cash was safely tucked away. They had lost touch when he moved higher up the pay scale and would never have met again if it wasn't for the freakish nature of fate.

A few months back Radebe had been in Joburg negotiating a drug deal with Gleason. The swanky hotel suite was full of his armed bodyguards, the atmosphere tense. They didn't like each other: the black guy from the streets, the white guy from a privileged background, all marble floors and chandeliers. But business was business, an unholy alliance, and if the cash flowed in they could just about tolerate each other. Gleason recognized the stain of ambition etched across his face, saw the confident way he carried himself. Radebe was someone to be wary of. He would have him watched.

On the table was a sample of the produce – Nyaope. A whitish powder, a mixture of low-grade heroin and rat poison or sometimes even crushed up medicine for people with HIV, if you sprinkled it on marijuana it was highly addictive, a life wrecking cocktail. At twenty-five rand a hit the streets were full of zombies stumbling through the traffic. Radebe wanted to take it to the Flats where Tik was still the prevalent drug. Gleason was worried about storing the stuff. The police in Joburg were snooping around everywhere, checking out warehouses on industrial estates. The press reaction to the effects of the drug on a certain stratum of society made it a hot political potato. They had to be seen to be doing something to remedy the situation. Radebe said he would find some quiet backwater en route from Joburg to Cape Town where they could hold the drugs for delivery. They talked money and shook on the deal, eying each other up like two boxers at the pre-fight weigh in. At the moment they needed each other but as for the future, who knows what it would bring?

Radebe left the building with a sense of relief. He slowly exhaled and lit a cigarette. He hadn't liked the way Gleason's minders had been eying him, it was as if they were measuring him for a coffin. Playing with the big boys brought a new level of danger, he would have to be careful. The higher up you went the harder it became. Back at his hotel in a different suburb he began to relax and poured himself a whisky from the mini-bar. He raised his glass and smiled, this deal would elevate him into the big league, the money would come rolling in, riches beyond his childhood dreams. He reached for his laptop and inserted his memory stick. Radebe didn't keep a diary or any details of his dealings on paper but everything was on that stick: contacts, some high up in the government or the police, some low-level dealers and a comprehensive catalogue of his transactions. You had to run a tight ship with the volume of money coming in and going out of his numerous accounts. He was always careful to erase everything from the hard drive of the computer. He kept the stick on a gold chain beneath his shirt.

***

The nature of impulse is hard to define. Who knows what made Radebe turn off the N1 onto Prince Albert Road? Sure, he needed a coffee and some lunch but there were plenty of other towns he could have stopped at. He parked his white Mercedes convertible on the main street outside Celestino's Coffee shop and took a seat on the veranda. He ordered a tuna panini with melted cheese and an espresso and thought of some of the deserted barns he had seen on the drive into the sleepy town. Ideal for storing the drugs, nobody would think of snooping around the middle of nowhere. Needing the toilet, he walked inside to settle the bill and there, behind the counter, was bloody Joseph. They instantly recognized each other and for a brief moment, they just stared, waiting for the other to initiate conversation.

"Well if it isn't Mr No Sweat Radebe of Cape Town. Gone up in the world I see."

Greg noticed the immaculately tailored suit and the gold ring, glinting in the sunlight. The youth on the bike was a thing of the past.

"What brings you to this neck of the woods?"

Radebe smiled, "I could ask the same question of you, Joseph. Last time I saw you was when you were helping out with my business dealings on campus." They laughed. As they reminisced, the germ of an idea formed in Radebe's mind. He wondered if Joseph was still malleable, still into drugs. It was worth a try.

"Is there somewhere quiet we can talk? I have a business proposition for you."

"Oh yeah?"

"You could make some serious money for doing very little, you interested?"

A small bird flew in the room, saw the sun through the window and clattered into the glass. They watched as it wobbled on the floor, disorientated. Charles picked it up and dropped it in the back yard. It staggered around in a daze.

"Come upstairs, I'm all ears," said Joseph.

"Charles, look after the shop for a few minutes, will you? I'm just going for a chat with an old friend."

They sat in the empty spare room and Joseph listened. Radebe was preaching to the converted. Greg had lost his moral compass years ago. A series of failed business ventures had left him virtually penniless. The coffee shop was barely ticking over, and this wasn't the UK where the benefit system provided a safety net. This was Sparta, only the fittest survived. The country was full of old men who had fallen on hard times searching for solace in the arms of rich widows. He just saw the dollar signs, if people were dull enough to blow their brains out on drugs that was their problem. The proposition was simple, all he had to do was store the drugs in transit, away from prying eyes. He owned an empty property on one of the back roads that fitted the bill nicely. He had spent his last savings buying it in the hope of renting it out, but the money had dried up and he hadn't been able to renovate it. It was set back from the road with no other buildings in its immediate vicinity, just the emptiness of the Karoo for company. They shook on the deal, both seeing no further than the financial benefits, each unaware that it would define their lives.

***

It was six hours later that Radebe realized that he had lost the memory stick. He was stripping off for a shower back in his penthouse apartment in Cape Town when he clasped the gold chain. A frantic search of the flat and the car proved fruitless. The thought of it falling into the wrong hands sent chills down his spine. Shit, it was 1,400 km from Johannesburg to Cape Town, he could have dropped it anywhere; by the side of the road where he had stopped a few times for some fresh air, at a service station, in Prince Albert or even in the hotel in Joburg. The chances of finding it were less than minimal.

***

Greg sipped his Klippies and coke, clinking the ice in the glass. He'd found the memory stick down the side of a cushion on the wicker chair when he was searching for his lighter. He plugged it into his laptop and, oh my Lord, he could not believe what he read. For the first time in a while, a broad smile spread across his face. This could be a passport to the Promised Land.

Chapter 14

In the feint world between dreams and reality, the seconds before wakefulness, Tom felt the bark of the tree beneath his hand. He heard the shout from up ahead, telling him to run. His feet crunched the ice below, his breath quickened. The sound of the playground had all but gone. There was just the two of them, making their way through the forest.

***

He wiped the sweat from his face and blanked it out, made himself a coffee and opened the shutters, the sunlight nearly blinding him. His feet felt cold on the tiled floor as he plugged his iPod into the hi-fi system. Music was his lifeblood. It took him to more pleasant pastures. He could chart events from his past by remembering the songs he was listening to at the time. A CD diary, formerly a beer stained vinyl one. Every gatefold sleeve told a story. He scrolled through the list and selected the Allman Brothers and sung along to *Ramblin man* in the shower, guitar riffs and all.

Sat on the veranda, he sketched out the next few days. The first thing was to rest and relax. There was plenty of time for soul searching over the coming weeks. He needed to get a feel for the place and have a look around the town, eat and sleep well, maybe write some poetry about what he saw rather than what he felt inside. As he was locking up a black guy in a Rasta hat opened the gate and shuffled towards him. He viewed him uneasily, but he was just trying to scrape a living and offered to wash the car. He didn't seem to want to take no thanks for an answer and said he would come back tomorrow. Tom was struck by the desperation in his tone as he watched the man weave his way up the street. This was a strange new world. The disparity in wealth and aspiration far more pronounced than back home, though you could see it there but it was more subtle. The glut of fast food outlets and betting shops on suburban streets told their own story but it was a sub text to life not front-page news.

Tom walked to the bottom of town and worked his way up. The OK supermarket was fairly well stocked, if overly full of meat and he would head back there later to pick up some essentials. Nearby was the North End township, he could hear the sound of laughter and African beats pumping out of a sound system. Every town, no matter its size, seemed to have a township attached to it, like a barnacle on a luxury yacht. He had noticed this on the long drive from Cape Town. As an outsider it was hard to comprehend.

He paused outside Prince Albert Correctional Centre and read the sign on the wall- "A place of new beginnings". He watched an inmate in a boiler suit sweep the floor, inches away from freedom, eyes dulled. Framed by a concrete arch, he was lost in his own world. The image stuck with him, gave him the seeds of an idea for a poem.

Most of the restaurants had alliterative names: Simply Saffron, The Lazy Lizard, Karoo Kombuis and Tom amused himself by thinking up some imaginary eateries- the Slurpy Spaghetti or the Pretentious Pasta. There was a smart gallery, showcasing a varied selection of South

African art. He was particularly taken by a set of photographs charting the development of a local black rugby team. The wonky posts in the background took him back to his childhood days. The town was obviously set up to snare the passing tourists. Off the main road the streets were mainly residential. He was struck by the wide variety of houses; some were old, Dutch gabled properties, others brick faced with thatched roofs. A far cry from the military style, uniformed terraced streets back home. The greenness of the gardens, irrigated by water channels, provided a counterpoint to the semi-arid expanse surrounding the town with its faded colours and dusty demeanour. He had read that the Khoikhoi people of South Africa had called the area the Karoo, or "land of thirst". It made sense. The warmth of the sun and the wide angled- blueness of the sky lightened his mood. The place had an airiness about it that was lacking in the humdrum of a city. There was room to move, room to think.

***

Tom sat on the veranda of Celestino's coffee shop and perused the menu. He ordered an Americano with hot milk on the side and a tomato and pesto panini. The place was empty and he watched the cars and lorries going by, interspersed by the odd tractor. It seemed surreal that twenty-four hours ago he was thousands of miles away staring at the four walls of his flat, the weight of the world on his shoulders. Now, sat in a different hemisphere, he had the opportunity to look at things objectively and piece his life together again. It would be painful, but this was the point of no return. He had to muster the strength to tackle his issues head on otherwise the future was bleak. The graveyards were full of drunks who couldn't stop drinking. He had seen their faces in countless pubs, their cheeks bloated bladders of discontent. He'd seen them wrestling with their own sorry back stories. Tom thought of his mum, she had won the battle of the booze but lost the longest war, that of a childhood scarred. He knew the root of his problem lay in his own childhood, that fateful blue-sky winter day when his life changed forever and nobody else knew anything about it. He had borne its burden all these years. The familiar chilled tingle licked his back.

***

Carla wiped the cup and watched the man on the stoep. He was quite good looking but a tad on the thin side. He needed a square meal and a bit of colour in his cheeks. She tried reading him but it wasn't easy as there was no reference point, he was on his own. Couples were simple, you could watch them interact, learn something from their facial expressions or body language. He had an air of vulnerability about him, but she sensed a certain charm. She smiled to herself. He had the look of a second-hand book, frayed around the edges but maybe a surprise inside. It had been a quiet day and he was the only customer. She had plenty of time for idle speculation.

He got up to pay the bill, fumbling in his pocket for his wallet, failing to notice the step. Losing his balance, he grabbed the table cloth as he fell. The cutlery came crashing down. He lay there like an upturned tortoise, embarrassed. He saw the smirk on her face as she came to help him. She tried to contain her laughter as he dusted himself down.

"You're supposed to walk to the counter not swim to it", she smiled as she said it. "You ok?"

"Yeh, I'll live, it's more my pride that hurts."

"Hi, I'm Carla, listen, I'll give you a coffee on the house, take a seat if you think you can stay in it." She smiled as she said it.

"Hello, I'm Tom." He gently eased himself onto the chair, rubbing his shin.

He looked at her for the first time. She had the most beautiful green eyes, deep as the sea. She brought the coffee and sat next to him.

"Well Tom, you here for the weekend?"

"No, I'm here for a couple of months actually, arrived yesterday, I'm renting a place." She was surprised.

"Got some work here?" He sipped the coffee, hesitated before replying.

"No, I'm taking some time out to relax, get some sun."

She looked at him thoughtfully, probably some mid-life crisis, on the run from something. Tom stood up; he wasn't in the mood to answer any more questions.

"Aren't you going to finish your coffee?"

"I'd better be going, gotta pick up some food for tonight, thanks for the free sip though."

"Pleasure."

"If I pop in tomorrow, I'll bring my snorkel."

"You do that, nice to meet you." She watched him walk down the main street, towards the Swartberg Arms, his frame slowly shrinking.

Prince Albert Correctional Centre

"A place of new beginnings"
But every new beginning
Is stalked by a sad, old end.
You stand in your Guantanamo orange
Boiler suit, gulping in the freedom
Through the archway,
Waiting to be corrected.
Not as simple as moving a misplaced comma
Or an errant full stop.
You carry a rucksack of rape
And regret.
A spillage of blood, money or the heart.
A timetable of tedium
Engulfs you.
Outside the incorrect world
Sweeps the streets.

Chapter 15

Joseph had signed his own death warrant the day he had resorted to blackmail, or strictly speaking, black email. Gone were the days of carefully cut out newspaper letters glued together in a threatening collage, posted by gloved hands. Now it was a faceless tinkle on a key pad and a click on the send button. The end result was the same though. Someone shit themselves and someone rubbed their hands with glee. There is nothing like anonymity to instil confidence in the perpetrator, nothing like fear of the unknown to torture the victim. A game of winners and losers played across the centuries. Joseph took on the role of internet troll, but not to harass a minor celebrity. He wanted serious money otherwise the Cape Argus would be celebrating the year's most sensational scoop; the unveiling of a budding drug baron and his clients in high places. The ramifications would spread far and wide, shattering lives and keeping the Police busy for months to come.

***

The blood drained from Radebe's face. It can take a long time to grow a tree but seconds for the fruit to fall. He paced the room, screamed and kicked a floor cushion, it sailed over the sofa, toppling the ornaments on the coffee table, scattering the pieces in all directions. Fingers tightening on the gold ring, he sat down and tried to compose himself. Nothing could be gained from mindless anger. He had to think outside the box. He re-read the email.

YOU HAVE UNTIL 12 NOON TO DEPOSIT 10 MILLION RAND INTO MY OFF-SHORE BANK ACCOUNT 637891239 CODE 34 65 18 OR I WILL GO TO THE PRESS WITH YOUR INFORMATIVE USB STICK. NO SWEAT WITHOUT TEARS!

Radebe knew, even with his contacts, that he wouldn't be able to trace the bank account. Off shore clients were assured of water tight security, that's what they paid for. He looked for any tell-tale giveaways in the text, not expecting to find any. The majority of it was factual apart from the last line-

NO SWEAT WITHOUT TEARS!

A throw away remark or was there more to it? No sweat was his Cape Flats nickname but most of those brothers were dead now. Nobody in his current circle ever referred to him as that yet there was something nagging at the back of his mind. He poured himself a brandy and coke and sat looking out at the ocean. The sea was calm and the moon cast a silvery path towards the horizon. A bird skimmed the water pursued by its shadow. As he watched it disappear it came to him, Joseph, bloody Joseph. He'd called him "No sweat" in Prince Albert when recollecting their earlier dealings at UCT. The bumbling amateur must have found his stick in Prince Albert and rushed into this stupid blackmailing scam.

Radebe leapt to his feet, gave Malherbe a call, time to inflict the kiss of death and retrieve the stick in the process, hoping that Joseph was too dull to have copied it. That was a risk he would have to take.

Chapter 16

The corridor was empty. Greg slipped out of the door and made his way to the fire exit, the smell of marijuana filled his nostrils. The sound of the students partying behind closed doors took him back to happier days. He passed each alcove in a nervous shuffle, scared someone would jump out of the shadows but he was alone, under the dim lights, slowly edging his way to freedom. He pressed the metal bar and gulped in the air, scanning the car park, everything seemed quiet.

Johnson watched him standing at the top of the fire stairs. The fool, thinking he could just walk out of here as if nothing had happened. There was a price to pay if you crossed Mr Radebe. He called Malherbe, told him to make his way to the back of the building. This would be easy; the car park was deserted, and they could bundle him into a car and be away in less than a minute. Johnson was tired of playing the waiting game, living out of the car and grabbing a sandwich here and there. He needed a shower and a good night's sleep. Let Malherbe do his work and he could head home. He grimaced, the problem now wasn't Joseph it was his colleague. He liked to prolong the pain.

Joseph made a run for it, car keys in hand and found the lock first time. He smiled as he swung open the door. Malherbe smacked the back of his head with a metal pipe. Johnson caught him as he fell and threw him in the back of the car; text book. Malherbe started the engine and drove off. Johnson stayed in the back seat and trussed up Joseph like a turkey, duct tape covering his mouth. Neither of them spoke until they reached the outskirts of town and took the road to Jonkershoek nature reserve.

Malherbe called Radebe, "we got the little shit boss, just going to dispose of him somewhere quiet."

"Good, cover your tracks and go through his clothes, he's got something of mine."

"What we looking for boss?"

"A red memory stick."

"A USB stick?" said Malherbe, exchanging glances with Johnson.

"Yup, call me if you find it, if not check out his student pad when you've finished with him, see if it's there."

They arrived at the empty car park near the gate for the reserve. The café was boarded up for the night.

"Wake the tosser up" said Malherbe. Johnson opened his bottled water and threw it in Joseph's face. His eyes opened and he tried to say something.

"Shut up arsehole, get out." said Malherbe.

They manhandled him and threw him over the gate, climbing over it themselves. A few kicks up the backside kept him stumbling on with only the thin beam of their torch to guide him. He cursed his own greed and stupidity and began to sob uncontrollably.

"Stop your fucking squealing," screamed Malherbe, "keep walking."

They reached the far end of the loop and stopped on the bridge. The soft clink of the water below was the only sound that punctuated the night.

"Free his arms Johnson it's time for some justice, an eye for an eye and all that, get him to lie down on the floor, hold his arm over the edge."

"Why don't we just shoot him and be done with it?" said Johnson.

"Where's the fun in that? You know me better than that."

Malherbe put down his bag.

"Let's warm him up first." He emptied a small container of liquid onto Joseph's hair. The pungent smell of petrol made him cough. He clicked his zippo lighter and laughed at the screams.

"Put him out and hold his arm, let's hear him scream." His voice was devoid of emotion. Johnson looked at him and wondered to what depths this man could sink. He was no saint himself but to see the pleasure Malherbe derived from inflicting pain sickened him.

"Please, just kill me; leave Carla alone, she's nothing to do with this." Joseph's mind was confused. The pain was unbearable.

"Who the fuck is Carla?" they said in unison.

The bag was open again; Johnson saw the glint of the machete blade caught in the beam of the torch. Malherbe cleaved the hand with one violent blow.

"You won't steal anything now will you, you fokker?"

Joseph screamed and fainted.

"For Christ sake Malherbe that's enough." Johnson pulled out his gun and shot Joseph between the eyes from point blank range; put the poor bastard out of his misery.

"Shit, you fucking idiot, we never asked him about the stick." Malherbe walked away, muttering under his breath; deflated game over. Johnson checked Joseph's clothing, keeping half an eye on his colleague in case he went berserk but apart from two sets of keys and a wallet there was nothing else of note. No memory stick. Now they would have to rummage round the student flat in the hope of finding it. It must be important. Sometimes life sucked. They dragged his body into the undergrowth and left him at the mercy of the local wildlife and peeled off their rubber gloves, dumping them in the bag.

They walked back to the car in silence. Back in town Malherbe stayed in the car, sulking, while Johnson turned the flat upside down. No stick to be found. He slumped on the bed, this killing game had worn him down. He had to find a way to walk out of this life and finally rid himself of that maniac Malherbe.

Back in the car Malherbe lit a joint, the adrenaline had dissipated, and he needed another buzz. Mr High and Mighty Johnson had spoiled his fun. He wouldn't forget that in a hurry. Johnson rung him to say he'd drawn a blank in the flat so he rang Radebe.

"Listen boss, Joseph is taken care of but there was no stick on his body and it's not in the flat. He did mumble something about a woman called Carla though, does it ring any bells with you?"

Radebe stroked his chin and rotated the gold ring on his finger, Carla, maybe she was a girlfriend in Prince Albert?

"No, its news to me, get rid of the car, I'll call you later, I may have another job for you, usual rate."

Malherbe dialled another number.

"Mr Gleason, it's Malherbe, I just killed a low life called Joseph for Radebe and I thought you might be interested in something I found out."

"This better be good."

"It seems Joseph stole a memory stick from Radebe and whatever is on it is hot shit. He's wound up big time. Joseph mentioned a woman called Carla just before he died, shall I check it out?"

Gleason smiled; his intuition never let him down. He hadn't trusted Radebe from the day he met him and now, maybe, he had the chance to bury him.

"You act normal and follow Radebe's instructions, keep me up to date with any developments."

***

Johnson and Malherbe drove the car to an industrial estate where they had parked up earlier.

"If you ever do that to me again, I'll fokken kill you, understand?"

Johnson stared out the window, said nothing. Any form of reply would set him off again. There was only so much shit you could take in one night. He checked his watch, 3am, half an hour and he'd be home. They parked up, doused the seats with petrol and set it alight. They could see the flames from the main road on their way back to Cape Town. Those township kids had a lot to answer for.

Chapter 17

Tom looked at the complimentary bottle of wine, sat on the work
surface like an unopened invitation. His hands were shaking and sweaty.
He rummaged through the cutlery drawer and found a corkscrew. It
was 8am but the urge to drink had consumed his every waking thought.
He removed the cork with an unsteady hand, poured a full glass and
held it up to the light. He swirled the contents and inhaled the heady
fumes, gripped the stem till his knuckles were white. Was he master or
puppet? The fucking battle scene lay before him; the wreckage that was
his life, the yes and no's vying for control. He was little more than a
hapless bystander. There was to be no cultured sip, he downed it in one,
refilled and did it again and again. The warmth, the familiar warmth,
flooded through him, shut down the pain. A line of red dribbled from
the corner of his mouth as if he'd punctured his lung. The phone rang
as he raised the glass to his lips. It made him jump and he dropped his
drink, knocking over the wine bottle in the process. The glass shattered
on impact, bled like a war wound. He stood there, legs spattered with
wine and screamed, cursed himself, the world, and every cunt in it. He
slid down the wall, slumped in the pool of wine and the tears came,
enough to fill a fucking wine cooler. It was a good hour later that he
jumped in the shower. The chilled needles of water jolted him. He
dressed and cleaned up the mess. The phone call had saved him from
himself but every day was a test of his resolve, whatever bloody

hemisphere he was in. He dialled up some blues on the iPod, something from *Clapton unplugged - Before you accuse me.*

***

Booze

Banjoed

Bollocksed

Blitzed

Blarney

Bluster

Bliss

Befuddled

Bedraggled

Bedevilled

Bloated

Bladder

Blunder

Barney

Blinkers

Banter

Blinded

Betwixt

Bar room

Brawls

Between

Bras

Bosoms

Buttocks

Bacon

Baked beans

Burgers

Belch

Black

Bin bags

Bathroom

Bleach

Broke

Bed

***

When he was a youngster, he viewed alcohol as a friend; a silent acquaintance with whom to conquer his shyness. Without drink he would have continued to cross the road to avoid girls he knew but, with the courage that beer gave him, he had entered the social whirl. Everyone in his circle drank as if there was no tomorrow, it was a cultural expectation. Nobody would risk being ostracised, it was social suicide. The mornings after were full of exaggerated tales of drunken debauchery which embedded him firmly in the group. He was one of the lads and the wild edginess of this life appealed to him, reeled him in. It began to define him as a character and he spent a lot of time and effort cultivating the image, but it was the hidden consequences of his actions that slowly dragged him down. The endless dark clouds of depression hung over him, the inner core of him was being eaten away but to the outside world he was a character, a player, life and soul of the party. He thought of himself as being a flash film set but when you opened one of the doors on the street there was nothing there, merely emptiness. He knew his outer mask of confidence concealed a deep-rooted insecurity. This morose sensibility seemed to echo down the generations of his family; the stench of a self-fulfilling prophecy. An image of his mum's gaunt body and dishevelled hair after weeks on the booze still haunted him. It always seemed to be the negative images that he was drawn to. He had returned, fresh faced from some rugby tour to view her in a darkened room. His dad had warned him that she was unwell, but nothing prepared him for the sight of her. It was only in the twilight of her life that she'd finally admitted what had gone on. The scars had never healed, as a child the curtains had been shut on her life, never to be reopened and the one man who brought a ray of light let her down.

Tom sat on the veranda, he knew that he lived too much of his life in the past, constantly looking back for excuses. It was time to man up and stop feeling sorry for himself. He needed some fresh air. He locked up the house and jumped in the car. Every morning he had looked up at the Swartberg pass, presiding over Prince Albert like some powerful overlord. Now seemed as good a time as any to drive to the top and take in the spectacular views. He drove up the main street, waved at Carla as she served some folks on the stoep at Celestino's and weaved his way out of town. He took a right, crossed a bridge and entered a steep- sided valley, walls close as two huge hands about to clap. The valley suddenly opened as the gradient increased, the sun glinting on the green flecked rock face. Near the top the road clung to the rocks in a series of switchback bends. At the summit Tom parked up and stood at the edge surveying the view in all its magnificence: barren, desolate, but imbued with an unearthly spirituality. It took his breath away. It was like he was the sole inhabitant of an undiscovered planet, free from the constraints of society, free from his straitjacket. He peered downwards and wondered if anybody had jumped, bones snapping like twigs on the rocks below. Once, in the fug of a drunken depression, he had wandered the streets of Walthamstow in the middle of the night and climbed a bridge over the North Circular and imagined jumping. He was too much of a chicken to actually do it but the very thought of it had set off the alarm bells.

Back in the car he thought how his mood mirrored the troughs and peaks of the hills and he was struck with the insignificance of man compared to the power of nature. The rocks would still be there when the moss was growing on his gravestone. He plugged in the iPod and deliberated between *American Interior* by Gruff Rhys or *New Frontier* by Donald Fagen, opting for the former. It seemed like the right sonic template for the terrain.

Tom weaved his way back to town, crossing the dry river beds that lay between the cliffs. He hadn't passed another car on either of his journeys and Prince Albert felt like a metropolis when he parked outside Celestino's. He called in there most days, primarily as an excuse to talk to Carla. He'd been summoning up the courage to ask her out, but the prospect of a negative reaction had, so far, dissuaded him. Today is the day, he thought to himself as he tentatively mounted the steps (mindful of his earlier mishap). He ordered his usual Americano with hot milk on the side and exchanged pleasantries with Charles, disappointed that Carla was nowhere to be seen. Charles was a nice bloke and he'd grown to like him. He was from Zimbabwe and had moved to the gold pavements of Cape Town to better his life. The reality hadn't lived up to expectations. He'd been victimized in the township and distrusted as an outsider, supposedly depriving locals of their livelihoods. He left one night in fear of his life. Prince Albert offered quieter surroundings in which to gain a foothold.

Carla appeared twenty minutes later carrying some bags of local produce. Tom helped her take them to the kitchen. "How are you this fine day?" she said, pleased to see him.

"Good thanks." He was an accomplished liar: Lying, a drinker's best friend, apart from the bottle itself.

"Just been for a drive up the Swartberg Pass, amazing views."

"I'm going to cycle up there soon, I've been training for a few weeks, fancy coming with me?"

Tom saw her smile and wondered if she was joking; his only recent regular exercise was lifting a pint. He had a muscular left arm but the rest of him was spindly.

"Jeez, it's hell of a steep. I'd need to do some serious training and there's another problem."

"What?"

"No bike."

"I've got a spare one, come for a ride tomorrow and I'll put you through your paces, assess your fitness, unofficially of course."

"Mm, allright. No harm in a trial run I suppose. I have to warn you though, I don't own any Lycra, it'll be strictly shorts and t shirt."

"You can borrow some of mine", she said, the look on his face was priceless. There was no way he was stuffing his leek (mini-courgette) and broccoli into any stretchy material. They laughed.

Tom walked home thinking the best laid plans rarely materialize. He had intended asking Carla if she would go to the cinema with him but now he was booked in for a morning bike ride, best get some rest to avoid the embarrassment of puffing like a steam train and disappearing in a cloud of dust as she sped into the distance.

One Squeaky Shoe

One squeaky shoe
punctuates the night
as he ambles along the avenues.
Isolated in a world of closed curtains,
illuminated by the harsh street lights.
The cold concrete steps beckon.
Pause.
Freeze frame.
Out on the ledge.

An arc of madness,
A swallow's dive.
The headlights are shattered bones.
The tail lights are streams of blood.
Grid lock,
ambulance windows,
horns ignite.

Press play.

Chapter 18

Tom had the dream, the dream that had stalked him through the shadows all these years. Filmed in technicolour, the soundtrack amplified. The trees parted, the leaves crunched under their feet. A bird eyed them warily from the roof of the tree top canopy, wide angled lens monitoring their teenage footsteps. It was lunch time; just the two of them had climbed the fence and entered the woods. They ran and laughed, covering each other with pretend guns, popping out from behind trees, forward rolls through the leaf litter. Climbing the fence had become a ritual for class 4L, a collective great escape, taking a pleasure from flaunting the rules, living on the edge. But on this day most chose the concrete playground and a game of football with imaginary crossbars that caused heated debates. It was a cold winter's day; the ice hadn't yet melted as they moved onwards, the sound of children playing diminishing with every step. Within the next few minutes the fingers of fate would strangle them, and the world would forever be a different place.

Chapter 19

Tom put on his old pair of shorts and looked down at his thin legs, 'the devil on tooth picks', he thought. He crossed his feet and stretched his hamstrings. It reminded him of all those rugby warm ups, dad waiting pitch side, snug in his sheepskin coat, cigar smoke swirling higher than a drop kick. The last time he had regularly ridden a bike was as a kid in the seventies, he remembered the expression on the shopkeeper's face when they bought fifty ice poles to quench the thirst at the summit. 'Fatty' trailed behind them and they'd finished most of them by the time he found them, lying on the grass, laughing. They made that kid suffer, poor bastard; nothing as cruel as childhood.

***

The main road was quiet this early in the morning as he made his way to Celestino's. Carla was waiting on the steps, both bikes pointing towards the mountain. Tom glanced to the hills, "we're not going up there today are we?"

She laughed, "No, we'll just do the first few slopes, test out the heart and lungs". They adjusted the seat to his height and he paid full attention when she gave him tuition on the art of gear changing.

"The wheels are still round and a pedal is a pedal, I should be ok", he said but above all he didn't want to lose face, be left roadside, wheezing like a pensioner. They set off at a good pace and Tom got into a rhythm. They passed the last buildings and turned onto the dirt road, the mountain rising before them. He watched Carla's calves tighten with each stroke of the pedal and wondered at the vagaries of life, two people thrown together by chance, alone in the quietest of valleys. He realized he knew nothing about her and she knew even less about him. So far they had lived on a diet of small talk but there were questions to be asked and that time was drawing nearer. What he would say, how much was he prepared to reveal?

Carla glanced back; he was doing well, his face seemingly showing no pain. He was fitter than she expected, maybe his competitive instinct was driving him on. She turned a bend and the gradient increased. The hills were covered in a blanket of silence. Carla stopped at 'die tronk', the steepest part of the climb. Tom caught up and wiped the sweat from his brow.

"Jeez, that's blown away the cobwebs." He looked up and saw the switchback bends meandering towards the peak, high above.

"Bloody hell, we're not even half way up, it's a beast."

"I'm impressed, I didn't think you'd make it this far. Let's turn around, I've got some sandwiches and a drink we can have at the bottom of the valley."

"Sounds bloody good" said Tom, his breath slowly coming back.

"For every uphill there's a downhill." The breeze chilled the sweat as he screeched round the bends like a teenager.

They found a picnic table next to the dry river bed and leant the bikes on a tree.

"That was more fun than I expected. I was worried I'd be left trailing in your dust but I guess I'm in better shape than I thought."

"Exercise is a powerful drug" she said looking at him a bit too closely for his comfort.

"Didn't you exercise much back home?"

"I used to do a lot of sport, mainly team games, when I was younger but not so much lately, I should do more, I miss it."

She poured Rooibos tea from a flask and they ate ham sandwiches. The mustard wasn't to his liking, but he didn't say anything, though his lips tingled. A small bird, sat in the branches of a nearby tree, eyed the crumbs accumulating on the table. Tom watched a lizard slowly snaking through the stones that were scattered across the dry riverbed.

"So, what are you doing here?" The question broke the stillness and took him aback. He paused, weighing up how to respond. He felt the shutters sliding down. He was adept at 'peeling someone's onion' but averse to revealing anything about himself. Carla looked at him expectantly. He hesitated, not sure what to give away

"Let's just say I'm taking some time out."

"From what?"

"I just need to find myself, I know it sounds like some hippy shit but that's the way it is."

He felt better for offloading something honest for once, even if it was just a minor revelation from the cupboard full he owned. Carla didn't say anything; he could imagine her trailing through the possibilities – drugs, crime, and debt. Maybe she was thinking he was a foot soldier in the bad lads' army.

"I haven't done anything bad" he muttered bleakly. She turned and looked at him, he half expected a put down and a swift exit.

She smiled. "I had to escape too; with me it was to release myself from the mundanity of my life. We've got something in common then, both of us off grid, both of us navel gazers." She laughed

"Let's head back; I need to open up the Coffee shop in an hour or so." He was glad of the reprieve, there was only so much he was prepared to give away before bolting for cover.

They rode side by side until they reached the tar road and turned left, the church spire in the distance.

***

As they turned downhill to freewheel home, looking forward to a cooling shower and a change of clothes, two men emerged from the back door of the coffee shop, their feet crunching the grains of glass strewn on the floor. They reached the safety of their vehicle, parked in the empty side street and drove away. They hadn't found what they were looking for. The boss would be seriously pissed off.

Chapter 20

Jo Myburgh's legs were thinner than those of her dogs. It was 8.30 am in Jonkershoek, six legs whirring, heartbeats raised. On her arm a monitor collecting the data. She would pour over it later, assessing her fitness in readiness for the upcoming triathlon season. In the afternoon she would pound the lengths in her pool and follow it up with an early evening bike ride. Exercise was the drug that fuelled her, if she wasn't on the move, she was thinking about it. The poor dog was wheezing like an old hoover but she didn't notice. Her mind was fixed on Paarl two weeks hence and the thrill of the opening race of the season.

It was hot, but the sun hadn't yet crept above the mountains. The valley was in shadows, the silence engulfed them. At the apex of the loop she stopped as she always did and checked her time. The fastest yet, she smiled and sat on a rock next to the bridge. Bolt wandered into the shrubs, probably to lie down, she thought. She heard him bark, an eerie echo rattled around the hills. She half expected to see some form of wildlife scuttle past with the dog in pursuit, but he didn't appear and the barking intensified. Checking her watch, it was time to move on, she gave Bolt a loud call and saw the vegetation waving ten metres away. Impatient, she hollered again, time was marching on, the sweat on her body was beginning to chill and her muscles were tightening up. She saw his nose poking through the leaves; he had something in his mouth. Irritated, she bent down to remove it. Ever since Bolt was a pup he had a habit of picking up sticks and stones, presenting them for her to throw. "Drop" she called but, unusually, he wouldn't. She grabbed his mouth and felt something cold and limp. Finally, it fell to the floor. Jesus Christ it was a hand. She screamed, stepped back and ran faster than she had ever done or ever will in any triathlon. Bolt stared at her wide eyed as she disappeared around the bend. One last chew of a finger and he set off in pursuit. He caught her near the dam, but she didn't acknowledge his presence.

Chapter 21

Carla waved to Tom as they parted at the top of Mark Straat. He nearly crashed into a parked car as he returned her wave. The look on his face made her laugh. He intrigued her; all chirpy duck on the surface but feet probably thrashing wildly below the water line. She felt like she wanted to get to know him better, delve deeper. She cycled up the side alley and saw the back gate wide open but she distinctly remembered she'd locked it. The keys were in the pouch of her cycling shirt. Looking down the path, the back door was slightly ajar, shards of glass on the floor. The place wasn't alarmed. Greg had said the town was safe but clearly it wasn't. She stood there for what seemed an age, heart thumping through the flimsy cycle shirt, and considered her options. What if the intruders were still inside? The open gate and back door gave the impression that they had left but she couldn't walk in and take that chance. As luck would have it, the problem was solved almost instantaneously. A police car was crawling up the road on routine patrol. She walked towards it and flagged it down. An inordinately fat cop with an airbag of a belly wound the window down.

"What's the problem lady? he said in a backwoods drawl.

"I think the coffee shop has been burgled, the gate's been forced open and I can see broken glass by the back door."

He listened to her accent, looked her up and down and immediately dismissed her as an annoying foreigner. He'd seen her round town. The place was increasingly full of them with their bags of money and fancy ideas.

"You seen anybody lurking around?"

"No, I've just got back from a bike ride."

"Get in the back of the car; I'll go take a look."

He pulled his gun from the holster, fat fingers all but enveloping it, and disappeared through the gate. Carla sat in the back picturing the coffee shop as a bomb site, her possessions, limited as they were, tossed around her bedroom. An old couple walked by and looked at her disparagingly. They must have thought she was in custody. She waved at them, demonstrating a lack of handcuffs but they had clearly filed her away as a criminal.

The policeman, Smit was his name, returned within a couple of minutes, gun back in the holster and not a hair out of place. An out of control smirk riding rough shod over his face. There had indeed been a break in. He blamed it on the township kids seeking a cheap thrill. Nothing appeared to be missing and nobody was hurt, the till was untouched. He left Carla with the number of a locksmith and the job of cleaning the place up, so much for roadside manner, she thought. He couldn't get out of there quick enough.

***

She found it strange that downstairs was exactly as she left it but they had ransacked Greg's room, emptied the cupboards and the drawers of his desk, scattered his papers. A photograph frame smashed, triangles of glass protruding, plant pots tipped, the soil littering the floor boards, filling the cracks. She sat on her bed, running her fingers through her hair, a friend of hers had been burgled once and they'd crapped on the floor, emptied her knicker drawer and wanked on her underwear. She'd burned all her clothes and ended up moving. It was the violation of personal space and possessions that prayed on the mind. Your own house ceased to be yours, it was forever tainted. She tried to ring Greg but he didn't answer her calls. She sent him an email, but nothing came back.

Carla lay on the bed in her cycle gear, part of her felt like packing up and moving on. She hadn't signed up for this, didn't need the hassle but could she really walk away, let Greg down? Then the idiots win. If we run at the first sign of trouble, when will we ever stop? Still, there was no way she felt like opening the coffee shop that morning. She called Charles and Sheila, and gave them the day off, told them she was unwell. After a quick shower she packed an overnight bag. Rifling through a drawer for some underwear, she felt something small and hard in the back corner. It was a red USB stick, probably left behind by some previous guest. She popped it in a side pocket of her rucksack. Maybe she'd check it out later, there might be contact details on it and she could post it to the rightful owner.

With the coffee shop locked up and a rucksack on her back, Carla walked down the main street. She had no idea where she was going to stay for the night but definitely not above the coffee cups. She needed to work out what to do, perhaps it was time to hit the road and put this place behind her. The morning heat was slightly eased by a soft breeze drifting over the mountains. The landscape was parched; they'd not seen rain in weeks. She took a left up Bergsig Straat and climbed the gentle slope to the top of the Koppie. There she sat overlooking the town; a splash of green in a sea of beige dryness. The leaves on the

Eucalyptus trees lining Kerk Straat were swaying gently and the church spire shimmered in the sun like a religious rocket ready to take off. Somewhere along the line, Carla realized, she had fallen in love with the town and its quirky artiness. It would be a wrench to leave its gentle palm. Maybe the break in was just a bunch of kids messing about. Wherever there are people there is always crime, for every saint there is a sinner. She sat up there for half an hour, her mood lightening under the sun. It was gone twelve o clock when she hit the tar at Crosby Straat. She walked up Mark Straat thinking about which B&B she was going to stay in when she saw Tom sunning himself on his stoep, the smooth grooves of Steely Dan in the background. She opened the gate and walked up the path towards him.

"Come to wash my car?" He had a smile on his face as he said it.

"No, there's been some trouble at the shop."

He could tell by the expression on her face that she wasn't joking.

"Shit, what's happened?"

She pulled up a chair and told him the news.

Chapter 22

The odd couple were reunited. Mr Psychosis and the reluctant criminal sat in unamiable silence on the stoep of the Swartberg Arms drinking ice cold Windoek lager. Their fragile relationship had taken an irreparable turn for the worse since the incident at Jonkershoek. The life of Greg Joseph had been terminated but not in the way the chief executioner wanted. Malherbe was not one for hiding his feelings and Johnson could feel the hatred lurking behind the sunglasses. The drive from Cape Town had been tense. They couldn't even agree on the choice of CD. Malherbe liked Afrikaans music; Johnson preferred the mainstream appeal of a Coldplay or Bon Jovi. Bok Van Blerk was the victor; Johnson tried his best to block it out. The journey had seemed interminably long. The brief intermissions of dialogue were, at best perfunctory. It was what was left unsaid that hung over them like oppressive cloud cover. There wasn't much life left in this unholy alliance, both of them instinctively knew that. Both had thought of exit strategies, one rather more violent than the other.

A small black kid in dirty shorts was hanging around the steps on the cusp of begging. A Jack Russell barked at him angrily and he sloped off back towards the township. The stoep was nearly full. The tourists were tucking in to 300g rump steaks or Calamari combos. Wine was flowing as freely as the anecdotes and the sound of laughter echoed down the road.

Malherbe and Johnson sat apart from the revellers and reviewed their morning. It hadn't gone well. They had followed Radebe's instructions and broken into the coffee shop in search of the infamous red USB stick. They'd seen a woman, must be Carla, lock up and head off on a bike with some dude. It didn't take her long to move on from Mr Joseph they thought wryly. When the coast was clear, it had taken them less than two minutes to get in through the back gate and door. Upstairs in Greg's bedroom, they'd turned the place over, looked in every nook and cranny but found zilch. Malherbe wanted to rummage through what appeared to be the girl's room, a pink bra was hanging from a handle on a cupboard, but they thought they heard noises coming from the front of the property so they left swiftly, to be on the safe side. These small towns were full of nosey okes. They had plenty of time to come back, prolonging the trip meant more pay after all.

Radebe hadn't taken the news well. Malherbe had never heard him sound so fucking agitated.

"You bloody stay there bru, turn the place over again and keep an eye on this Carla chick, see who she hangs out with, you might have to pull her in, find out what she really knows."

"What's this all about boss, is the stick that important?" Malherbe gently probed.

"Let me worry about that, I pay you to do what I want, not to think, just do your job man." He put the phone down abruptly.

Malherbe sat alone in his room. Whatever was on the damned stick must be explosive stuff. He quickly rang Gleason and updated him. The old man was interested, very interested in the latest developments. He even said he was thinking of sending some of his guys down from Joburg to help out. Shit, there would soon be more criminals in Prince Albert than law abiding folks. The lid was going to blow off this town. He rubbed his hands and smiled, he loved a good dust up.

Chapter 23

Jeff Morgan sat quietly at the back of the class, avoiding eye contact with the teacher, his mind was elsewhere. He was in a mobile classroom overlooking the playing fields, still covered in a thin film of frost, the goal posts framing the caretaker trying to paint white lines on a white pitch. Suddenly he saw a zebra burst through the fence, blood oozing from a wound on its flank. Either side it was flanked by wild dogs, mouths agape, snarling.

Chapter 24

Driving from murder to murder was becoming routine for Captain Dirk Steyn of the Stellenbosch SAPS but two within a couple of hours was stretching the point. They were very different though. The first was a gang fight on the platform at Stellenbosch station; one fatality, just a young kid, about the same age as his son, throat slit, a pool of blood dripping onto the track. He thought of Freddie, safely ensconced in Paul Roos, probably running around the playing fields without a care in the world and thanked his lucky stars. The second was more unusual. A body found up at Jonkershoek nature reserve, up near the loop. A white guy, hair burnt, hand cut off and a bullet between the eyes; a Hindu special. No fingerprints on the body, no wallet, no means of identification at the scene of the crime; a professional job and a sick one at that. There must have been at least two of them. The hand was severed in one clean blow; someone had to be holding his arm down. It reeked of underworld retribution. Somebody had tried to put one over the boss and been caught in the act. Serial killers, by nature worked alone, liked the anonymity of the city. All this, of course, was mere supposition but twenty years chasing the bad and ugly had taught him a thing or two.

He knew he wasn't well liked by his colleagues, no partner ever lasted more than a couple of weeks. The only one he had ever bonded with, Corvier, had let him down. He'd caught him taking bribes to supplement his meagre income. It came to a head one afternoon when Dirk read him the riot act, reminded him of his responsibilities and threatened to report him if he didn't get his act together. That night the idiot had blown his own brains out. Suicide was the resultant verdict of the enquiry but his colleagues distanced themselves and pinned the death on him. He got nothing more than perfunctory grunts from them and the glazed look of indifference. No matter, it was a results business and he got results. He liked working alone anyway, cutting corners and dispensing with all that bureaucratic crap that was dragging them all down. Alone against the world, that was his mantra; hard-nosed but fucking effective.

***

Steyn parked his car in an opulent street near the university. He could smell the cash behind the security fences with their sharpened prongs and packs of patrolling dogs. He pressed the intercom, "Captain Steyn SAPS, Mrs Myburgh I need to talk to you, it won't take long."

She saw him through the security camera, standing there impatiently. He walked up to the tall, antique door. You could have built a shack out of it. A tall, lithe woman opened it. She was as thin as a poor man's wallet. He noticed thin rivulets of mascara leaving a feint trail from those high cheekbones. She'd dispensed with the running clothes and was wearing designer jeans and t shirt; her breasts, two moles poking out of a summer lawn. She offered him a drink, but he declined. They sat in leather chairs and she poured a shaky whisky from a cut glass carafe. As he looked at two Irma Stern's on the wall she began to talk in a tremulous voice.

"Look, I don't want to get involved in all this stuff, Bolt found a hand in the bush and brought it out to me, when I realized what it was I just panicked and ran, that's it."

"I understand Mrs Myburgh, this must be very distressing for you but I have to do my job, did you see anybody else on the loop?"

"The place was empty as far as I can recall but I wasn't paying much attention, all I could think of was the hand, the veins and the blood." She shuddered.

"I don't really want to talk about it anymore", she began crying and reached for a tissue from a silver box. Carol Boyes, no doubt, thought Steyn.

"Ok Mrs Myburgh, I can see you're upset, and I won't prolong this, but you need to go to the police station tomorrow and make a formal statement. That should be the end of it, if it comes to court you won't have to make an appearance, let me assure you of that."

"Who was he?" she asked as he left.

"We don't know as yet but we'll find out, we usually do".

Steyn sat in his car and made a couple of calls; first Botha at the station, no ID from the photo of the victim, not on the database, local or international. Next, he rung Mbani at forensics, the answer was what he expected. A trawl through the root canal of dental records was the only viable option; someone somewhere had capped that gold tooth. On the way back to base he wondered if Mrs Myburgh had named the dog after the athlete or the canine in the film.

Chapter 25

Tom wasn't used to being a counsellor. He was normally sat in the opposite chair talking shite. He was a master in the art of deception, secrets neatly folded and covered in dust. He was, however, a good listener. Carla told him about the burglary and he kept his eyes firmly on her, noted the nervous inflections in her voice. When she'd finished, he went over to her and put a reassuring arm around her shoulder. It seemed natural and the right thing to do. She smiled at him.

"Tom, I know it's a bit of a strange request but can... can I stay the night here, I don't want to stay in the coffee shop on my own, especially tonight?" She hadn't come there with that intention but just blurted it out.

He was taken aback and averted his gaze to conceal his surprise. He looked at her overnight bag. He couldn't really pack her off to the hotel. It would be like disowning her and showing a complete lack of empathy.

"Of course you can, you can have my bed. I'll sleep on the couch."

"Are you sure? I don't mind the couch, I don't want to kick you out of your own bed."

"Listen, it's no problem, it'll be nice to have someone to talk to."

They walked inside and she dumped her bag near the kitchen table. She picked up his iPod and flicked through the list of artists.

"Jeez Tom, there's some good stuff on here, I'll give the Zappa and Beefheart a miss though, a bit too leftfield for me."

"What, not a fan of *Trout Mask Replica*, you haven't lived" he said, reclining on the couch, laughing. "Put something on."

She picked Steely Dan, Michael Macdonald singing his smooth backing vocals on *Peg*.

"It's funny how we are drawn to the music of our youth isn't it? I suppose that's when we form our identity, nail down who we are."

"I hadn't thought of it that way but I know what you mean. I look at it more as a musical diary."

They spent a couple of hours choosing alternate tracks filling in back catalogue moments from their lives. Tom explained how he couldn't listen to *Who's Next* without remembering reading *Dune* at the same time when he was teenager, supposedly revising for exams. Carla recalled listening to *Blood on the Tracks* by Dylan when some guy gave her the push at university. There's nothing like jilted love to spin you towards the record deck. Mid-afternoon Tom rustled up some sandwiches, they sat at the table and Carla poured them some tea. She noticed a book wedged by the sugar bowl and leafed through it.

"Tom, are these your poems, she read the latest one called The Steel Flower in the Karoo."

"Ah yeh" he winced. "I've been writing them since I was a teenager." In truth, he was a bit embarrassed; he didn't like to broadcast his poetic leanings, preferring to keep it as his own private world. He felt exposed letting someone else inside.

"Mm, I like it, you ever had any published? Music lover, poet, you're a renaissance man, any other talents I should know about?" He wondered if she was teasing him.

"I've had a few published here and there but I'm not really driven by ambition. They're not really intended for public consumption. Sounds a bit pretentious but it's my way of making sense of the world. Sometimes I'm not so great at communicating with people and I like to recoil into my shell."

She looked at him thoughtfully, weighing him up. "Well, you seem to be communicating freely enough with me."

Tom laughed, "Maybe you're the exception to the rule. Listen I've got an idea, we can't sit in all night, why don't we grab something to eat at the Gallery and then go to a movie? They're showing North by North West at the showroom tonight."

"Cool but I need a shower first and a change of clothes, are you going to wear a Cary Grant suit?"

"No, but I think I can muster a loud shirt, more Elvis in *Blue Hawaii*."

She headed for the shower and he dived in his bedroom to quickly change into faded jeans and beach party shirt. A quick squirt of the old Giorgio Armani and he was ready to go. Strange days are these he thought as Carla zipped by wrapped in one of his towels. She reappeared in a white linen dress cut just above the knee, it was a bit crumpled from being shoved in the bag but God she looked good. A splash of lipstick and they were off.

The restaurant was above the art gallery in the Seven Arches, a Victorian style building on the main street. They climbed the wooden stairs and found a table near the window. The waitress introduced herself, she was as tanned as a mahogany table and had the air of an ex tennis pro. Carla ordered a Bergwater white wine and Tom pushed the boat out and had a red Grapetizer.

"Don't you want a beer?" Carla said.

"Mm…. no thanks, I'm teetotal Tom" it's a long story.

"Go on." She sipped her wine, God, how he wanted to guzzle it down himself. He hid his hands under the table so she couldn't see them shake.

"It's a familiar tale, I'd be the last man at the party, jabbering on, repeating the same story over and over, falling off chairs. It was embarrassing, the world was crashing down around me but I'd still be propped at the bar till the lights went out."

He realized he was giving more away than he was accustomed to but he felt like he could trust her.

"Did you start young?"

"Not really, sixteen I suppose but I've downed some barrels since."

"Was there pressure to drink, you know, when you were with your mates?"

"Damn right there was, where I'm from, if you are sober on a night out you're the odd one out, the weird one. Some people can handle it, know when to stop but it got a hold of me and when I hit some hard times it got a whole lot worse."

"How bad did it get?"

"Believe me, you don't want to know." He grimaced, a thousand shitty flashbacks raced through his mind. Or that's how it felt.

"Did you get any help?"

"That's why I'm here to be honest, to sort myself out, make a fresh start." Now the truth was out there, rearing up like an angry Ostrich. He watched her closely, trying to second guess her reaction.

"Well at least you recognized there was a problem Tom, a lot of people never do. I admire you. It's brave to look inwards. We don't always like what we see."

She didn't know the half of it.

"So Carlie, what brings you here, nothing as sordid as my predicament no doubt?" Tom was keen to remove himself from the spotlight.

She sighed. "I'm on the run from an overdose of mundanity. Steady teaching job, steady money, steady decline into old age."

"Steady boyfriend?" said Tom, it was his turn to look under the stone.

"Not for a long while, too busy marking books."

The place was full, mainly with the grey hair and money brigade. Some were perusing the art for sale on the wall. Lots of the men had their jumpers draped over their shoulders as if they were strolling around a golf club in Berkshire. Carla ordered duck and cherry pie and Tom chose lamb chops, Karoo style. The meal was excellent, and they talked about movies they liked. Over their dessert, Malva pudding with custard, he made her laugh when he recounted a teenage visit to the cinema with a girl. They had gone to see *Apocalypse Now*, hardly romantic fare to begin with. One scene, late in the film had frightened him. A head had been thrown into a cage and he'd kicked the chair in front, possibly inflicting whiplash on a fellow viewer. The next week the girl gave him the elbow.

"Don't worry" he said, "I won't be kicking anybody tonight. I've seen the film a few times."

They walked the short distance to the cinema, the red and white fluorescent lights shining like a beacon for the arts. It looked rather incongruous in the context of the town but it was an impressive building. Tom had peaked inside during the day but never actually been in. It took your breath away; polished marble like floors, stylish tripod tables with gleaming metal legs, expensive looking chandeliers and comfortable white leather couches.

"Wow, we've stepped back in time, I should be wearing a flapper dress" she said. Tom felt a bit out of place too in his beach bum regalia. The theatre itself was just as impressive, it was beautifully decorated and the red seats were sumptuous. They sat back and lost themselves in the film. The iconic scene where Grant is waiting to be met on a deserted road in the middle of rolling wheat fields is a cinematic masterpiece. Shot in one long take, no dialogue, with the crop-dusting plane swooping down, Grant scurrying for cover in his immaculately tailored suit. The film really came into its own on the big screen, Mount Rushmore loomed above them. They hardly talked, both enthralled. At the end the audience burst into spontaneous applause. It was definitely worth the thirty rand they'd paid. On the way home they talked animatedly, debated the minefield of mistaken identity and marvelled at the beauty of Yves Marie Saint.

When they got home, Tom made them a coffee and Carla yawned.

"You should get some sleep girl. It's been a tough day for you."

"I think I will Tom, I really appreciate you putting me up like this and I've had a lovely evening, thanks a million."

He got himself a spare duvet and spread it on the couch. She kissed him lightly on the cheek and closed the bedroom door. Tom lay in the darkness mulling over the day. It was a tale of the unexpected, but he'd enjoyed it nevertheless. If life was a movie, he would be that alpha male, open the bedroom door and swagger on in, waving his boxers in the air, confidence oozing from every pore but that was not him. He was more epsilon male, waiting for life to come to him rather than chasing it. The prospect of rejection always loomed large, he always thought first about what could go wrong, saw doom and gloom before boom.

He drifted off to sleep. Carla lay on the bed, still in her dress, and smiled. They'd had fun, he was a bit mixed up but there was something about him that intrigued her; that tinge of melancholy coupled with a sense of humour, the tortured artist, a man of hidden depths. She laughed at herself. She'd made it sound like the opening chapter of a romantic novel.

***

The sound of piercing scream woke her up in the early hours. She sat bolt upright. Her first thought was another burglary, but she heard a gentle sobbing. She realized she'd fallen asleep in her dress and got up, gently opening the bedroom door. In the dim light she could vaguely make out Tom's body silently shaking.

"Are you ok?"

"I've had the dream again, except its true." She sensed he was semi-comatose and possibly unaware of what he was saying. He was waking now and shaken up.

"What dream?" she said calmly.

"The only one I have, it stalks me, always does, always will." His eyes were adjusted to the light now and he saw her standing close by.

"Have you ever tried dream therapy?"

"No, I refuse to tell anyone what happened, I've kept it in all these years" He was sailing in uncharted waters and the stormy seas were enveloping him. She lay next to him.

"You can't keep all that shit in Tom, whatever it is, it'll eat away your soul and you're worth more than that." He was struck by her tenderness and her close proximity to him. He could feel the heat of her body. She stood up as if to leave but peeled off her dress and climbed in with him, holding him.

"Tell me about it honey."

It had been so long, festering within that he couldn't just blurt it out but he felt something inside breaking up.

"I can't now Carl, but I promise I will in the morning"

"Promise?"

"Yeh I promise" he said, and he meant it.

She spooned him and kissed his neck, sending shivers down his spine, he could feel her breasts rubbing against him. She slid down his back gently licking his skin. He could feel his boxers becoming a tented village and soon a hand slipped under the material. He could resist no longer and turned, kissing her with force. His hands eased off her panties and soon they were writhing in sweat, fingers tightening in each other's hair, bodies pressed together.

It was well after dawn when they awoke, arms and legs still entangled. They looked at each other, smiled and kissed again.

A Steel Flower in the Karoo

Alone,
like an only child.

Perched upon four
metal poles,
converging.
Blades shaped
as the palm of a hand,
offset angles,
the poetry of geometry,
ready to catch
the merest breeze
Or harness
the rancorous displeasure
of the wind.

They guard their circular dams
With a sun lit jealous glint
And pump the fruitful juice
That slakes the thirst
Of sheep so hardy.

A silent whirr
whispering power.

Chapter 26

The main street was deserted in the emerging light. Johnson was up early, glad to escape the metronomic snoring of Malherbe. He'd drunk too much last night and passed out on his bed as soon as they'd gone back to the cramped room they were staying in at a mid-price B&B on the outskirts of town. The coffee shop showed no signs of life and there were no lights on. The lock on the back gate had been changed; the girl had been spooked by the burglary. She'd probably gone to spend the night with some friends. She'd sounded English when they'd seen her talking to the guy on a bike; they weren't used to crime from the northern hemisphere. He'd read the police didn't even carry guns in England. There wasn't a problem, she couldn't have gone far. It wasn't as if she could blend with the masses and slip away to some innocuous suburb. This was a small town and there was nowhere to hide. Maybe he had done her an injustice. Perhaps she was the British stiff upper lip type and would open the coffee shop later on that day. Either way, they would find her soon enough.

Johnson didn't feel like going back to the room. The prospect of listening to Malherbe's endless tales of torture, the way in which he took delight in inflicting pain, filled him with disgust. He wondered how it had all come to this. He hadn't chosen crime as a career path, he'd somehow let himself be sucked into it through his own weakness. A few years back he'd had a steady job as a mechanic but the garage went bust. He needed a job and started as a security guard at a factory. It was tedious but it paid the bills. One night, when he was dozing on duty, three guys jumped him, one with a knife at his throat. They threatened him, made him say where his old folks lived, scared the shit out of him. Then they made the proposition, they needed a guy on the inside to turn a blind eye when they regularly came to turn the place over, taking small enough amounts to pass under the radar. He should have told the boss and the cops but all he could think of was his mother, partially blind, holed up in a flat in Durbanville. He couldn't let anything happen to her. Late that summer, the boss did some stock taking and the figures didn't add up. He was fired on the spot, dumped on the scrap heap, accused of stealing and he offered no defence. The next few weeks he drowned his sorrows, sat in the same seat in the same bar, sinking in a fog of depression. Most days he could barely talk and hardly ate. One evening a rough looking dude in a faded suit pulled up at the bar stool next to him and asked him if he wanted to earn some cash. He must have looked like he needed some. All he had to do was make a few deliveries, pick up some packages and ask no questions. He'd lost his way, was on the bones of his arse and, like a fool, he'd said yes. By the time he'd sobered up he was in up to his neck and the money was so good that he couldn't turn it down. Nothing, if not reliable, he got more work, more money and unfortunately, mad Malherbe came with the package.

Johnson lit a cigarette, turned at the thatched rondawels and walked down a dirt road. There was a sign post to Gamkapoort dam. He kicked some stones and moved to the edge to avoid a dust cloud billowing behind a bakkie that was loaded with farm workers in their blue overalls. To the left he saw a small building, it looked like a tiny church, the work of someone with faith and fortitude no doubt. It stood there like a lost disciple. The door was slightly ajar. He walked in, sat in a pew and looked at the brown wooden cross. He wasn't a religious man but he got down his knees and prayed, prayed for forgiveness, prayed for a way out of the darkness into the light. He lit a candle and watched the light flicker amidst the unlit wicks. In his heart he doubted God would roll out the red carpet to redemption. It was a journey he would have to make on his own.

On the way home, he shuddered at the thought of what Malherbe might do to the girl, who knows what lurked in that bag they'd loaded in Cape Town, it seemed heavier than usual and, through the partially opened zip, he thought he'd seen the glint of a silver drill.

The room was empty and the car had gone. Malherbe wasn't one for walking.

Chapter 27

His mouth was as dry as the Karoo, head pounding. Malherbe glanced around the room and was pleased to see there was no sign of Johnson. He'd had enough of the soft fokker's attitude, whose side was he on for Christ sake? He made himself a black coffee to clear his head and cursed the little plastic container of milk that was impossible to open. In the end he jabbed it with a key, spilling a few drops on the tiled floor. It was time to get things going. He was already tired of the tin pot town with its arty shops and drive through tourists. It wouldn't take long to track down this Carla chick and squeeze out the information. She would squeal like a baby. It had been a while since he'd had fun with a woman. He smiled at the prospect.

The bag of tricks clunked in the boot as he hit the gravel near the Bush pub on Pastorie Straat on the outskirts of town. A quick drive around the town itself had come up blank, she was lying low but it was still early in the day and now he was looking for something else. The girl would surely turn up at the coffee shop sometime soon but if they grabbed her there he had a problem. Someone would hear her wail when he got down to business, small towns were full of busy bodies with big ears. He needed somewhere more remote, and then she could scream for all she was worth, with only the wildlife as an audience.

Malherbe lit a cigarette and drove slowly over the undulating ridges, scanning either side of the road for something suitable. The vegetation was sparse and clung to the earth for dear life, kralbos dotted around like clumps of unkempt hair on a balding head. At the top of a small hill he saw an old derelict barn, about fifty metres off the road, in a hollow. He drove in and was careful to park behind the building so as not to be visible from the dirt track, even though he hadn't seen a vehicle since leaving town. The door was hanging off rusty hinges and squeakily protested when he opened it. Inside was an ancient Massey Ferguson tractor, faded red, with flat tyres and some old farming tools that wouldn't be out of place in a museum. Two old wooden chairs were wedged under a shelf stacked with a dusty container of engine oil and a roll of twine. He jumped up onto the hard metal seat of the tractor, lit another cigarette and inhaled deeply. Jeez, this place was fit for purpose. He imagined the girl tied to the chair, face pale, hair full of sweat, and the smell of fear emanating from her every pore. He would make her bleed, burn that sweet skin. The thought of it aroused him.

Chapter 28

The coffee tasted good that morning. They had had a shower together and now Carla was making them scrambled eggs. Tom was sat at the kitchen table watching her whisk the eggs in the pan. They played some Josh Rouse on the iPod and all they needed was the Sunday papers to add to the relaxed atmosphere. She looked at him and smiled.

"Tales of the unexpected hey?"

He nodded in agreement, buttering the toast.

"Life's full of surprises but Jeez that was a nice one." They ate quickly, both of them ravenous. When he was loading the dishwasher, she looked at him with those big green eyes and he knew what was coming.

"Tom, last night when you were upset you made a promise, remember?"

He half thought of feigning ignorance but already, in the little time he'd known her, he knew she was worth more than that. He sat on the couch and ran his fingers through his hair. It was hard to lift the lid on a secret that had been boiling away, unattended for decades. It had ruled him, governed his daily and nocturnal thoughts for so long that he'd come to believe in its permanence. Countless counsellors had tried to winkle it out of him with their tissue boxes at the ready, ambient music in the background but he had always pulled the shutters down, deftly steering the conversation to calmer waters. The truth, the bald truth, was too painful to confront. He feared it. Part of him had been sealed off for more than thirty years, like a contaminated island. Here, thousands of miles from the drabness of his London existence and his world of self-pity, he was close to finally letting go. His hands were clammy and he could feel a nervous tick pulsing in his cheek. Carla was staring at him, expecting a reply. He stood up and paced around the room. Through the window he saw a Cape girdled lizard squeeze between the rocks looking for shelter from the sun. He returned to the couch and looked at the woman he barely knew. What would she think of him if he came clean?

"Tom, you've gone pale, it can't be that bad can it?"

She sat next to him and stroked the back of his neck.

"Carla this is hard, I haven't told a living soul what happened all those years ago. I've lived with it for all this time." She saw a small tear roll down his cheek towards the corner of his mouth.

"Just tell me love" she said, the gentle warmth of her tone bringing him to the brink of confession.

"I… I can't. I'm not ready." He stood up, walked to the window, turned away from her. "I don't want to ruin everything. I'm just getting to know you."

She could see it wasn't the time to press him.

"Ok honey, I was just trying to help. It's none of my business. Sorry if I've been insensitive."

"Don't apologize, it's me, I'm a complicated fucker. I've stewed in this shit for a long time and it's hard to let go." He sat next to her.

"I was close then." He cuddled up to her.

"Shit, this is weird, I feel like I can tell you anything and I've only just met you. Give me a couple of days and I'll spill the beans." He meant it. He could feel the shackles loosening.

"Maybe our stars are aligned." She smiled at him.

"Don't tell me you believe in all that astrology bullshit?"

"Not really but sometimes it's the right place, right time, right people."

He looked at her. It was the first time he'd felt alive in a long while.

Tom made coffee and they sat on the stoep. Some colour had returned to his cheeks and he felt a tentative pull towards the future rather than his customary urge to trawl through the past; new ground indeed. His mind turned to more immediate matters.

"What are you going to do about the coffee shop?" he asked.

"I'm going to open it up. Will you come with me to check its ok?" She was understandably nervous.

"Sure but I meant more long term, are you going to stay for a few more weeks?"

"Yeh, as long as there are no more burglaries, I'll try and get in touch with Greg to see how long he'll be, he's an elusive bugger, I haven't heard a word from him since he left."

Tom stood up and poured more coffee from the pot.

"Were you two an item back in the day?" He regretted it as soon as he'd said it, it sounded juvenile.

"Is that a hint of jealousy from the dark Welshman, showing your true colours are you?" He liked her sense of humour even if she was having a slight go at him.

"No, no. I'm curious, that's all."

128

"He was just a friend at university but he was too busy chasing busty blonds with buck teeth to register me on his radar. I liked the more reserved types. He was a bit full of himself."

"Billy big head, was he?"

"I suppose he was. To be honest, he was shocked when I turned up on his doorstep. He's changed."

"In what way?"

"Well, more world weary, like there was a huge weight on his shoulders."

"That's what time does to you, youth don't last forever." He cleared the table while Carla washed the coffee cups and laid them on the drying rack.

"What about you Tom, have you left a trail of women in your wake?"

He blushed, "bloody hell, I'm no Hollywood heart throb, no Richard Burton. I'm a shy boy. When I was a teenager, I would cross the road to avoid girls, I was terrified of speaking to them. That's what attending an 'all boys' school does for you."

"But surely you hooked up with some as you got older?"

"Yeh, I did but I never played the field, I'm a loyal fucker, not that it did me any good."

She could see she'd touched a nerve.

"Why, what happened?"

"Well I was married but it didn't work out. We drifted apart. I've got two kids, a boy and a girl. They live with their mum, I see them on weekends."

It was better to tell the truth, there was nothing to be ashamed of. Most people of his age came complete with baggage. You weren't twenty-one forever. He waited for her reaction. She seemed unperturbed.

"Was it an amicable split?"

"Not initially but things have settled down. We've tried to put the kids first and protect them. It's not their fault. My boy, Jeff, took it badly. He's the youngest. Lizzie's been more resilient, she's close to her mum and that bit older."

Tom realized he'd been so wrapped up in himself that he'd hardly given his kids a thought. It was uncaring of him.

"Lots of my friends are divorced; it's the scourge of modern life. Sometimes I think I'm lucky I never married. Being left on the shelf has its advantages." She laughed as she said it.

"You are definitely not shelf material." replied Tom.

"I'll take that as a back handed compliment young man."

They went inside and Carla packed her bag, she put her arms around him and kissed him.

"What am I going to do with you, my lost Celtic soul?" she whispered in his ear. He could think of a good few things, but that coffee shop wouldn't open itself.

They locked up and wandered onto the main street, oblivious to the outside world, paying scant attention to the traffic or the parked cars pointing north and south.

***

Malherbe and Johnson, sat in a Toyota Hilux double cab, watched them stroll together hand in hand towards the shop. She took the keys from her bag.

"We'll have to take the two of them", Johnson grimaced as he said it.

"All the better, double the pain" replied his partner, barely containing his excitement.

They got out of the car and crossed the road. They were armed and dangerous, one infinitely more than the other.

Chapter 29

Steyn was driving to the station when he got the call. It was Mbani from forensics. "Hey, Dirk, my man, got a result on that body from Jonkershoek, he had a load of dental work done at Somerset West a few months back, gold tooth 'n all."

"Who is he?" Steyn turned into the car park behind the building and turned off the aircon.

"Botha checked him out bru, his name is Greg Joseph, some English dude, did post-grad studies at UCT, ran a couple of unsuccessful businesses in town then ran to the hills, opened a coffee shop in Prince Albert."

"In the Karoo?"

"Yup, been hanging out there for a couple of years brother. No criminal record here or back home in good old England, clean as a tootin' whistle."

Steyn never ceased to be amazed at Mbani's verbal meandering, that kid watched too many Yankee cop shows.

"Wife, girlfriend?"

"Nope, unmarried."

"What the fuck's he doing in Jonkers having his hair permed and hand cut off?"

"Don't know bru, that's your department, I paint the scenery you fill in the people." He hung up.

Steyn took the lift to the third floor and ignored the frosty stares. His desk was a mess, papers strewn everywhere. On the corner was an old photograph when his wife was thinner and they were happier. Always look at the mother, the old man had told him. True enough. He poured himself a shit coffee from the machine and sat in his chair. Something stunk about this case. An apparently law-abiding citizen brutally executed four hours away from home, a professional job, these were no chancers chasing a few bucks and a cell phone. What was this Joseph involved in? The fact that he had a clean record was immaterial; a whole load of shady underworld characters went to the grave without anybody ever knowing they were criminals. There was an ugly underbelly of society that forever remained faceless. It was underneath the leaf litter that the vermin crawled.

"Hey, Sikosi wants you in his office pronto", Wiese shouted from the other side of the room. Steyn sauntered through, he was still wary of Colonel bloody Sikosi, he'd been transferred from Durban, rumour had it, to weed out the deadwood. He looked at the white guys as if they were foot soldiers from the apartheid era. The fact that he bore an uncanny resemblance to Idi Amin served to further lessen his appeal. He was a big man who more than filled his shirt. His desk was ordered, everything at crisp ninety-degree angles. Steyn sat down and waited. The silence was interminable.

"Captain, I've observed that you are not a team player."

"Look boss this isn't a popularity contest, I'm here to do a job not to be sociable. I presume you've checked out my record."

Steyn was irritated but knew it was best to keep calm otherwise he could be swept out with the garbage, the latest from the old school to be dumped on the scrap heap.

"I want a cohesive task force, good communicators who share information, do you understand?"

His tone was patronizing, and Steyn could feel his hackles rising. It was a deliberate attempt to provoke him but he wasn't going to fall for the bait. Best play the game and make all the right noises, not provide the hierarchy with the requisite ammunition to shoot him down.

"I understand boss, I haven't been myself lately, been having a few problems at home and I've been a bit irritable at work."

He could see that Sikosi didn't believe him, but he'd unsettled the boss. It was clearly not the reply he'd been anticipating. Serve the bastard right for trying to goad him.

"Well sort it out, a stable home life is essential if you are to function properly at work, anyway I didn't call you in here for a marriage guidance session, there's some important police work to be done. This murder up at Jonkershoek, we've had a positive ID, Greg Joseph from Prince Albert, owns a coffee shop. I want you to get up there and look into it."

"Really?"

"Yes, it's your case, remember? This guy must have been caught up in something serious. I've rung the local police; Smit is the officer you need to talk to when you arrive. Oh, and don't upset anyone when you're there, remember it's all about communication."

He opened his diary and picked up his phone. Steyn took this as his cue to leave. A road trip to the backwaters wasn't what he expected but at least it would provide a temporary respite from the toxic atmosphere at work and a limp, failing marriage. Nobody raised their heads as he left the office. The house was empty as he packed a bag. He tried calling Christel but she didn't answer. A brief text message telling her he'd be out of town for a few days probably brightened her day. It was gone one when he finally hit the road. He smiled. It was sad. Lately he was happiest in his own company.

Chapter 30

It was like town mouse and country mouse but with added mistrust. Steyn sat in an office in Prince Albert police station, Smit, the local cop, lounged the other side of the table, all paunch and Brylcream hair. Steyn, despite his advancing years, was athletic, possessing a body honed by countless pursuits down back streets and regular gym sessions. It was one of the defining parts of his identity. He doubted whether Smit could run five yards without puffing like an asthmatic. It was obvious from the first limp handshake that this wasn't going to be easy. Steyn had seen it all before, backwoods cops liked their ponds to have no ripples, liked the easy life. Getting up was a strain for some of them. He counted Smit among their number. Dispensing with idle small talk he got straight to the point.

"What can you tell me about Greg Joseph? We found his body at a nature reserve near Stellenbosch; he'd been tortured, nasty stuff."

Smit tried to stifle a yawn but failed.

"Not much really, he's a foreigner, English, turned up here a couple of years ago and opened up a coffee shop on the main street, keeps himself to himself."

"Kept himself to himself" said Steyn, "he's past tense now. Did he have a girlfriend or friends?"

"Look, we weren't watching him but a girl turned up a couple of weeks back, she's running the shop for him. Rumour has it he had to go back to England for some sort of emergency."

Rumour has it thought Steyn, towns like this thrived on rumours, careless whispers shared by those with nothing better to do and the fact that it involved foreigners fanned the flames no doubt. These remote towns harboured a dislike of the outsider; saw them as a threat to the local community, buying up their properties with their fat bank accounts clanking behind them like tin cans tied to a wedding car.

"Her name's Carla, I talked to her yesterday, there was a minor break in at the coffee shop", Smit didn't seem perturbed.

Steyn raised his eyebrows, "what happened?"

"Some township kids broke in and ransacked one of the rooms but nothing was stolen, the till was untouched."

"Which room did they turn over?" asked Steyn, he thought he already knew the answer.

"I think it was Joseph's, they must have started there but been disturbed"

It didn't seem a particularly convincing explanation to Steyn, it smacked of lazy police work.

"Why do you think it was the township kids?"

"Because they're responsible for the petty crime round here, we catch them all the time but we can't lay a finger on them", he barely concealed his disdain.

"Is that so?"

"You bloody know it is" said Smit, raising his voice.

Steyn stood up but Smit remained seated, red faced.

"I'm going to check out the coffee shop and talk to Carla, does anyone else work there?"

"A couple of people from the location, I don't know their names", Smit looked at his watch as if he had other pressing matters to attend to. His complete indifference was palpable.

Steyn left the building resigned to the fact that he was on his own with this case, par for the course but that was how he liked it. Working with others slowed you down. He had the feeling Smit could be obstructive and perhaps it was a good thing that he seemed so disinterested.

***

The heat was oppressive; he wiped the beads of sweat from his brow and walked up the gentle incline of the main road, stopping at the chemists to buy some Nicorette chewing gums. It was hard to kick the habit and the gum cost more than the cigarettes but at least his lungs were grateful. He paused at the exotic cinema and looked at a poster of Lizanne Barnard who was performing there in April. Her tousled hair and enigmatic smile made him laugh, what with the strapless dress and seductive fingers caressing the keyboard, necklace dangling tantalizingly. There was a small market near the church that had attracted a fair-sized crowd. The smell of a braai dragged him in, but he opted for the sugar rush of some koeksisters, paying the old lady with some small change in his pocket.

The pavement was quieter further up the road. The stoep of the coffee shop was deserted. Steyn tried the door, but it was locked. There were no signs of life around the back either. The lock on the back gate looked new, probably fitted as a result of the burglary. He circled the building, peering in the windows but there was no sign of life. The tables were set up, cutlery neatly arranged, tablecloths ironed but the place was empty. He knocked the door and shouted but there was no response. Steyn sat on the steps and ran through the scenarios. Carla was frightened by the burglary and, running scared, had gone to stay elsewhere in the town or even left the place completely, or, and this was the worst-case scenario, she was implicated in Joseph's problems and had been abducted. The former seemed most likely, why should a visitor put up with the discomfort and unease of a burglary when she had no permanent ties to the place? But it was the darker option that troubled him. Over the years he had learnt to trust his instinct and, much to the annoyance of his colleagues, he was mostly right. Not every time of course but a high percentage of the time he was on the money. He would have to find out Carla's surname, get Botha to check her out to see if he could come up with anything, give some sort of insight into her world. Steyn looked at the wooden steps and saw some scuff marks, three or four people, an altercation or just some irate folks needing a coffee? The cogs in his brain turned and clicked, they didn't need oil. They were well lubricated.

As he sat, lost in his private thoughts, a couple approached the shop. He realized by the way they were dressed that it was the two people Smit had said worked there. Steyn greeted them and showed his ID. He took them to Lah di dah farmstall for a coffee. They would hopefully be able to shed some light on Greg Joseph and Carla. At present, Steyn thought, the investigation was clothed in darkness and he was blindfolded. What was new? It was the start and things had a habit of opening up.

Chapter 31

A bubble of bliss can be pricked at any given moment. One second he had an intimate hand on her shoulder, the next he felt the cold blade of a knife graze his throat. A world turned upside down in the time it takes to sneeze.

As Carla opened the coffee shop door Tom placed an early order for an Americano with hot milk, she laughed. He sensed the presence of someone behind him but before he could turn to check he was felled by a heavy blow behind his knee. He tried to grab a chair to save himself but pulled at the table cloth instead. The cutlery rattled to the floor. Face down, a boot pinned between his shoulder blades, he was unable to move. Carla was lying next to him, a small cut was leaking blood above her eye, she must have hit her head on the corner of the table when she, too, was thrown to the ground.

"Stop the fokken wailing Carla or we'll blow your brains out, save us some time and effort." They both heard the metallic click of a gun.

"Just take the money, please, leave us alone." Her voice was thin and reedy. Tom wondered how the hell they knew her name.

"We don't want your money, we want information, we know you were working with Joseph, we're not stupid, girl."

"What? I'm just running the coffee shop for Greg, doing him a favour that's all. He had to go back to England."

"Bullshit honey, Joseph's in the morgue in Stellenbosch, bullet between his eyes, burnt hair, one hand missing. We put him there."

Malherbe gestured to Johnson, it was time to go.

"Listen up, outside is our car, you're gonna walk out nice and easy and get in the back, any noise and it'll be the last you make, understand?"

Tom felt the nozzle of the gun pressed in his back. He nodded in silent agreement. His mind was numb and he was incapable of stringing two thoughts together. He risked a glance at Carla. Her face was ashen. One of the assailants moved the curtains and peered out of the corner of the window, checking if the coast was clear. The other one pointed a gun at them and they shuffled towards the door, Carla still carrying her overnight bag. Within seconds they were in the back of the car and lying under a blanket, like two celebrities escaping the paparazzi.

"What the hell are you mixed up in Carla?" whispered Tom.

"I've no idea, you've got to believe me", she hissed.

Tom didn't know what to believe. The brief ray of hope that had shone on him seemed to have been extinguished. He craved the warmth of a drink, it was the only coping strategy he had. He tried to dampen the rising panic, close his mind to the fearful uncertainty, but he couldn't. If it was fight or flight, he always ran. His whole life he had baulked at confrontation, avoided it at all cost. He was the sort of guy who got angry an hour after being beaten up. Carla gripped his hand tightly; he could feel the pulse racing in her wrist.

"Shut the fuck up." The nozzle of the gun pressed the base of his spine.

They lay there quietly, breathing erratically, sweating. The car bounced over low, undulating hills, they must be on a dirt track heading away from town. After a few minutes the car turned right into a hollow and came to a halt. They couldn't have gone far. In a blur of blinding light that scorched the retina they were bundled into some sort of derelict old barn.

"Sit on those chairs, tie 'em up Johnson, nice and tight."

It was pointless to resist with a gun pointing at you, less than a metre away. He looked at Carla, trying to reassure her but neither could hide the fear in their eyes. The rope bit into his arms, made him flinch.

"Listen, you've got the wrong p…" Tom was cut off mid-sentence, his mouth sealed with duct tape. He tried to continue but the words rolled into a meaningless wail, a trail of slime oozed from his nostril.

"We're not interested in you bru, you're a nobody that never was. It's this beauty we're after."

Malherbe turned his gaze towards Carla, running his eyes up her long legs, lingering on her firm breasts. Tom saw the way he was looking at her. He was sickened.

"It's this chick who's got the answers and I'm going to take it real slow, make her squeal."

His hard, blue eyes were iceberg cold, thin lips gashed in a smile. Tom noticed Johnson avert his eyes to scan the arid Martian landscape framed by the glassless window.

"What's in the bag honey, sex toys, soiled underwear?"

Malherbe emptied the contents on the floor. He ignored the make-up and toothbrush and picked up the pink panties.

"Mm nice, matches the pink bra in your bedroom, what you got on today honey?"

He knelt and forced her legs apart, staring at her crotch.

"Fuck you, you pervert" she screamed and aimed a kick at his face. He moved his head to avoid the blow and grabbed her leg, sinking his teeth into her flesh.

"Don't fuck with me sister, show some respect", a thin sliver of blood trickled down his chin. "Nobody fucks with me, nobody", his hands were shaking.

Carla's scream punctured the air. A Pale chanting goshawk, startled, took flight from a nearby tree and eased itself up on the wind. Tom tried to shout, his mouth filled with bile and he retched.

"For Christ sake Malherbe, go easy, let's just ask the questions and we can get out of this place." Johnson was still at the window, he looked uneasy.

"Look Johnson, I don't know what's got into you, you've gone fokken soft in the head. I'll do this my way and if you interfere like you did up at Jonkers there'll be consequences, understand?"

"Let's just do the job Malherbe, that's what we're paid to do."

Their eyes met, neither prepared to give ground or debate the matter further.

Malherbe picked up Carla's bag and checked the side pockets. The first was empty but in the second was a red USB stick. He held it in his palm.

"Well, well, look what we have here Johnson, do you still want to join the UN peace keeping force? This must be Radebe's memory stick, the girl's a fucking thief, she was in it with Joseph all along. What do you have to say for yourself now, you stupid bitch?"

Tom waited for Carla's response. His brain was scrambled. What the hell was she mixed up in, what was with the stick, who was Radebe and who were these two heavies, one of whom made Jo Pesci's character in *Goodfellas* seem like Jimmy Stewart in *Harvey*? He wished he was back in London, drunk out of his mind in the pub, just one of the pasty faces repeating the same stories to people who never remembered them. At least that was a crawl to the grave, laced in melancholy, but he'd be suitably anesthetized. He looked at Carla, could he have misjudged her so badly? It was hard to fathom.

"I found that stick in my underwear drawer this morning when I was packing. I've no idea how it got there, I just picked it up out of curiosity, I was going to check it out later", she said.

"You expect us to believe that bullshit, can't you come up with something better than that?"

"It's the truth" she said, looking Malherbe straight in the eye then glancing at Tom for support. She couldn't tell what he was thinking; there wasn't much to go on apart from the widening of the eyes and a raised eyebrow. She couldn't blame him for doubting her, her explanation sounded unconvincing despite it being truthful.

"I'll be the judge of what the truth is honey, I'll be the jury and the fokken executioner", he replied, lighting a cigarette and slowly exhaling the smoke.

"The boss will be pleased we found his stick and I'm sure he'll want to know why you are walking around with it, you'll tell the truth alright when I get down to business, you'll squeal like a fokken baby, but do you want to hear the bad news girl, do you? I'm in no rush, I like to take it real slow, watch you squirm and writhe, watch you beg like the tramp you are."

Tom closed his eyes and tried to blank out the nightmare. He cursed his self-indulgence. Why couldn't he have faced up to his problems back home, his hindsight had always been better than his foresight, but nobody could have expected this to happen. One minute you find a saviour, the next she disappears like a beautiful apparition, turns to dust in your hands and you yourself are a rotting carcass to be picked at by vultures in some barren field. It was an ill wind that had brought him here and the prospects looked bleak.

Chapter 32

Steyn steered through the stands laden with tourist knick-knacks. Chipped enamel plates going for two hundred rand, the world had gone mad. It was so hot even the mosquitoes were sweating. He found a quiet table in the corner, away from the other customers. They were foreigners, boasting about the ludicrous exchange rate, bags bursting with presents ready to disperse around the world. The waitrons from Celestino's sat opposite him like two errant pupils in front of the headmaster, he could tell they were apprehensive, to them he represented old school authority, and he moved swiftly to allay their fears.

"Look, don't worry guys, you're not in any trouble, what's your names? I'm Captain Dirk Steyn from Stellenbosch police and I'm hoping you can help me out."

They introduced themselves as Charles and Sheila and sat there, impassive, waiting for him to continue. Steyn decided to spare them the darker details, there was no use in putting the fear of God into them.

"Your boss, Greg Joseph has got himself in a spot of trouble, when did you last see him?"

Sheila sat as if transfixed, but Charles answered.

"He left a couple of weeks ago, Carla's been running the coffee shop with us. She said Mr Joseph had to go back to England, is he ok?"

"Yeh, he's in a stable condition." Nothing more stable than death thought Steyn. He continued his probing.

"Can you tell me something about Mr Joseph, what was he like to work for?"

They looked at each other but it was still only Charles who spoke.

"Crap."

"In what way?" said Steyn.

"When we first started working for him he was ok but lately he hardly talks to us, just to tick us off. If it wasn't for Carla, we'd have left."

"You feel the same way?" Steyn looked at Sheila and she nodded.

"This Carla, is she his girlfriend?"

"No" she said, it was the first time she had spoken.

"How can you be so sure?"

"Trust me, I'm a woman, we know these things."

Steyn had no answer to that and didn't want to debate the merits of women's intuition. He quickly changed the subject.

"Look this is important, did you notice anything unusual in the past couple of months, anything out of the ordinary?"

The coffee finally arrived. The waitress had been swooning around the foreigners maximizing the opportunity for a sizeable tip and had forgotten about them. Steyn shook the sugar sachet and tapped it on the table and watched the two of them, more in hope than expectation.

"No, I can't really think of anything" said Sheila. She sipped the froth off her coffee and looked like she'd be pleased to get away. Charles looked on the verge of saying something though.

"It's probably nothing but there was something strange a while back."

"Go on, what happened? Don't worry if it's something trivial. Anything, no matter how small, could be of help."

"A black guy, well dressed as far as I can remember, turned up and ordered a meal. I served him on the stoep. I gave him the bill and he went inside to pay. Mr Joseph was behind the counter and they recognized each other, it seemed like they was old friends, laughing and joking then Mr Joseph asked me to look after the shop when they went upstairs for a chat."

"Why was that odd?"

"Well Mr Joseph never left me in charge before. I didn't think he trusted me."

"What were they talking about at the counter?" asked Steyn.

"I don't know, I was the other side of the shop clearing a table, I couldn't hear anything."

"What did this guy look like?"

"He was a tall, fit, like a basketball player."

Steyn was all ears now. Was this some innocent reunion or was it something with more sinister undertones? There was a faint chance this could lead somewhere interesting.

"How long were they upstairs?"

Charles hesitated, "it's hard to remember, not too long, maybe twenty minutes. They came back down, shook hands and then the black guy drove off in his fancy car."

"Fancy car?"

"Yeh, a white Mercedes convertible, it looked brand new."

"Thanks Charles you've been very helpful." Steyn took down his cell number and told the pair of them he would inform them if there were any developments. As he got up to leave Sheila put a hand on his arm, "what about Carla, where is she, she didn't open the shop this morning?"

Steyn told them about the minor break in at the coffee shop and said he thought Carla would be lying low for a couple of days but imagined she would re-open for business in the near future. In truth, he had no idea where she was, but he had a horrible feeling she was in a whole load of trouble. He left the restaurant in a state of restless unease, the heat didn't help, his shirt was clinging to his body. He watched Charles and Sheila head down the main road towards the location; a whole new world that was completely alien to him. They had to work all hours to rub two fifty rand notes together, it was a precarious existence, living hand to mouth with kids to feed.

Steyn crossed the street and walked to Celestino's at the top end of town; still no signs of life at the front of the building. Around the back he checked left and right but the street was deserted. He scaled the fence and dusted himself down. There were no electric fences here or beams or lasers. The endemic fear of crime that ruled the city suburbs had yet to reach the rural backwaters (it was on its way though). A kitchen window was open and he slipped through, careful not to kick over a tray of cups that were next to the sink. He knew he should have informed Smit before entering the premises but time was of the essence. Police protocol was never high on his agenda anyway.

The kitchen was readied for business, the cutlery and crockery laid out neatly next to the coffee machine. All seemed as it should be. He walked through the archway into the main room. The first sets of tables were set for customers but near the door a chair had been tipped over and a table cloth pulled to the floor, spilling the cutlery. There were a few scuff marks on the tiled floor. Steyn pictured the scene; Carla, keys at the ready, unaware of one or two assailants behind her, they pushed her to the floor and she tried to grab the table to break her fall. To his practised eye it had all the hallmarks of abduction. She was either in collusion with Joseph or inadvertently mixed up in his murky world and the bad guys had caught up with her. This, of course, was all supposition on his part but it echoed a grim pattern he'd been unfortunate enough to witness on countless occasions.

One man dead, an English woman missing and all he knew about her was her first name. A mysterious black dude in an expensive Mercedes but he could be an entrepreneur or a university lecturer, a symbol of the new South Africa, the rainbow nation, a disaffected local policeman with an attitude problem. The avenues of investigation weren't aligned in his favour but, in some weird way, that's how he liked it. There was nothing more satisfying than piecing together fragments of information until the truth was revealed. It's what drove him on year after year. It's what made all the other associated crap somehow bearable.

Steyn went upstairs to check out the bedrooms. Greg's had been tidied up after the break in. there were still some small grains of dirt between the bare floorboards and one of the plant pots had a jagged crack in it. The desk drawer was full of letters, mainly bills and nasty reminders from the bank. Mr Joseph had some serious debts. The cupboards were full of clothes but a search of the pockets proved fruitless. Under the bed, hidden by some empty shoe boxes, were some drugs paraphernalia; pipe, cigarette papers and a large bag of cannabis. Not in itself a sign of being heavily involved in the drug world but Steyn was beginning to have his suspicions. He turned his attention to the other bedroom which was evidently Carla's. Her clothes were folded neatly in the drawers and tucked underneath the jeans he found her passport - Carla Thompson, DOB 21.10.1968, birthplace Crouch End, London. He took down the details and rang Botha, asking him to run a check on her. Now he could put a face to the name and begin the more onerous task of trying to find her, hopefully alive.

Chapter 33

Tom watched the two men through the window. They were too far away for him to hear what they were saying but he could tell by the way that they were waving their arms that they were arguing. Malherbe and Johnson, they had revealed their names. Apart from satisfying his curiosity this was a bad thing, they would never have divulged their identities if they had any intention of freeing the pair of them. The prospect of an imminent death swallowed him up. If this was a film set the ropes would be loose and they would free their hands. Carla would grab a bottle and knock Malherbe unconscious. He, himself, Tom the pacifist, would strangle Johnson with his bare hands, watch the life slip from his eyes and they would walk hand in hand into the sunset accompanied by some romantic soundtrack. But this was no film, there was to be no Hollywood ending. He closed his eyes and in his mind he was in a deserted cinema watching a film of his life. It was in black and white. A lurch from pub to pub, error strewn, laced with humour from the dark side but beneath it all, fundamentally, there lay a decent man; a 'what if man', a 'could have been' man, flawed but worth an investment. It was the things that he was in control of that had let him down, the hedonist within. The old booze had clouded his thoughts, hampered his judgements and, ultimately, destabilised him. The irony, the twist of sobriety, was that the faint glow of the future was to be extinguished before it had a chance to catch light. When he had finally turned a corner that didn't have a pub at the end of it, met someone who could lift his spirits, empathize with him, the road stopped; death in a foreign field. Not even an unmarked grave, just a body in a run-down barn in the middle of nowhere. Tom wished he was sat on the veranda with Carla playing her *Tonight the streets are ours* by Richard Hawley but the reality was too bleak to contemplate. He was sucked back from his ruminations by the sound of her voice.

"Tom, it's the truth, you have to believe me. I've no idea what the hell Greg was mixed up in but whatever it was, it has nothing to do with me."

All he could do was nod, she was pleading with him, her tone desperate.

"These guys hate each other Tom, it's obvious. Maybe we can play one off against the other. I think Johnson believes me, I could see it in his eyes."

Tom nodded in limp affirmation, he admired her wild optimism but he was a born pessimist.

Malherbe walked in, mumbling to himself. He was carrying a bag that was rattling. Johnson followed in his wake, looking peeved. Tom didn't envisage the bag contained tools to fix the old tractor. He tried not to think too much about what it might contain. The heat was unbearable. Sweat from his brow had irritated his eyes and he was desperate to rub them.

Malherbe sat on the tractor seat and smiled. He lit a cigarette.

"Right, enough of this fokken around, let's get down to business, they say the truth hurts; time to find out."

He circled Carla and ran his fingers through her hair.

"Some pretty chick hey, it's a pity I am going to have to ruin your looks honey. You'll be fit for a freak show when I've finished with you. I want the truth not some bullshit, now spill the beans you whore."

He grabbed a chunk of her hair and pulled it hard. She screamed. Tom shouted at him to stop but it was a bloodless gurgle muffled by the tape.

"Listen Carla just tell him the truth, make it easier on yourself", said Johnson.

"For Christ sakes I am telling the bloody truth. I'm travelling round Africa for a few months, I knew Greg in university and I just intended to stay a few days to recharge my batteries. He had some sort of emergency, or so he told me, and I offered to help him out till he got back. As for the stick, I don't know how it got there. Presumably other people have stayed in the room why don't you ask them? I found it yesterday after the burglary when I was packing. I don't know why I put it in my bag. I should have just left it there. I suppose I was curious but I haven't looked at it. I haven't got a clue what's on there."

She was jabbering away but it was a lost cause. Tom's head slumped forward, and he stared at the floor.

"Nice speech honey but really, do you expect us to believe that and who is this jerk you're with?" Malherbe nodded towards Tom.

"He's a friend I've met since I've been in Prince Albert."

"A bit more than a friend I'd say judging by your canoodling outside the coffee shop."

"Yeh he is but what's that got to do with you, it's not a crime is it? You're the pair committing the fucking crime. We're fucking innocent and you should let us go, talk some sense into him Johnson."

Tom watched Johnson to gauge his reaction but his eyes were ambulance windows, giving nothing away. He stood there like a witness at an execution, gaunt and impassive. He lit a cigarette and Tom detected a slight tremor in his hand as he raised it to his mouth. It was a feint seed of hope, and maybe he was imagining it, but he had to have something to cling onto, however tenuous it was.

"You're like a busted record honey, needle tripping on the same old groove. I guess we'll have to do this the hard way, time for some fun hey Johnson?" Malherbe opened up his bag and pulled out a small blanket, which he laid on the floor. He took his time organising the tools of his trade and arranged them neatly, like some old army doctor in the field; scalpel, assorted knives, knuckle duster, pliers, hammer and an electric battery-operated drill.

"Why the wide eyes guys, what did you expect, a picnic hamper?"

All Tom had was his eyes; the blinds were down on the rest of his world. All his previous trials and tribulations were irrelevant, all the self -analysis worthless; death in the company of strangers. He closed his eyes and from within the darkness remembered a morbid poem he'd written in the early hours of some drunken, depressive night.

The Quiet Room

All the silver slug trails
In the garden of life
Lead to the quiet room.
I'm sat here now in the glass cube,
Backside planted on a see-through plastic chair.
It is a wordless room.
They hand me a black framed iPad and press play.
There's dad, cigar smoke swirling,
Playing 'On top of old smoky' on that Spanish guitar
He bought down Cathedral road.
Mum's pouring herself a glass of wine
And missing the glass.
My kids are waving at me from a tent
Perched on the cliff at Durdle Dor.
I stand, try to leave but they restrain me.
I see the four seasons,
One through each seamless window.
It's Autumn to which I turn,
I come from there
And I will return.
I watch the brown leaves harden
And crinkle, turning to dust,
Embers of light
Slowly extinguished.

Chapter 34

Jeff sat in a side office behind reception. It was a windowless room with just a table and two chairs. He'd been there for twenty minutes, waiting for the learning mentor. She was overworked. There were too many problems in the school for one person to deal with. It was like spinning plates on sticks at a circus, a constant run around to prevent them crashing to the floor all at once. He looked at a poster on the wall about levels of well-being but couldn't be bothered to read it. Eventually she arrived, flustered, a stack of unkempt papers in her hand, an ink stain on her fingers.

"Morning Jeff, I'm surprised to see you here, what's the problem?"

"You tell me", he replied.

She was unnerved by his attitude and sullen stare. He was normally a happy go lucky sort of a kid, popular with his classmates, not the sort of child that was usually on her radar.

"Listen Jeff, if you don't talk to me, I won't be able to help."

He sat there in silence.

"Your teachers are concerned about you, they say you've become withdrawn and take little part in the lessons. It's unlike you. Is there anything happening in school that's upsetting you, any bullying?"

"No."

"Is that all you've got to say Jeff, is anything happening at home?"

He could feel the tears welling up and he tried to hold them back. She saw his shoulders shake as he lay his head on the table.

"Jeff, talk to me, you can't keep it inside, what's going on and I'll try my best to help, it's something at home isn't it?"

She was conscious of not pushing him too far or putting words into his mouth. The disclosure had to come from him. He nodded.

"Ok Jeff I realize it's difficult, but you just have to tell me. Today it's confidential but if what you say is of a certain nature other people may have to be involved. Do you understand?"

She hated saying this but, by law, she had to make it clear. Every step had to be done by the book, carefully logged for future reference.

Jeff raised his head.

"What do you mean of a certain nature?"

"Well", she tried to choose her words carefully, "if something was happening to you at home, I'd have to do something about it."

"What, like abuse, it's nothing like that", he was mortified.

She breathed a sigh of relief. Lots of people live behind middle class curtains but you never knew what was going on behind them. Abuse spanned the spectrum from poverty to privilege.

"Glad to hear it Jeff, now take your time and tell me what's bothering you, is it about your mum and dad?"

She'd checked his admission form and noted that his parents had divorced though they had joint custody. He primarily lived with his mum. In some ways he was lucky because he presumably saw his dad on a regular basis. Half the school were single parent families, invariably with the mum, and a fair percentage of the dads disappeared for good. It was a cruel world.

Jeff looked at her and hesitated. He didn't like sharing problems and preferred dealing with them himself. He was a closed book and found it hard to express his feelings, even to his nearest and dearest. He sometimes confided in his sister but lately she was all hair and make- up, her with her pink sheets and Justin Bieber poster. She had little time for him. Mum was stressed with work and preoccupied with her new man and dad, well, he'd legged it to a different hemisphere and he was pissed half the time anyway. He'd tried hard to supress his emotions in school but they'd spilled out, not in the form of anger but he'd been rumbled through self-enforced solitude. Here in the now with Miss Stevens, it was the day the sky finally caved in. Silence was no longer an option.

"It's my dad, I think something's happened to my dad."

"Give him a ring after school, I'm sure he's fine, he lives in Walthamstow, he's not ill is he?"

"He's gone away; I've not seen him for a few weeks."

"Gone away, what to prison?" -Common enough in the building, she thought.

"No, he's gone on a long holiday to South Africa to clear his mind, that's what he told me."

"Has he been in touch since he left?"

"Yeh, he's been sending me a text every day but I haven't received anything for a couple of days."

"He's probably just lost his phone, Jeff, or travelled to a part with poor reception. If anything was seriously wrong somebody would have informed your mum, have you talked to her about it, what did she say?"

"She says he's probably gone on a bender, typical of him. He likes to have a drink, my dad, but he's gone to sort himself out, that's what he told me, said he'd come back a better man."

Miss Stevens looked at the vulnerable child in front of her and felt his pain. She put her arm on his shoulders and gave him a squeeze. There wasn't enough love in the world.

"Do you want me to give your mum a ring Jeff?"

"No, please don't do that, she'll go mad and panic."

"Alright Jeff, it's easy to say but try not to worry, I'm sure your dad's fine and he'll be in touch very soon. In the meantime, try to focus in school and join in more in class. Get back to being yourself, have fun with your mates."

He stood up and walked past the desk.

"Remember my door is always open, you know where to find me if you need me"

She watched him disappear down the corridor, one blazer amongst the throng. Her eyes were drawn to a poster of a Larkin poem on the wall outside the English room. The lines slagging off parents were all too appropriate.

Chapter 35

Steyn left Celestino's via the front door, if anybody questioned him he could always flash the police badge and send them on their way. He'd spent the last ten minutes inside thinking of his next move. Botha was efficient and it wouldn't be long before he had more information about Carla Thompson. His gut feeling was that she would have a clean record but that didn't necessarily mean much. Greg Joseph was apparently a law-abiding citizen but he was lying on a cold slab in the Stellenbosch morgue with a tag tied to his toe. As he walked down Kerk Straat Steyn grudgingly accepted the fact that he couldn't be the lone ranger. This wasn't the suburbs of Stellenbosch where he had connections, a network of informants that he had cultivated and sustained over a number of years. He was a stranger in the backwoods and couldn't rely on his reputation to open doors. Help was required if he was to trawl the murky depths and unravel the unholy mess. He couldn't exactly knock every door in town like Mary and Joseph looking for a place to stay. He needed other feet on the ground, people he knew and trusted. It was worth a try, he called Colonel Sikosi.

"Colonel Sikosi speaking."

"Hi boss, Steyn here, there have been some developments in the Joseph case."

"Ah, Steyn, glad you've rung, saves me the bother, there's been a complaint about you."

"Complaint?" Steyn was mystified.

"Yeh, you didn't listen to my pep talk did you, remember the buzz words, communication, teamwork? Well Captain Smit in Prince Albert has personally told me you were surly and aggressive. What the hell are you playing at? He's one of us man."

"Christ boss, that's a load of crap, he's just some jumped up country bumpkin who's had his nose put of joint."

"Is that all you've got to say for yourself?"

"Look, he resents an outsider creeping into his precious little kingdom. I promise you sir that I was professional at all times. I was only with him for a couple of minutes and he was disinterested to say the least. It's me who should be bloody reporting him."

Steyn could feel his hackles rising but tried to keep a lid on them. He knew Sikosi was itching to exploit any grievances levelled against him.

"Update me on the case Steyn, you're not doing my blood pressure any good, I thought you'd be less of a pain in the arse the further away you'd be but it's unfortunately not proving to be true."

Sikosi glanced at his watch, lunch time was beckoning.

"I checked out Joseph's coffee shop. No major finds there. I rifled through his desk, it seems he was heavily in debt. There were a load of irate letters from the bank. I found a small drugs stash. It's possible he was involved in drug related activities. A woman was staying with him, an English girl, but she's disappeared. I found her passport and Botha is checking her out. The worrying thing is there were signs of a disturbance in the coffee shop. A tablecloth and cutlery looked to have been dragged to the floor and there were scuff marks near the door. I think that this girl, Carla, may well have been abducted. I reckon there must have been at least two of them otherwise how would they get her in a car without looking too suspicious."

"All of that is supposition on your part Steyn what does Captain Smit think?" said Sikosi.

"I went in alone boss, Smit was busy. Can you send up a couple of guys to help me out? I can't do this on my own."

Sikosi was apoplectic.

"No, I bloody can't. Now you listen to me Steyn, get your arse down to the local police station and sit down with this Smit and work with him. He knows the fucking area, he bloody lives there. No more shit from you, sort yourself out, do you understand?"

"Yes boss." Sikosi hung up.

Steyn could imagine the veins throbbing in his temple. This was a thin tightrope he was walking, and he didn't want to fall deeper than the Fish river canyon. There was no longer any other alternative other than a slow walk to the police station and an attempt to build a bridge of reconciliation with the aforementioned Captain Smit. Complete arse that he was.

He strolled slowly down the road, picking up a cool drink from one of the seemingly endless supply of cafes in town. Two guys were going at it hammer and tongs on the tennis courts. The ball was an apt metaphor for how he felt, smashed between Sikosi and Smit with no control of the force or the trajectory. For a long time now, he had thought about resigning from the police and becoming a private detective. At least he would then be master of his own destiny and not some political pawn in the wider scheme of things. The problem was he couldn't see himself trailing the husbands of rich wives down the avenues of infidelity. It was the edginess of policing that enraptured him. The thrill of chasing hardened criminals, the blood and guts of it. He might be a flawed character, irritable and hard to work with, but he knew the difference between right and wrong. People could say whatever they liked about him but he knew his moral compass was intact. It was us against them and he approached his job with an almost religious zeal. Trying to locate some distant relative of a client to inform them of an inheritance would never be enough for him. As much as he sometimes hated it, he was a cop through and through, there was no disguising the truth.

The reception desk at the police station was empty. Steyn sat down and waited. He could hear the drunks wailing from the cells at the rear of the building. Botha called.

"Hi Captain, I checked out Carla Thompson, she's clean as a whistle, no criminal record. She's a primary school teacher on a sabbatical. She's been travelling round Africa. No obvious connection with Joseph but we are working on it. Hey boss she's a bit of a looker isn't she?"

Steyn ignored the comment. He defined people in two categories; victims and perpetrators. It didn't matter to him what they looked like.

"Thanks Botha, call me if you find out anything new."

He watched the minutes clicking away on the police issue clock hanging on the wall next to a smiling photograph of Jacob Zuma, must have been taken before they started investigating the renovations at Nkandla. There were a couple of empty police cars parked outside. He picked up a local paper that had been left on a chair and browsed through its pages. Nothing much seemed to happen in this godforsaken town. The adverts were bigger than the news.

"Can I help?"

Steyn looked up, a police officer had finally plucked up the courage to stand behind the desk.

"Yes, I'm Captain Steyn from the Stellenbosch police, I was here earlier and I need to speak to Captain Smit urgently, where is he?"

"I am afraid that won't be possible sir, he's out and about."

"You call him and tell him Steyn wants to see him now, I'm not leaving here till I see him face to face."

Steyn sat down again. He hated wasting time. It was a valuable commodity and it was running out.

Chapter 36

There was a trail of urine running down Tom's leg, wetting his laces. An ever-expanding wet patch discoloured his shorts. He'd tried telling them he needed the toilet but any attempt to talk became a meaningless drone behind the tape. Anyway, they were looking at Carla. He was an inconvenient side show. Malherbe stood next to her and started to spout off again.

"Well, plan A clearly didn't work but it rarely does. A man of my experience has a plan for every letter of the alphabet. I am the dictionary of destruction."

He laughed at his own pathetic joke. This man was worse than psychotic, he was completely insane, the rest of this longest day stretched out ahead but it didn't bear thinking about. What he would give now for the dull anonymity of London.

Malherbe turned his attention to Tom.

"Pissed yourself have you? Shit scared no doubt. So you fokken should be. Let's see how much Carla really likes you."

He lit another cigarette and lent over, blowing smoke in Tom's face.

"Women like her chew up guys like you and spit them out on the floor. You're no more than a notch on her headboard. Or are you?"

He stabbed the lit end of the cigarette into the back of Tom's hand, ignored the muffled scream, and looked at Carla.

"What do you say to that miss pretty panties? I could make a nice symmetrical pattern around his eyes, a circle of weals, a ring of fire, whatever you wanna call it."

"For Christ sakes leave him alone, this has nothing to do with him. Don't hurt him anymore. How many times do I have to fucking tell you? We're innocent."

Carla sobbed, the bite on her leg hurt like hell and she feared what might happen next. She had a horrible feeling he was going to rape her with Tom forced to watch and Johnson weakly acquiescing, too scared of his colleague to intervene. Bullies always had a passive gang that hid behind the main man. They liked the safety and anonymity of the shadows.

Johnson spoke. Carla was startled; she'd had him down as an elective mute.

"She could be telling the truth, she'd have cracked by now. Call the boss, ask him what he wants us to do. We should have told him as soon as we picked them up, but you didn't listen to me, did you?"

Malherbe turned a wrathful gaze on his partner and gave vent to his pent-up anger.

"What the fokken hell has gotten into you man? You've gone soft in the head, taken in by the ways she looks. Well let me tell you, she's guilty. She's a lying bitch. As for this other idiot, he's just thinking with his cock like the rest of us."

"But the boss might want to talk to her. We've no idea what's on that stick or why it's so important to him. I'll call him", said Johnson

"No you fokken won't."

Malherbe pointed a gun and his fingers were twitching, sweat dripping off him. Tom watched the two of them stare each other out.

The criminal population of the barn was about to lose fifty per cent of its population, assuming Carla was innocent. He knew, in his heart, she was. The problem was that Johnson was the only one of the pair capable of displaying a modicum of reason. Without him there was no hope.

"Christ Malherbe, calm down, just remember who we work for, who pays us. He won't be happy if he's not kept in the picture."

Johnson kept his eyes on the gun and backed away. He sat down by the door, trying to diffuse the situation.

"If you interfere one more time, I swear I'll kill you. Now let me get on with my work. The boss likes answers and when I have them, I'll call him, understand?"

Johnson nodded, stone faced.

Malherbe lit another cigarette and slowly inhaled, the packet was nearly empty. He surveyed his tools laid out on the carpet and weighed up his options; a sharp knife or the drill? The sound of that would get them squealing. He wanted blood, to feel it on his fingers, taste it on his lips. Drill through the finger nail of Tom, that would make the bitch blab the truth then he'd fuck her senseless, spread those long legs wide. The thought of it made his cock harden.

The sound of the drill had them writhing. They were both straining at the ropes, eyes bulging like bullfrogs on steroids. He stood at the top of an ugly triangle and felt the power coursing through him, a step closer, the rhythmic hum of the drill reverberating around the room, he waved it in their faces like a small kid with a toy light sabre. Walking behind them, he bent to his knees, inching the drill closer and closer to Tom's shaking fingers.

"Stop, stop, I'll tell you everything."

Tom looked at Carla, what the fuck was she going to say? He felt his chest tightening up.

"Well the little bird can sing."

Malherbe turned off the drill and pulled up a chair close to Carla's.

"OK songbird, what's really been going on, what've you and dead Gregg been up to?"

Carla closed her eyes and Tom hoped she was cooking up a cock and bull story that was believable. He didn't doubt she would be lying but he realized it was an attempt to prolong their stay of execution. In the short term it had saved his fingers.

"Come on, stop fokken about with me."

Malherbe was irritated by the slowness of her response and he tightened his grip on the drill.

The world seemed to have stopped turning. All their eyes were trained on her. The only sound was that of a gentle breeze rustling the bushes outside. Life and death were arguing between these four walls, but which was it to be?

"It was a scam, we…"

Carla was interrupted by Pharell Williams launching into *Happy*; it was the ringtone of Johnson's phone bubbling away in his top pocket. He answered.

"Hello boss, yes we have her, but we had to pick up a guy she was hanging around with. We've got them in a safe house out of town."

"Yup she had the memory stick in the bag."

"She's not told us anything yet but Malherbe's just getting her to open up. What do you want us to do with them when we've finished?"

"Ok boss, see you later today, I'll tell Malherbe to do that, where should he meet you?"

"I understand. Bye."

Johnson smiled.

"There's been a change of plan Malherbe, the boss wants to speak to Carla himself."

"You're winding me up."

"Nope, there's an airstrip nearby. He'll be here in a couple of hours."

"What about these two?"

Malherbe was fucking annoyed.

"I just have to keep them locked up here until he arrives. He wants you to check out the building where the stuff is stashed before you collect him. It's on the gravel road to Leeu-Gamka. I'll tell you where exactly when we are outside."

Malherbe closed his eyes and ran his fingers through his hair.

"Fuck it."

He left for the car with Johnson in tow.

"Shit, Tom, thank God for mobile phones. My mind went blank. I was struggling to think of a bullshit story to stop him from hurting you."

All Tom could do was nod like a plastic donkey in the back window of a car. Now they had a temporary reprieve but shit, what would the boss be like? If there were incremental steps of evil, what if he was further up the stairs than Malherbe? A couple more hours of life had opened up but the long-term prospects hadn't changed. Christ, if they didn't hurry up, he would die of thirst. His mouth was as dry as the river beds that crossed this barren land.

Chapter 37

Steyn looked at his watch; the minutes were stacking up in a wasteful pile. Two hours sat here and still no sign of Smit. Where the hell was he? Probably lecturing some down and out for stealing a bottle of Klippies from the OK Store, threatening to lock him up with the other drunks to join the wailing hordes. The cells sounded as if they were full of women giving multiple births. His phone beeped, it was a text from Christel-

'Gone to stay at my sisters in Paarl for a few days. Freddie's away on a cricket tour not that you'd know about it. When you get back call me. WE NEED TO TALK.'

We need to talk. He knew what that meant, another request to attend marriage guidance sessions, listen to some stranger prying into their lives with a tissue box between them and a glossy brochure to take home and read over breakfast. At some point he would have to agree, they couldn't go on like this, barely speaking just existing. He was about to reply when Smit walked past him with no sign of acknowledgment, face flushed.

"In my office, Steyn."

They sat either side of a bare desk. 'In' and 'Out' trays were clearly surplus to requirements in Prince Albert. Steyn broke the ice.

"I need your help Captain Smit, I've reason to believe that Carla Thompson, the girl staying with Joseph, has been abducted."

"What?"

"I think it's related to Joseph's murder. My hunch is that its drug related, and her life is at risk."

"Hold on Steyn, you've only been here five minutes, don't get carried away with your wild ideas, things like that don't happen in Prince Albert and if they ever did I would know about it first. Joseph was murdered in Stellenbosch so you should pursue your investigations there and stop poking around my town."

Steyn wanted to grab him by the throat and rattle that fat belly of his, the pompous arse, but he restrained himself. Assaulting a fellow police officer would give Sikosi the green light to sack him without the need for a prolonged tribunal and Lord knows South Africa had enough of them on the go. He had to somehow circumnavigate the road block and get this idiot on his side, shock him to his senses.

"I was in the coffee shop today. There were signs of a struggle, cutlery everywhere, tablecloth pulled to the floor, scuff marks near the door, drugs under Joseph's bed and a drawer full of debt letters. What do you think all that means Captain Smit?"

Steyn could tell he'd riled him, his cheeks had reddened and he'd lost the power of speech, albeit momentarily.

"Pardon? You stroll into the coffee shop and turn it over without bothering to tell me and then have the cheek to come in here spouting off your crack pot theories. Sikosi will love this."

"Hold on Smit, I was passing the coffee shop when I heard a noise. I didn't have time to call for back up but I'm telling you now. We need to work together. This girl's life may be at stake."

"So you keep saying."

"If the press get hold of this they'll be swarming all over this town in a matter of hours and you will have to answer a lot of awkward questions. As a matter a fact I know a few journalists who'd be very interested in a story like this."

Smit swallowed hard, trying not to give his emotions away. Steyn was a devious bastard clearly capable of being under- handed.

"Look Steyn I'm bogged down with work but I can spare you a couple of guys for two days max and, listen to me, you are not to do anything without informing me first. This town is under my jurisdiction and I will not tolerate any more 'fly by night policing'. We do things by the book here. Colonel Sikosi doesn't like you and neither do I. Don't make your life any harder than it already is. Do you understand?"

"Yup, it seems clear enough."

Steyn sat back and folded his arms. They'd sunk to the level of veiled threats, each trying to out manoeuvre the other without losing face. It was an unholy alliance which failed to mask their mutual distrust, but it gave him something to work with.

"Thank you for releasing the officers to work with me. Needless to say, I will inform you of my every movement. Let's hope we can find this girl before it's too late. We'll comb the town first, check out the hotel and B&Bs and take it from there."

They parted with their customary limp handshake and Steyn sensed that Smit's mind was somewhere else. He'd seemed preoccupied throughout their brief meeting, unable to disguise his disinterest. If some drug ring was exposed in his small town it would put a gold embossed certificate on his wall, even bring promotion but, by all accounts, he wasn't bothered. He was probably just thinking about what to put on the braai tonight and what to drink for sundowners.

Chapter 38

Tom had fallen asleep. Carla didn't have the heart to wake him.

He was lying in the comfortable bed of a dream, a nostalgic trawl through childhood memories back in Wales. He would always be Welsh despite living in London for thirty years. Part of him would always be that child, exploring the hills and woods, meandering the terraced streets that were dwarfed by the coal tip and its newly sprouting grass carpet. He remembered blackberry picking with his grandad and endlessly pulling the long toilet chain in the empty train station just because he wanted to, him and gramps laughing like drains. These trips always ended in the pub where he once gave himself a Guinness moustache whilst propped on the bar, aged three. Fell about laughing they did. It turned out to be a portent of things to come. A love affair with Guinness and its siblings, destined to end in tears. God, how he loved grandad, him with the gentle ways and twinkle in the eye, the way in which he accepted the defeat of life with dignity. The way in which he stayed strong when the mines shut and a day's work was taken from him. Those days, cradled in his arms, listening to the stories of a lifetime underground and now, deep in the tunnels of his own mind, Tom remembered a poem he'd written about him, years ago, not long before he died. It was a testament to a hard life. Most of his poems seemed to deal with a sense of loss and this one was no different. Poetry from the dark side had always come more easily than the sugar-coated verse of hearts and flowers.

Maerdy Gras (Little Moscow)

The shafts of his mind were coal mine black. Dust lay on dust. Lungs bloated hoover bags ready for recycling. Wheelchair sat square to the view, brakes on, always the brakes on, just the eyes were rolling, remembering, reminiscing and kissing the past, holding it like a youthful lover, caressing it with fingers maimed deep beneath the earth.

But the scars live on. The 'blue tattoos' permanently etched and inked by that old fossil time, legs stiff as chair legs, heart trapped beneath the surface, buried with the memories. There was no more Mrs Evans from number 77 with her lips as red as the commies that once bedecked these streets; her washing line empty save the plastic pegs.

Loose change rubbed shoulders with the odd note in his threadbare pocket. He gently tinkled the contents and listened to the sounds spilling like froth off a fresh −un, glasses clinking, amplified laughter, pub brimming with the unemployed drinking their dole checks like there was no tomorrow but it always comes and so does the day after.

Call it a carnival of destitutes. It's a long way from pit head to death bed, stumbling slowly step by step, past the firedamp and the flint mills, the coal mine canaries and pit ponies put out to grass. Blame the butcher of Grantham for this slaughter and rile at the absurdity of her state funeral. Forget T.S.Elliot. This   is   the   fucking wasteland.

Chapter 39

He could see grandad's smile caught in the cricket photo from 1924; Zion cricket club, Pontypridd and district league champions. There he was, far right with his Elvis quiff thirty years too early. The photo, still in its original frame, took pride of place on his bedroom wall back in London. He looked at it every day, kissed it sometimes.

***

Tom awoke. He checked the wall for the photograph, checked the bedside table to see the time, tried to wipe his eyes with his hands but he couldn't move them. In that fleeting moment between dreams and reality, that sudden step off a cliff, he was lost between worlds. As he slowly came back to his senses it all slipped back into place. The dilapidated tractor was still there, as were the instruments of torture, the sun reflecting off one of the sharp blades. He remembered Malherbe driving off and hoped he'd never see that bastard again. Johnson was nowhere to be seen but couldn't be far away. The noose had been slightly loosened but they were still rooted to the hangman's podium, permanent fixtures on death row. He tried talking to Carla, but he sounded like *Chewbacca*. He'd forgotten about the bloody masking tape. Tied and gagged, a blindfold would complete the unholy trinity. Shit, what a mess.

"Tom, Tom, listen, I'm going to get Johnson to take that tape off you. I'll tell him we need to drink some fluids. I think we can work on him. He doesn't look comfortable with the way things are developing. Did you see his face when Malherbe had that drill?"

She'd lost it now, rabbiting on and on. All Tom could do was nod, his communicative skills confined to an affirmative or negative shake of the head with no elaboration possible. She kept harping on about Johnson as if he was as malleable as wet clay. He felt her optimism was futile but he'd try his best to back her up. He was hardly the world's best ally. A lifetime spent avoiding his own problems had taken its toll. Failure fuelled failure. Fate blew him around like an empty plastic bag on a windswept street. Yet meeting Carla had changed his outlook, made him see opportunities for change. He'd taken a step, albeit a tentative one, towards some form of redemption. The first strides towards reassuming control over his life and he couldn't just give up. He winked at her. She smiled.

Johnson walked in, puffing on a cigarette. He looked tired.

"We need water. Can you take the masking tape off? He can hardly hurt you with his voice can he? Have a heart."

Johnson took out a couple of bottles from his bag and removed the tape. Tom took in a lung full of air and spat out the bile.

"Fucking hell Johnson how can you stand around and watch this happening? Have some self-respect man."

Johnson raised the water to their lips but said nothing.

"How can you let that arsehole push you around? I could see you weren't impressed by the violence. I saw you flinch. He'll kill you too one day, you know that don't you?" Carla was watching him carefully for any reaction, but he was giving nothing away.

"Give us a chance. Christ, you must see that Carla's telling the truth, we're not from your world, we're just two innocent people caught up in this mess. Do you really want our blood on your hands?"

Tom paused for breath. He'd given it his best shot for what it was worth. Carla smiled at him.

"Tom's right, we don't deserve this, neither do you. When I look at you I can see a decent man trying to crawl out, do you really belong with scum like Malherbe?"

"Shut up, you've no fucking idea." Johnson was angry and agitated. He paced the room.

"There's nowhere I can go where they won't find me. There is no way out."

Carla watched him closely; he was close to breaking point.

"I can tell Malherbe wanted to rape me. I saw it in those cold eyes. He's probably thinking about it now and he'll be back. Are you going to stand there and watch like some pervert in a mac, can you live with that?"

He snapped, jumped up, screamed.

"I'm going to end this shit once and for all."

He cut the ropes that bound them and waved his gun in their faces.

"Turn around, face the wall, now!"

Tom held Carla's hand and focused on an old oil can and its line of dried dribble. The sound of the gun ripped the air.

Chapter 39

The lump on Malherbe's head had swollen to the size of an elephant's bollock. The call from Radebe at such a crucial time had driven him to the edge, not that he was ever far from it. The urge for blood is what drove him on, pleasure from pain soothed him. Every squeal of anguish excited him. The thought of shagging that icy English chick consumed him. He was raw, a savage and he fucking loved it. That girl would get it alright, but he would have to wait and by God, he didn't like waiting. He lived for the thrill of the now.

As he drove the car back to Prince Albert, and attempted to calm himself down, he took some solace from the fact that it was only a matter of time. In a few hours Radebe would get what he wanted and be gone. The playing field would be empty, and he could finish the job at a leisurely pace. With a bit of luck Johnson would fly out with the boss and he'd have the barn and the girl to himself. A bullet in that guy's head would loosen her up.

There was a crack in the side window where he'd smacked his head in frustration, but it didn't obscure the wooden sign to the Bush pub. He checked his watch, plenty of time till he had to pick up the boss from the airport. A couple of sundowners were in order to calm the nerves and lift his spirits. It wouldn't take five minutes to check the drugs stash before going to the airstrip. The light was fading and it would soon be dark. He parked up next to an old Volkswagen combi and walked in. The Stormers were playing the Sharks at Newlands. A group of men, some in kit, were hollering at the tv, swearing at the ref. The rest of the place was empty and in need of a clean. There were empty glasses and bottles littered on the tables. It must have been some late-night party. The pub was a mile or so from the town and he could sense it didn't belong there. The genteel tea rooms of the main street would disapprove.

Malherbe got himself a chilled Windhoek lager and picked up some cigarettes from the machine. He made his way outside where it was quiet. Dusk was falling and it was humid. He scanned the sky, there could be a thunderstorm brewing. By an old dead tree he noticed an archaic dentist's chair covered in a thin film of dust. He pictured Carla strapped to it, legs apart, begging for mercy. Lord that girl had it coming. His mind was full of her, billboard full, like a garish advertisement for an exotic foreign movie. He lit a cigarette to calm his nerves. It was time to get his head together and work out what the hell was going on. The whore was obviously guilty but Radebe didn't want her divulging any secrets about the memory stick. Whatever was on there must be big news. Mr Radebe didn't chart himself a plane and hot foot it up here just to take in the Karoo scenery. He was shitting himself big time. Malherbe smiled. If he boxed clever, he could catapult himself into the big league. Walk tall in Jo'burg with the main men.

Gleason answered after a couple of rings.

"It's Malherbe here. Things are bubbling up baas. We picked up the girl and she has the memory stick. Radebe won't let us interrogate her. He's flying up himself to talk to her. Whatever is on the stick must be toxic stuff."

There was silence at the other end. Malherbe could imagine him rubbing his chin, weighing up his options.

"Interesting, leave it with me. I'll send some of my guys down, they'll be in touch." He hung up. Shit, he was a man of few words.

Malherbe sat back; a twenty second phone call and life may be forever changed. He'd wanted to discuss his new position, but Gleason was a busy man. There'd be time for that when the dust had settled and this crappy little town was history. He sipped his beer and thought about the future, the past was bricked up, any nagging memories blocked out. It was the only way he could cope. The endless childhood beatings were banished from his mind, anaesthetised by his own violent disposition. Every blow and scream empowered him. He checked his watch, better go and check the drug stash before picking up the boss, follow instructions and act normal. He finished his drink and threw the bottle into the undergrowth.

***

The gravel road to Leeu-Gamka was empty. The small barren hills that bordered it, quiet. Darkness was on its way, the light fading fast. Malherbe parked up behind the building out of sight from the road. There were a few tins of paint in the corner and some boxes of tiles as if to give the impression of someone moving in but it was the pile covered by tarpaulin that he was interested in. He lifted it gently. The drugs were still there, enough to keep the Cape Flats high till Easter and beyond, the street value incalculable. Mr Radebe was a rich man, for now. Propped behind the door he noticed a baseball bat. He picked it up and trialled a few swings; ideal for cracking a knee cap or two. He tucked it under his arm and left the place as he found it. The clock in the car said 6.30, with full beams on, he headed for the airstrip. Things were about to get interesting around here. A sleepy town awakes.

Chapter 40

Jeff was at the bus terminus in Walthamstow waiting for the number 97 to take him to school. The place had been done up, the whole area being slowly gentrified, coffee shops springing up everywhere populated by the yummy mummy brigade with snotty nosed kids called Caspian in tow, ill mannered, unkempt hair. Houses in the village, small terraced places, were going for a million. The world had gone mad. This ethnic mix, this melting pot, was home, all he knew. He thought of dad's childhood, roaming the hills in his Welsh village, home by dark, knowing everyone. It was a different planet. He checked his phone for the hundredth time; still no texts. He'd listened to Miss Stevens, tried to take heart from her reassurances but it wasn't her dad who'd disappeared off the face of the earth was it? He was sick with worry. Something must have happened to him, he could feel it deep inside.

The bus arrived, the masses charged as if to push it over, but he stood back. He couldn't face school, not today. The crowd jostled, moving as one. Heels clicking the steps, tap dancing underground, bound for the Victoria line. Jeff stuffed his blazer in his rucksack and put on a sweatshirt. He sat in a quiet carriage at the end of the train and checked the tube map. He wanted to lose himself in the city, be just another face with story untold.

***

The gorilla behind the toughened glass viewed the public with distaste. Tourists ignored the camera warnings and clicked away. It was like a circus freak show. Jeff wandered past the empty elephant enclosure and climbed the stairway. He watched the giraffes with black tongues nibble the leaves. It wasn't under African skies but it was as close as he could get. His phone buzzed. It was a text from mum.

'ARE YOU OK? WHERE ARE YOU!!! CALL ME. SCHOOL SAID YOU ARE NOT THERE?????'

He unzipped the side pocket of the rucksack and pulled out his mum's Barclay card. It had been easy to slip it out of her purse when she was showering before heading off to work earlier that morning. The pin number was written in his school diary; she'd been pleased when he'd offered to go food shopping at Sainsbury's with her and had been too busy jabbering with the checkout girl to notice him hovering next to her when she punched in the four digits.

It was a slow walk to the exit, past a horde of tiny school kids in over-sized fluorescent council workman tabards; pack lunches swinging like elephants' trunks. He reached the tube station and sunk beneath the city.

Chapter 41

Steyn viewed his two new colleagues with the weary eyes of a veteran. They were barely out of nappies, their trousers neatly ironed, shoes polished to parade standard. He sighed. Smit had given him the new kids on the block. They were full of beans but he doubted if they'd be well stocked in the intuition department. At least they'd have some local knowledge and perhaps he could tap into their youthful enthusiasm. Six legs were better than two and time was of the essence. He introduced himself and briefly outlined the case as they made their way to the main street. Van Buren was to start checking B and B's at the top of the town, Strydom at the bottom. Steyn himself would check the restaurants, gallery and Swartberg Hotel. He gave them each a photo of Carla and waited for the expected comments but they walked off in different directions without saying a word. They arranged to meet outside Celestino's at eight.

Steyn's gloomy mood was dampened by the darkness. If his theory was right the search would prove fruitless, but you had to start with the basics to eliminate the faint chance she was right under their noses, chilling out after being scared by the burglary. If, as he thought, the bad guys had abducted her, she would be holed up in a safe house out of town or worse still, on the road to nowhere. What he would give now for a clue, no matter how small, something that would ignite the investigation and speed up proceedings. He drew a blank in the first few restaurants but a waitress in the Gallery recognized Carla from the photograph and said she'd dined there a couple of nights back. She was with a guy and she remembered them laughing a lot.

"Do you think they were a couple or just friends?"

The waitress paused a while, "judging by the way they looked at each other I'd say they were lovers in the first throes of romance, they were very animated and hanging on each other's every word. Definitely not an old married couple, they munch olives in silence."

Steyn thought of his last meal out with Christel. He'd watched the fisherman on the harbour wall and she'd been engrossed with some trivia on her mobile phone. They'd barely conversed.

"What did this guy look like?"

"Average height, about 1.70, slight build, well-tanned, dark hair with grey flecks, salt and pepper stubble."

"Was he South African?"

"No, I think he was from the U.K but he had a strange accent, I don't think he's English."

"Scottish, Irish, Welsh?"

"I've no idea; they all sound the same to me."

Steyn knew what she meant, he'd visited Britain in his younger days and had been confused by the wide variety of dialects in such a small place, every twenty yards they sounded different but were equally unintelligible.

"Are they ok?" The waitress sounded concerned.

"They're not in any trouble. We just want a chat with them."

Two cent lies were standard fare for Steyn. He didn't want to start a chain of gossip that would weave its way through the sparse streets. He thanked her and checked his watch. It was time to meet up the guys from police academy. As he left, the smell of Karoo lamb teased his nostrils. He hadn't had a square meal for twenty-four hours and he was tempted to turn around and place an order.

The main street was quiet. The tourists were holed up for the night in restaurants or drinking up a storm in their rental properties. One or two beggars had ventured from the location and a kid, no more than seven, stopped him, asking for money, saying his mum was "sick, very sick." He gave him a few bucks and told him to make his way home. The kid skipped down the street as if he'd won the lottery.

Van Buren and Strydom were sat on the steps of Celestino's waiting for him.

"Hello Oom, you're late" Van Buren smiled as he said it.

"Less of the Oom, just call be baas son." Van Buren paled and left the talking to his colleague.

"I think we may have something Captain. An old lady that lives across the road saw Carla and a man enter the coffee shop this morning."

"Was he average height, dark hair, designer stubble?"

"Yeh, that's him." Strydom was perplexed.

"They had a meal last night in the Gallery, all loved up by all accounts."

At last a picture was beginning to form. Steyn felt his customary rush of adrenaline.

"That's not all baas, she said two men were right behind them and that they went in together."

"Did she see them leave?"

"No baas, she had to go to church to light the braai for a fete."

"Shit, that's the bastards abducting them, what cars were outside?"

"There was a big white bakkie but she's not good with cars, she doesn't know the make or model."

Did she get a look at their faces?"

"No, only Carla and the guy with her. She just saw the back of the two men behind them. They were tall and well- built both wearing baseball caps."

"Good work Strydom, things are becoming a lot clearer around here. These guys are professionals. They've abducted Carla and her friend and taken them to a safe house. It won't be in Prince Albert itself, too risky. It's probably some deserted property fairly close to town, to avoid prying eyes."

Steyn was energized; cases were a closed box at the outset but when the lid opened, he came alive.

"Wouldn't they drive them back to Stellenbosch, get away from here as quick as possible?" Van Buren had plucked up enough courage to re-join the conversation.

"It's a possibility but they want answers and they want them quickly. My inclination is that they won't go far, and they probably welcome the anonymity this place offers. It would be easy to dump bodies in the wilderness and wash their hands of the problem before returning to familiar territory."

"Do you think they'd kill them boss?" Van Buren sounded shocked.

"Life is worthless to these bastards. They'd kill their own mothers if there was something in it for them. Do you honestly think they'd be worried if there was blood on their hands? If you do, you're in the wrong job."

Steyn glared at Van Buren, tired of his youthful naivety. The kid was acting like this was a scout outing. Dib, dib, dib, fucking dob, dob, dob.

"What's our next move baas?"

At least Strydom seemed to have his feet more grounded in reality thought Steyn.

"That's a bit of a dilemma. There's nothing much we can do now. At first light we'll scour all the properties in a five-kilometre radius of the town and hope we strike lucky. In the meantime, I'm going to get a bite to eat. I'll see you in the morning. Oh, Van Buren, call Captain Smit and inform him of the developments."

Chapter 42

It was the sound of sobbing that made them turn around and what they saw was a broken man. Johnson was slumped in a corner, head in hands. The gun discarded a few feet away, near the tractor wheel. Tom eyed it nervously, it was only a matter of seconds since it had been used and he shivered at the prospect of that bullet blowing the back of his head off. Where the bullet actually landed was immaterial, they were both still alive. He looked at Carla and she motioned him to pick the gun up. He did so, gingerly. His record with firearms was far from exemplary. He'd once been paintballing and shot a mate in the arse from point blank range when reloading but she didn't know that. There was a lot she didn't know about him but now they might have the opportunity to learn more about each other. He smiled for the first time in what seemed like a lifetime. Carla broke the silence; she hugged him and whispered in his ear,

"What about him?"

Tom glanced at Johnson. He was in a catatonic state, seemingly oblivious of their presence.

"Just leave him, we'd better get out of here before Malherbe gets back."

"Which way should we go?" Carla was looking for him to lead.

"We'll have to go cross-country, we can't go on the road in case Malherbe passes us. We'd best get moving, they could be back any minute, grab that torch it's going to be rocky."

Carla picked up her rucksack, her keys were still in it. She saw the memory stick on the table but left it there. If they took it, they would be guilty by implication. As they were just about to leave Johnson stirred, dusted himself down and stood up, staring at them blankly. Tom waved the gun at him but Johnson raised his hands in resignation, muttering away.

"I'm sorry, I can't live this life anymore."

Tom got the impression he was talking to himself. It was a surreal experience listening to a criminal reach Malcolm Gladwell's tipping point and put his feet back down on solid ground. A small victory for good over evil, played out in the wilderness. Tom felt a sudden warmth for him but he didn't know what to say. This wasn't the time to open the dusty pages of a confessional diary.

"What are you going to do?" Carla pressed him gently.

Johnson had a vacant look as if he'd moved properties but left his voice in the old one. He reminded Tom of the walking dead.

"See that door, I'm going to walk out of it, walk away from this town and this way of fucking life."

With that, he picked up his bag and paused at the door.

"Get out of here now before Malherbe gets back."

They watched him meld into the gloom, the sound of his feet diminishing with every step.

"Shit, no betting man would have put money on this happening, maybe there is a God after all. We need to move it, c'mon."

Tom packed a couple of bottles of water and they left via the back door. They were in a hollow and it was impossible to get their bearings. The ground was rocky and treacherous and without the aid of a torch they would have no chance. They were careful though, to keep the light beam close to the ground. It would have been stupid to illuminate the night sky with a 'come and get me' flare.

"Let's get well away from the road and up on top of one of these small hills, we should be able to see the lights of Prince Albert, it can't be far away, we were only in the car for a few minutes."

Tom was conscious he had been a bit of a passenger in this bloody mess and he knew he had to be more assertive. It wasn't natural for him to take the lead in anything. He was always on the periphery of parties ducking and diving, never confident enough to take centre stage; last of the sociable introverts. He was usually happy to plough his lone furrow but circumstances dictated a proactive rather than reactive role and he had to rise to the occasion. Perhaps there was an alpha male lurking in the depths, waiting to see the light of day.

They clambered to the top of a hill and saw the lights of Prince Albert in the distance, the feint silhouette of the church spire illuminated above the cluster of buildings. Now, a safe distance away from the theatre of screams, they sat down and shared a bottle of water.

"You weren't really mixed up with that Greg, were you?" It was an awkward question, but it had been praying on his mind. There was a small grain of residual doubt gnawing away at him.

"For fucks sake Tom, let's clear this up once and for all. I have nothing at all to do with him, I wish I'd never set eyes on him again. Weren't you listening back there?"

"It was a bit hard to focus."

"If you don't believe me leave me here, I can fend for myself thank you." She was angry and Tom tried to calm her down.

"Look I do believe you but I can't think straight. A few hours ago, life seemed hunky dory but then it got turned upside down. We can get through this if we stick together. You can't blame me for being confused can you?"

He hugged her and kissed her on the cheek. She didn't reply for ages and he wondered what she was thinking.

"Any meaningful relationship is based on a mutual trust. If we don't have that we don't have anything, understand?" She gave him the cold stare.

"Yeh, it was a stupid thing for me to say."

What do you think we should do next?" He was glad she'd changed the subject.

"We either make our way to town and jump in my car and head for the deep blue yonder or we go to the police station and explain everything." He rubbed the bristles on his chin and bent to tie his shoelaces.

"I agree."

"The second idea is probably the safest bet. My worry is that as soon as we set foot in town, we'll be sitting ducks. If we do go to the police station we'll have to skirt around the town to minimize the risks."

"The police station it is. We'll think of a plan on the way. Come on let's make a start."

***

It was a few hours before they approached the outskirts of town, both bruised and cut by numerous falls in the prickly bushes. Conversation was non- existent. The thin beam of the torch hadn't lasted more than an hour before the battery died. They'd stumbled blindly onwards, cursing every slip and stumble. Progress had been slow but they couldn't rush. If someone broke an ankle they were well and truly fucked.

They sat under some trees, exhausted, and watched a field of cows milling around without a care in the world. The question now was whether to wait for dawn and the bustle of people or to walk on in through the solitude of the night. In the end the decision was taken out of their hands, they fell asleep beneath the canopy of branches.

Chapter 43

The tube train was steadily filling up with suitcases bound for Heathrow; a mixture of travellers returning home and Brits heading abroad, judging by the mix of languages doing the rounds. Jeff took out the book of his dad's poems. He'd been reading them a lot in his absence. It made him feel as if he was close by. He read one about escalators, an old woman had wobbled at the top of one, just minutes ago and he'd clung onto her to stop her falling. It was his good deed for the day; a day in which he was breaking all the rules, stepping out from the shadows of despondency. If nobody could find dad, if nobody even cared, he would. He'd get on that plane, get a bus to Prince Albert and track him down. Seeing those daft kids bunk school, fly to Turkey and on to Syria, had given him the idea. Sitting in front of the six o'clock news he'd plotted his exit strategy. Number 1 kids detective, that's who he was.

The terminal was packed full of errant trolleys vying for the fast lane, he felt small ducking and diving between them in search of the BA flight desk. The security was tight; armed police patrolled in their bullet proof vests. The country was on high alert, an attack highly likely as the news reader always said. He stared at the mass of faces, he was nervous.

Half way down the queue at the flight desk, he rehearsed his spiel. He was off to visit grandad, he would meet him at the airport, and they'd go to the holiday house in Hermanus. It was amazing what you could research on the internet. One more couple to go and it was his turn. He pulled out the Barclaycard in readiness. A sudden thought crossed his mind, what if there wasn't enough money in her account? She was always buying lipstick and lingerie, especially since she'd hooked up with that idiot. He'd reached the front.

"Where's your mum and dad son?"

"Uh, I'm travelling alone, visiting grandad."

"Travelling light I see." She laughed and winked at him, thinking it was some kind of joke.

"Look, here's my credit card, I'm in a hurry."

The false smile had vanished and she reached for the phone. He grabbed the card and ran for his life, proper cross country speed, side stepping the open-mouthed and sped towards the nearest escalator.

Escalators

Arteries of access,
From the sunken world
To the sunburnt streets
And into the soup of the city.
Silver and chrome,
Parallel lines,
Steel spine running its loop.
A collage of conversations
Hang in the air.
Fifty jigsaw pieces
Tossed up high.
We move like tramps
Down below,
Picking up the dog ends of words.
Romance and retribution
Lie uneasily in an unmade bed.
Affection and affliction
Eye each other warily.
I fell down one once, inebriated.
Washing machine on spin cycle.
Bitten by the steel teeth,
My back was covered in unfinished
Sentences

Chapter 44

Radebe rotated the gold ring on his finger. He hated flying. The sky was for birds. His fear was compounded by the fact that he practically had to fold himself in half to fit into the four- seater. They'd had to skirt the thunderstorm hanging over the area but not without a brief dalliance with the turbulent air. He'd stretched out on the back seats and closed his eyes but couldn't escape the feeling of being locked up in a rattling egg box. He sensed the plane beginning to descend and thought of the few hours ahead. It was time for closure. Having the memory stick back in his possession would help him regain some sort of control but there were still nagging doubts praying on his mind. Was this Carla in cahoots with Joseph, was she familiar with the contents of the stick and were there other people involved? These were all questions that needed answering. One thing was certain. He had to find out for himself. Mad Malherbe was fast becoming surplus to requirements. Johnson said he was going off the rails, more interested in the art of violence than extracting the truth. It was time to sever the ties with him, find someone more reliable. Johnson needed a new partner and there were plenty of candidates ready to step up to the plate. This mess had to be cleared up as soon as possible. If Gleason got wind of this there would be hell to play. He shuddered at the prospect of his carefully crafted world coming crashing down.

Radebe looked out of the miniature window. Prince Albert was illuminated, a speck shining through the darkness. They dropped suddenly, buffeted by the wind. The buildings became clearer and he saw the orange flicker of a big fire, way out to the left of town. He braced himself for landing and saw Malherbe's white Toyota Hilux parked a convenient distance away.

***

Malherbe saw the plane drop through the clouds. He puffed on the last of his joint and checked his watch. Radebe was late. This was a futile exercise and he didn't need the boss to do the dirty work. That was his business and he'd have to try hard to conceal his indignation when Mr big shot got in the car. The slimy fucker must have something major to hide. Why couldn't wimpy Johnson have picked him up? It should be him, now, back at the base, slowly stripping Carla, his hand moving up her thigh, close to the honey pot. He closed his eyes, mentally rehearsing his every move, fuck, he wanted her bad. His phone beeped unexpectedly, bringing him back down to earth. It was a text from Gleason. His heavies were on the way. He smiled at the prospect of the mayhem that could well unfold. Poor, unsuspecting Mr Radebe wouldn't know what hit him. Serve him right for not paying enough, the tight bastard. The plane bumped its way down the so-called runway and he drove, like a servile chauffeur to the rich and famous, right up to the door. All that was missing was Mariah Carey's red carpet. The car radio was playing *Cars Hiss By My Window* by the Doors but Radebe was more of a Jay-Z man, black and upwardly mobile, so he turned it off.

201

The muscle-bound pilot jumped in the front, Radebe took up his customary position of authority in the back of the car. The greetings had been perfunctory. They eased past the golf course, if you could call it that, it was no Arabella with manicured fairways and sparkling golf carts, it was a wasteland, peppered with rocks, tin cans and bottles. The odd war-torn flag barely visible in the gloom.

"There's a big fire to the left of the town, we saw it from the plane. Did you see it on the way here?"

"No baas, it must have happened in the last half an hour or so."

"Did you check the drugs?"

Shit, Radebe was one never-ending question; Malherbe tried hard to conceal his annoyance.

"It's all safely stashed. I was there an hour ago."

"The drugs are not stored over that side of town are they?"

Malherbe paused, there was a chance to really wind up the main man but he decided against it.

"They are out that way boss but it's a big place, the drugs are unlikely to have gone up in smoke."

"Drive us there now." Radebe slid the ring round his finger and tried to think calmly. No use getting wound up like a top until you knew the score. Chances were the fire was nowhere near the damn drugs. He was getting more and more paranoid; the loss of the memory stick was playing on his mind.

They drove in silence, the fire looming ever larger till it almost filled the windscreen. As they drew closer what had seemed a feint possibility became the truth. Malherbe turned into a side road and spun the car round, accelerating back to town.

"What the hell are you doing?" Radebe screamed from the back.

"Sorry boss, that's your drugs gone sky high, we better get out of here. The place will be swarming with cops any minute now. Let's get you safe, back with Johnson and the usual suspects."

"Fuck, fuck, fuck, what the hell's going on?"

Radebe was raging in the rear-view mirror. Malherbe kept his smile on the inside. They slowed as they approached the town. A couple of police cars drove by. The first driven by an officer as fat as a sofa, his eyes touched with madness. Malherbe swerved to avoid him.

"Fok that oke's in a hurry."

The main street was quiet at this time of the night. Radebe kept his own counsel as they drove past the sign for The Bush pub, 'bulging biceps' was a blank stare. Malherbe recognized another robotic hitman fresh off the assembly line, primed for action but not interaction; sweet, infinitely better than 'socially conscious' Johnson. He was for the scrap heap.

Malherbe jumped out first and jogged to the building.

"Johnson, stand to attention, the baas is in da house."

He opened the door. The place was empty. The chairs were upturned and the ropes lying on the floor.

"Fokken hell. Baas come quick."

The three of them stood in a dumfounded triangle,

"Jesus Christ Almighty, I knew Johnson was a weak link, he's been acting strange lately", said Malherbe.

"What do you mean?" Radebe had sat down on the tractor seat; a cold sweat had come over him. He saw the fucking memory stick in amongst Malherbe's torture kit and pocketed it.

"Well he's gone all soft, said that the girl might be telling the truth, told me to go easy on her. If he had picked you up none of this would have ever happened, nobody, escapes on my watch."

"Ring Johnson." Radebe was trawling through the worst-case scenarios, what else could bloody go wrong in this tin pot town?

"Get Mr muscles from Malmsbury to do it, I'm going to find them. They can't have gone far without a car."

Malherbe was seriously pissed off, just standing about wouldn't achieve anything. Every minute was precious.

"Wait. He can't. His tongue was cut out in a gang fight."

"Found comfort in the gym, did he?"

Malherbe rang but there was no answer, not that he expected one.

"If Johnson's behind this, I'll kill him", said Radebe.

"No you won't, he's mine. I'll dispose of him, the fokken idiot."

"Maybe they jumped him?"

"What? Burst the ropes like the Incredible Hulk and squashed him in a limp sandwich, hit him with my hammer? Where the fuck is his body then? No way. He let them go."

Radebe interlocked his long fingers.

"Look, we can't waste any more time. We've got to find them, silence them for good. I wish I'd never set eyes on this town and the sooner we're out of here the better."

Malherbe agreed. Rock abs nodded. The problem was they had one car in the wilderness and it was darker than the deepest shaft in a diamond mine.

Chapter 45

The Calamari combo was tasty but Steyn couldn't enjoy it to the full. His mind was preoccupied with the intricacies of the case. He hated inactivity, especially when the investigation had begun to move forward. He'd rung Charles and asked him if Carla had a boyfriend and found that she'd been spending time with some Welsh guy, Tom. This dovetailed nicely with the waitress's description of the couple in the Gallery. It was highly likely that Tom was the man with Carla at the coffee shop door, both of them bundled into a car a matter of minutes later. Steyn was an intuitive cop; his gut feeling was that they were just in the wrong place at the wrong time but that did nothing to lessen the danger they were in. If he was back home in Stellenbosch he could have organized a blanket search with plenty of feet on the ground but here, in the backwoods, he was a lone wolf with two cub cops at his disposal and a stroppy red neck Captain to deal with. The town was locked in the box of the night and there was nothing much he could do until first light. Sometimes cases like this hinged on luck, you could be in the right place at the right time. Retiring to bed for an early night seemed wasteful, Steyn paid the bill and walked to his car. A drive around the compact streets and outlying area would give him time to think and help him make a plan for the next day. He checked his phone. No messages. He should have replied to Christel but she'd either be asleep now or drunk, listing his inadequacies to that Gollum of a sister.

The main street was quiet, the back streets even quieter. Whatever fun was happening in town was hidden behind closed doors. Steyn kept his eyes open for a white Toyota Hilux but he drew a blank. He drove out of town past the location, the jumping beat of jive music boomed from big speakers. It was party time there every night, not that they had much to celebrate but then, what did he know? A sign pointed to a golf course that didn't seem to exist and there was an airstrip to the left, a small plane parked up by a shack. Probably the air doctor tending to an elderly patient, the nearest proper hospital would be in George. He turned around and headed back to town. The dirt side roads feeding off the tarmac were probably the best option.

Steyn checked the sat nav. The first turning was the R353 TO Leeu-Gamka. He hit the gravel and scanned the odd building en route. There were no signs of life. Professionals would look for somewhere that was partially hidden from the road. He slowed down to look more carefully but it was hard to pick out buildings in the darkness. Despite the good intentions, he knew this was a fruitless exercise, but God loves a trier. The road stretched ahead, a steep incline followed by a bend to the right. The top of the hill would be a good vantage point and a suitable place to turn around. His eyes were tired and he had the beginnings of a headache, born from frustration.

The blaze of light took him by surprise. The building was engulfed in flames, smoke billowing skywards. Two police cars, blue lights flashing, were at the scene, parked a safe distance away. Steyn drove down towards them and wound down the window, the smell of street drugs hit him full on, it made his eyes water. Smit was standing with a couple of other officers. He didn't look too pleased when he saw who got out of the car.

"What are you doing here? This is none of your business." His tone was as inflammatory as the fire raging before them.

"I'm just checking out the area in preparation for my work tomorrow. I presume Van Buren filled you in on the developments?"

"He did, too busy to tell me yourself where you?"

"Sikosi advised me to be a team player. Just following orders, delegation is the name of the game. That's a lot of drugs gone up in smoke there. A bit of a coincidence don't you think?"

"It might not be drugs, it could be chemicals."

Steyn had to stop himself laughing, Smit was out of his depth.

"Look, I reckon Joseph was involved in some sort of drug ring, Carla was abducted because of her association with him. They want closure. Then a drug stash goes up in flames nearby, Christ, it doesn't take much of a leap of faith to make the link, surely even you can see that?"

Smit wanted to belt the shit out of him, the interfering fucker but he managed to restrain himself.

"You've watched too many movies Steyn. Crack pot theories are fine in a cheap film script but they don't stand up in the real world. You've got no hard evidence and you're clutching at straws because Colonel bloody Sikosi is breathing down your neck. Now get the hell out of here and let me get on with my job."

Steyn backed down. There was no point antagonizing the idiot any more. He couldn't appeal to Sikosi for extra help either, he was stranded in no man's land with two rookie cops with a combined age that didn't even add up to his own.

"If that's the way you see it Captain, I've got nothing more to say to you."

With that, he turned on his heel and drove back to town.

Smit watched him disappear into the distance and spat on the floor. He'd give him one more day and that would be it. An aggrieved call to Colonel Sikosi, even if it was totally unfounded, would rid him of Captain fucking Steyn. Prince Albert, and the police force, would be better off without him. Mavericks, with their fancy Dan ideas; there was no place for them round these parts.

Smit left a couple of cops to keep an eye on the fire and drove back to the police station. He couldn't face going home. A night sleeping on the couch in his office beckoned. The dawn of a new day would hopefully see this whole, unfortunate chapter come to an end.

Chapter 46

Tom was woken by heavy breathing on his face. It wasn't Carla. A cow had lent through the fence and taken a shine to him. Its breath gave vegetarians a bad name. He stood up and stretched. It had been an uncomfortable night. Carla was asleep and he didn't want to wake her. The sun was up. He thought of light as the symbol of freedom but they weren't safe yet. They were tantalizingly close to the Police Station but it would be foolish to walk directly there. Malherbe and his gang were sure to be wandering the streets in pursuit of them. He shuddered at the prospect of ever having to go through this all again. If they had their mobile phones it would be simple; a quick call to the cops and they'd be picked up in a couple of minutes. The trouble was, the phones were on his table, next to an unmade bed. The night of passion with Carla seemed a lifetime ago. For the first time in ages he thought of his kids back home. Jeff would be worried. He'd been sending him jokey texts every day to keep him amused and the sudden break in communication would make him think dark thoughts. In the family tradition, he was another half empty rather than half full sort of a guy. It wouldn't take much to push him over the edge.

Carla stirred and opened her eyes. They smiled at each other and the world suddenly seemed a happier place.

"It was hardly glamping, honey, but we live to fight another day." Tom hugged her and ruffled her hair.

"You've got campers hair." He said.

"I feel like I've spent three nights at Glastonbury on the booze", she replied, yawning.

Tom remembered all those Reading festivals: jumping off the Caversham bridge into the Thames, getting squashed between two police horses when he moved a cone in the road, hitting a dwarf in the head with an apple, white t shirt stained with red wine, long hair matted with mud from rolling on the floor, Guns n Roses blaring in the back of a cramped van, wine, women and song. He'd been a wild bugger alright. He missed those lost days of youth. Short hair with grey flecks, sober, was the now, but the iPod diary could tell some stories, fill in the missing blanks of all those years. *I'm going to live forever (if it kills me)*, William Tyler was damn right, even if his album was instrumental, the song title spoke the truth.

"Tom you're miles away." She'd come to recognize that look.

"We should be on the move, let's get this thing done."

She was right; he had his head in the clouds again. He'd spent half his life up there.

"Sorry, I was lost in my own thoughts."

"I think we should skirt round the back of town, maybe along the Koppie trail and cut down a side street to the Police station. That way we avoid the centre of town."

"Sounds like a plan", he said.

Both of them stared at the hills. They were scared, though neither admitted it. Luckily, the smallness of the town made it easy to work out where they were. They edged past Gay's dairy and cut across some fields running parallel to the main road, the Swartberg pass looming in the distance. They passed a posh bed and breakfast on their right and jumped over a small stream. The traffic was sporadic and they waited till all was clear, darting across the main road. Nobody had seen them and they walked quickly for a few hundred metres on the Weltervrede road before veering off and heading to the slopes of the Koppie. At the top they paused for a rest, Prince Albert laid out before them like a picnic blanket. Tom took out the last water bottle and they shared it.

"If we carry on walking along the top here we'll come out on the dam road, it's just a few hundred metres to the Police Station from there. I love it up here but somehow, not so much today."

Tom looked up at the vast expanse of blue sky, life seemed so simple up there. The birds flew free. He quoted some poetry at her.

Midnight waters
Burning skies
Interspersed
With countless lies

"Which miserable bastard wrote that?"

"It was me, sat in my comfortable bedroom overlooking the Welsh hills, back when I was fourteen."

"Ah, teenage angst."

"Cynics can never be disappointed, that's the way I look at it. I'm in the Dylan Thomas camp, he once said - 'poetry is statements made on the way to the grave.' He was in it soon enough too."

"Well I could do with a dose of happiness right now. Life's not all about getting jump started in the back of an ambulance."

She had a point.

"What are you going to do when we get out of the mess?" He almost said if but some of her positive mind set was rubbing off on him.

"I'm going to lie on a beach in the sun with you beside me, how does that strike you?"

"Tidy."

"Tidy?"

"It's a Welsh expression, means fucking great" Tom did his Richard Burton impression and they cracked up laughing.

"Elizabeth, I've bought you another diamond and a small island, just big enough to house your jewellery."

They reached Magrieta Prinsloo Street and ran to the Police Station, it wasn't time for a cautious walk and they half expected to hear the sound of bullets rattling around them but they opened the door, breathing hard, unscathed. The place was empty but they could hear the drunks wailing from the cells at the rear. There was no bell to press so they stood at the counter, Tom eyeing the door nervously.

"Hello, hello." Carla shouted. There must be somebody on duty. A fat guy appeared, she recognized him. It was Smit, the arse who had supposedly come to her rescue when the Coffee Shop was burgled. He looked like he'd seen a ghost.

"Carla?" His bull frog eyes were bulging.

"Are we glad to see you officer Dibble." Tom was relaxed.

"It's not safe here; you'd better come with me." Smit motioned towards a side door.

"What do you mean it's not safe here, it's a bloody police station?"

"There's no time to explain. I'll tell you when we get to the Coffee Shop."

They sat in the back of the police car, bemused. Smit wouldn't answer any of their questions. He parked at the rear of the building and ushered them in through the gate, scanning the street when Carla fumbled for her keys.

"Sit down" he said, a bit too forcibly for Tom's liking.

"Hold on a min...." Tom's sentence was cut short. Smit was pointing a gun at them, his fat trigger finger twitching.

Chapter 47

Malherbe and Steyn were faced with the same dilemma, if viewed from either side of the great moral divide; they both wanted to find Carla but were equally under resourced. Radebe dropped the man with no voice in town with instructions to steal a car. They needed to be able to split up to maximize their chances of tracking the girl down. Malherbe couldn't help feeling it was a wasted exercise. He suspected she was long gone. They could easily have hitched a lift and be half way back to Cape Town by now. That's what he would have done.

***

Steyn had breakfast early, Strydom and Van Buren turned up in one car. He'd been hoping to have three vehicles at his disposal, his own included, but Smit had declined his request. Steyn took the east of town, leaving the west to the local cops. Tweedledum and Tweedledee were chirping away like excitable parrots when he left them at the petrol station. There was a long day ahead and a crucial one at that. If they didn't make any headway before dark, it was curtains. He might as well drive back to Stellenbosch with his tail between his legs. The prospect of a ceremonial grilling in Sikosi's office was unpalatable.

***

Malherbe checked his phone. Gleason's cronies should be in town soon. If he got away from Radebe for a while he could enlist their help and increase the slim chances of finding the whore and her dim-wit side kick with the weird accent. He cursed Johnson for the hundredth time that morning. That guy would pay with his life. No matter how long it took him, he would track him down. They split up, Radebe and Bismarck-biceps taking the outlying areas and he was to patrol the streets of the town.

***

The opposing camps were like two planes circling a hub airport but both unaware of each other. Steyn searched a number of properties near the gravel roads but found nothing of any significance. Malherbe completed endless loops of the town, but the streets were quiet and there was no sign of Carla. Radebe checked some abandoned houses on the Welterfreede road but they were as empty as a tramp's pocket. Strydom and Van Buren drove on out past the Swartrivier olive farm but had nothing to report for their efforts.

It was mid-morning when Malherbe drove down a side street and noticed a police car parked at the back of Celestino's. He parked a safe distance away and kept an eye on the back gate. The cops were searching for clues, they'd rumbled that Carla had gone missing. He pictured them, handling her silk panties that he'd seen draped on the back of a chair. He should have pocketed them when he had the chance, kept them for future use. He knew she'd never have gone back to the coffee shop, she was cleverer than that. The town was unsafe, she'd be well away from the place, laughing at them all, dreaming of a bright future. Well, it wasn't over yet. His phone buzzed. It was the Gleason mob. He arranged to meet them in the car park outside the OK supermarket. He flicked through the gallery on his phone looking for a photo of Carla to show them. There she was, the Queen of bondage. He wished he'd taken a shot of her with legs splayed wide, her eyes begging for more.

***

At 10.30 Steyn called a temporary halt to the search. They met at the Lazy Lizard for a coffee. Comparing notes took precisely ten seconds. Not a sniff, no leads, the prospect of another long shift looming ahead.

"How long do you reckon we've got baas?" said Van Buren.

"We might have run out of time already, we have to find something soon otherwise its game over."

Steyn hated saying it. He couldn't stomach failure and he took it personally.

"Isn't it pointless carrying on?"

Strydom cringed; his colleague wasn't blessed with tact, or brains for that matter.

"Jesus Christ, get a grip man, someone's life is at stake, and we're not stopping until we bloody find her. If you've not got anything sensible to say then fucking shut up."

Steyn raised his voice and every gaze in the café was on him.

"You two check out the dam road, I'll try the Seekoegat dirt track. Let's go. If you spot anything call me straight away."

Van Buren took his advice and kept his mouth shut.

Chapter 48

The Gods were against them. It was the second time in twenty-four hours that they'd been held at gunpoint by a madman. This time it wasn't a hardened criminal but a red faced, sweaty cop, the man who, in theory, should be protecting them. Tom sat still, trying to fathom out what was going on. The guy was off his trolley, any sudden movements could summon a bullet.

Smit walked closer to them.

"How long have you been working for Joseph?"

"A few weeks, I've just been helping him out in the coffee shop, why the fuck are you pointing the gun at us? We've come to you for bloody protection."

"The coffee shop is a scam and you know it. Let's be more specific, how long have you been involved in the drug trade?"

Carla was irate.

"I've no fucking idea what you're babbling on about. I wish I'd never set foot in this town. Listen to me. Two guys, Malherbe and Johnson; Malherbe is one evil bastard, a tall guy, blond, think Gestapo, they picked us up, tortured us but we got away. Their boss, Radebe, is flying in here. They'll be looking for us. We need your help for Christ sakes."

"You're lying, tell the truth."

Smit was up close now. The red mist had descended. He jammed the gun into Carla's temple. Tom kicked him hard in the bollocks and punched his jowly cheeks and he doubled up in pain. He pinned him down and belted him again.

"Carla, grab the gun from the bag, quick."

She found it and Tom man- handled the punch-drunk hulk onto a chair. Christ, he weighed more than Ollie le Roux. Carla gave him the gun. Tom looked him straight in the eye.

"One move and I'll blow your brains out, you fat cunt. Carla, find some tights, stockings, belts, anything, we need to truss him up and get out of here."

She returned with some rope she found in the stock room and a pair of her black tights. Smit came round just as they finished tying him up. They gagged him with the tights and ignored his feeble wailing. Tom gestured towards the kitchen and Carla followed.

"What the hell is going on?"

"I've no fucking idea."

We need to get out of here sharpish." He could hear Smit moaning in the other room.

"What about your car?"

"Nah, it's too risky, shit what are we gonna do?" Tom could feel the panic setting in.

Carla looked out of the window and saw Greg's bikes. They filled a couple of rucksacks with food, drink and jumpers; nothing too heavy to carry. Before they left, he found a piece of card and printed a message with an arrow next to it- BENT COP. He placed it on the table next to Smit and left.

Carla tied her hair up and with their helmets and sunglasses they would hopefully pass as two random cyclists. It was the only chance they had. She adjusted the seat for him. A back spasm was the last thing they needed. The prospect of freedom lay behind the garden gate but neither of them wanted to be the first to open it. Every door seemed to lead to further trouble. Tom took the first step. He popped his head round the gate, the street was quiet.

"Let's try and head over the pass, nobody would think we'd go that way. Keep a reasonable pace, not too fast as to attract attention. Look straight ahead and pray we don't get any punctures because then we are fucked." She nodded in agreement.

They kissed, glasses clashing together. It was just a few hundred metres before they were on the main road and they stuck lucky. Chance, that fickle bedfellow, finally fell in their favour. Some private cycle group was passing through and they tagged onto the peloton, heading past the graveyard and the final buildings on the outskirts of town. There was a gentle incline up the open road. Thankfully they were going at a steady pace so there wasn't any danger of becoming detached from the group. They turned right onto the dirt road and there before them was the mighty Swartberg pass; the long and winding road, stairway to the stars. Fuck the song titles, they were in with a chance.

Tom had cycled the initial slopes a few days previously, but it was a different matter weaving your way to the very top. They settled into a steady rhythm and the collective energy of the group spurred them on. They crossed the dry riverbed a couple of times, lush vegetation flanking them on either side, but he had no time to take in the beauty of the surroundings. He was all fucking ears, waiting for the sound of a car, come to drag them down. There was a limit to how many lives they had. He tended to put the p in pessimist at the best of times. Doom and gloom were always in the room as far as he was concerned.

The group came to a sudden halt at a picnic spot. Tom didn't want to stop but it made sense to stay in the pack and make use of the anonymity it provided. He sat on the floor with Carla at the back of the group, furthest from the road. They ate some bananas and dried fruit, getting their breath back. Tom noticed the cyclists break into small groups, probably an organized tour uniting a bunch of strangers under a banner of exercise. It was more than likely their first day and they hadn't got to know each other yet. They fitted in nicely and no-one bothered them.

"We're no way near far enough away."

"I know." Both of them were watching back down the road as they were talking.

"The problem with these bikes is that we can only make slow progress. A car can chase us down in no time. Even if we see a police car, how do we know we can trust them? For all we know, the whole police force in town could be corrupt."

"Yeh, but all we can do is carry on. If we hear cars behind us, we'll have to get in the middle of the group for cover and hope for the best. Once we reach the top there'll be a long downhill and we can pick up pace."

"What's on the other side of the mountain?"

Tom had no idea of the geography of the area. It had been a miracle that he'd been able to work the satnav and find Prince Albert in the first place.

"I think Calitzdorp is the nearest town, Greg used to go there for supplies."

"What, cigarette papers, bongs? Calitzdorp, it sounds like a German prisoner of war camp."

Carla smiled.

"We can go to the police there; the whole country can't be bent."

The group were packing up, there were a few worried faces looking at the precarious switch back bends up ahead. There'd been no sign of any cars yet but that could change in an instant. Tom immersed himself in the rhythm of the wheels and focused on his breathing. A few days back he'd written a poem imagining cycling to the top of the pass. He could never have envisaged it becoming a reality. But this was no joy ride. It was head down and hope. He was in no mood to take in the stunning scenery that had captivated him on his previous ride. Instead, he shut down his mind and recited the poem under his breath. It was time to dig deep.

Cycle up Swartberg pass 2152 m

To be read upwards

in God's gallery.

hanging like paintings

are fading silhouettes

Here the distant hills

summit bound.

take the yard

I grind the inches,

With desire and will

it lurks in the valleys of the mind

the reach of mere physicality,

but triumph lies beyond

gears, calibrate, lubricated chain

revolutions, whirl of spokes,

calves taut as banjo strings

hammer on steel

Pulse pounding

stiffen in silence.

These green embroidered hills

like hot snakes.

sweat oozes through the undergrowth

Beneath the bandana

rise and fall of feet.

pressure, pedals

Caught in the cadence,

Chapter 49

Smit stewed in his own piss. He should have shot the bastards, disposed of the gun and cleared his name in one fell swoop but it was too late now. He cursed his ill luck. Why did he have to stop that fateful night? Ok, there'd been a light on in the deserted barn, he'd seen it from the top of the hill, but would the world have stopped if he'd driven past? Joseph was inside moving the boxes of drugs. He should have arrested him there and then, end of story but no, the slimy pom had sweet talked him. The dollar signs had flashed around the one-armed bandit that was once his brain. He'd left with his pockets stuffed full of notes, with the prospect of a bulging bank account dangling in front of his smiley face. The whole thing was like a series of crossroads and he'd taken the wrong turn every time. Weak, weak, weak what an arse but the money had rolled in; life was a box of chocolates until Joseph went and got himself killed. What the hell was he doing near Stellenbosch? Then Sherlock had to turn up didn't he? Mr Steyn, the righteous fucker. He'd played him well, reported him to his boss but the bastard was still here, looking under every bloody rock, stone and pebble.

What a difference a few hours can make. Last night he'd thought he was a free man. He'd driven slowly down the Leeu- Gamka road with a can of petrol; an oily rag and matches were on the passenger seat next to him. There was something liberating about preparing to commit a crime. As the drugs went up in smoke his guilt would burn away, leaving just the ashes as a testament to his idiocy, untraceable. He could wash his hands of this sordid mess. In his heart of hearts he realized it wasn't as simple as that but, Jeez, it would make him feel a whole lot better. He realized he wouldn't be in the clear until Steyn was safely back in Stellenbosch and Carla was found, dead or alive, preferably dead. If all avenues of enquiry were exhausted, he was in the clear and he could park his conscience in some deserted side street.

The road had been empty. The strain was beginning to tell, his wife had noticed how quiet he was and had asked him if he was feeling ill. He'd fobbed her off with claims of tiredness and over work and she didn't press the matter. He'd donned a pair of police issue rubber gloves and got down to work. Once the bonfire was lit and he saw the initial flames grow he was out of there, long before the fire took hold of the building and it became visible on a grander scale. His braai lighting skills had nearly deserted him, and his hands were shaking but the flames lit up the interior.

He remembered checking the rear-view mirror for the expectant glow. It hadn't taken long for the building to be engulfed by flames. The place was as dry as an old wooden chapel.

Chapter 50

Malherbe pulled up next to the Jeep and climbed in the back. Gleason had sent three of them down, he wasn't taking any chances. The two in the front were the silent types. Cloete introduced himself and got straight to the point.

"Mr Gleason's pissed off. He wants to cap this leak pronto. What's the state of play?"

"Carla is still on the loose. Radebe and his sidekick have arrived. They're searching the outlying area and I've been looking around town for her" said Malherbe.

"What sort of outfit are you, letting a woman escape?"

Malherbe didn't like his tone, the jumped up Joburg bastard.

"Hold on, nobody escapes on my watch. It was Johnson's fault, he was in charge and he's disappeared."

"It strikes me that Radebe needs to be careful who he employs. There's no amateurs in the Joburg operation." He smirked and lit a cigarette, took a long inhale.

Malherbe wanted to strangle the condescending fucker but, as pleasurable as it would have been, it wasn't the way to step up the ladder into the big time. The two guys in the front would have something to say about it as well. He had to look at the bigger picture and tread carefully.

"Let's not waste time worrying about Radebe's recruitment policy, we need to find the girl, then you can deal with him."

"We can't do any worse than you can we? We'll give it a go for a few hours but we're really interested in the memory stick. Mr Gleason wants it and Radebe doesn't come with the package."

"Why all the fuss about the fucking memory stick?"

Cloete smiled.

"That's for us to know and you to ponder my friend."

Malherbe held his tongue. It wasn't going to be easy working with these idiots.

"Radebe has got the memory stick, it's round his neck."

"That's not the only thing he's going to have around his neck before we are finished. There's a good length of rope in the boot."

Malherbe didn't bat an eyelid. As Radebe hung from a beam, the life squeezed out of him, his own stock would rise. Dog eat dog, call it what you will, it was onwards and upwards. A bounce on the trampoline of life and he would be swinging on the stars and he wouldn't let go.

Cloete watched him, his eyes narrowing.

"What's in this for you Malherbe?"

"That's between me and Mr Gleason."

Two could play at that game.

Chapter 51

Two hours driving around the area and he was none the wiser. Steyn refused to admit defeat but it wasn't looking good. He drove up the main street, took a right after Celestino's and turned down a side street to double back on himself. There was a police car parked by the back of the coffee shop and the gate was wide open. It struck him as odd, who the hell was in there? Maybe Smit had finally woken up and dragged his fat arse into gear and become a real cop again, perish the thought. He parked up and braced himself for the possibility of another verbal spat. The back door of the coffee shop was wide open too but there was silence within.

He pulled out his gun and stepped into the kitchen. It was as he remembered it. Steyn inched in, listening for any signs of movement. He peered through the serving hatch, careful not to disturb the coffee cups that were stacked neatly on the counter. There was a guy slumped in a chair, asleep. It was Smit. He was tied up and gagged. Steyn saw the sign pointing to him- BENT COP. He looked in a bad way, battered and bruised, blood oozing from the nose. Steyn slid gently to the floor; it could be a trap to lure him in. Whoever had done this could be lurking in an alcove, waiting to take him out. If they were there, they were bloody quiet. All he could hear was a tap dripping. He reached for a coffee cup, lay on the floor and lobbed it in. It smashed on the tiled floor, fragments splintering in all directions. Steyn heard the muffled wail of Smit, he'd probably shat his pants, and they'd certainly take some filling. He listened to the sobs and the snorting, checking for any other noise but it appeared it was just him and lard arse in the building. He picked up a bread knife and, gun in the other hand, walked in. Smit's bloodshot eyes registered a friendly face. He mumbled something in the muffled language of the gagged. Steyn cut him loose and removed the tights from his mouth.

"Jesus Christ, am I glad to see you, get me some water and a towel, will you?"

Smit rubbed his wrists and stretched his fingers, quickly throwing his BENT COP label under a table.

"Who thinks you're a bent cop then?" Steyn smiled.

"It's nothing to fucking laugh about. It was Carla and that guy."

"They've been back here?"

"Yeh, I was checking out the coffee shop when I saw some movement inside. It was them. I was just explaining to them that they'd be safer in the police station when they bloody jumped me. They're involved in this drug ring, fucking foreigners messing up our country."

Steyn wasn't sure he believed him. Smit hadn't behaved naturally since he'd first met him; his mind seemed to be permanently somewhere else. He got the distinct impression he was hiding something.

"What did they tell you, I presume they engaged you in conversation before beating you up?"

"She came over all innocent, some cock and bull story about being kidnapped but let me tell you, she's behind this, her and Joseph and that thug with her, Tom."

Smit was back on his feet again.

"I find that hard to believe Smit. We checked Carla out. She's a primary school teacher travelling for a year to fight off middle age. Hardly drug baron material."

"Why the hell did they attack me then, explain that?"

Steyn gave him a withering look.

"Only you know the answer to that Smit."

"What the hell are you suggesting?"

"It just doesn't add up, we have a witness who saw Carla and Tom being bundled in here and apparently abducted, they supposedly escape and attack a cop, the very man they should be running to for help, a bit weird don't you think?"

The veins in Smit's temple were pulsing, his skin blotchy and red.

"Don't you question my credibility you fucking city-slicker. I am the law in this town and I do things by the book. Do you understand?"

Smit squared up to him, swinging his weight around.

Steyn sat in a chair. It was an old trick, made the aggressor look like a childish delinquent.

"Calm down, we're on the same side remember? We're wasting time. Did Carla mention any names?"

"You believe that bullshit she told me?"

"I have to fill in the picture, look at all the possibilities. That's my job."

Smit couldn't think straight, his head was throbbing, Steyn was a clever bastard and it was difficult to pull the wool over his eyes at the best of times and these were the worst.

"Come on Smit, did they mention any names?"

"Uh, Malherbe, Johnson and Radebe."

Part of him wanted to confess but he was too scared. The only hope was that the bad guys caught up with Carla first and killed her. What a bloody idiot he was.

Steyn rung Botha to check the names out. It wasn't much to go on, but it was worth a try. One fruitful lead and it would be game on.

"Which way did they leave?"

"Through the back door" Smit checked his watch, "about an hour and a half ago."

"Jeez, if they're in a car they'll be half way to Cape Town by now."

"She didn't have a car. She used to borrow Joseph's. I used to see her driving round in it."

Smit had regained his composure. The best policy was to be more conciliatory, deflect attention from himself.

Steyn ran his fingers through his hair and rubbed his head. Carla and the guy were still alive, but had he badly misjudged them? If Smit was to be believed, they were involved in the drug ring but deep down, he doubted that; a goody two shoes primary teacher on vacation, drug dealer? Come on. These cases demanded a clear thought process, subjective, logical, and rational. Why would Carla go back to the coffee shop? It would be the first place the criminals would look. He sometimes put himself in the position of the victims, what would he do if faced with the same circumstances? If they didn't have access to mobile phones the sensible thing to do would be to hand yourself in at the nearest police station. The BENT COP sign had got him thinking. If they roughed him up and legged it, why take the trouble to write a bloody caption? What if it was Smit involved in the drug ring, what if he brought them here to cover his tracks? Low pay, disillusionment, dead end in a sleepy town, the prospect of easy money would appeal to the morally weak. He'd seen it all before, cops on the make. Look at bloody Corvier. It would explain Smit's reluctance to help him since his arrival but now was not the time to grill him on the braai. If he could find Carla, alive, the truth would come out soon enough.

Steyn gazed through the kitchen window. There was something different from his last visit. The tables were still there, with their green sunshades and Celestino's logo. He saw the spanner on the floor. It was the bikes. The two bikes had gone.

Chapter 52

Tom was finding it hard to stay with the group. A life on the ale had sapped any endurance he once possessed. Carla looked back at him and waved him on. He focused on the immediate road ahead. He daren't raise his head to check how far it was to the top, his heart was screaming stop but he kept the slow rhythm going, somehow. The only sounds he could hear were the whirr of the wheels and his laboured breathing. They turned a bend and the gradient steepened sharply. He passed a sign (Blikstasie Tronk) at the speed of an arthritic pedestrian and the whole valley opened up. The track flattened out for a while and he could see the stone packed walls clinging to the mountain in a series of zig zag bends. The top was visible for the first time and still there was no sign of a car in either direction. Maybe they had a chance. He caught up with the group and glanced back, the worst of the climbing was over. They stopped at a turn off for a water break. Tom's hands were shaking and his legs had liquefied.

"Fuck that nearly killed me."

Carla opened a bottle and gave him some water.

"You did good Tom, it's just a gentle climb to the top and then it's all downhill. I've been listening for cars all the way. Do you think we're safe?"

Tom didn't want to make her more nervous than she already was.

"We've got a better chance than we did a couple of hours ago."

The group were getting ready to move again, their mood lightened by the feel-good factor of conquering the mountain. They were nearing the peak now, Tom glanced back but there was no vehicle in sight. His left leg was beginning to cramp up and the top couldn't come soon enough. Carla motioned to him. The leader had taken a sudden sharp right, the pack following him in an orderly line. Tom saw the sign, Die Hel, as the last cyclist hit the dirt road.

"Christ, what do we do now?" Carla stared at him.

It was just the two of them, exposed on the mountain top, at the crossroads in more ways than one. He'd taken too many wrong turnings in his life, most of them while blind drunk, but faced with a sober decision, his brain invariably froze. The sound of a car engine coming up the valley forced his hand.

"We'll have to stay with the group; it's too risky to stay on this road on our own."

The adrenaline kicked in and they caught up with the pack within a few hundred metres. The valley flattened out but there were twists and turns ahead and steeper slopes in the distance.

"Die Hel, it sounds ominous." Tom was trying to make conversation. They'd both been listening for the car but it had stayed on the main track and headed downhill.

"It's some sort of hidden valley. I think there was a community that lived there, undetected for over a century. The road was only built in the sixties. Greg told me about it."

"There is a road out the other end isn't there?"

"Uh.., I'm not sure but we're going to find out one way or the other."

234

They were a few kilometres down the road and there was clearly no point in turning back. A startled Klipspringer shot across the track in front of them and the group stopped to take some photographs. Tom surveyed the surroundings; the aloes were standing like soldiers, watching the road, the ground parched. The silence engulfed them. This was ancient land, untouched by the ugliness of civilization. The weakness of man had no place here. The place gave him a faith in the firmness of life. All things must pass but each small rock had more significance than the transient dealings of the disaffected. People had a lot to answer for. We crawl all over the planet eating each other but it was here before us, and will be, long after we're gone.

Carla recognized that look in his eyes.

"You've gone bloody AWOL again, c'mon, let's keep up."

She rubbed his arm and they were off, it was getting very hot as midday approached. As each hour passed, the further away from Prince Albert they got, the more confident she became. She surprised herself by imagining a future with him. When all this mess was behind them, they'd have some serious talking to do. He needed someone to steer him through life and maybe she was the one. They'd gelled almost instantly. It was unlike her to see life as *an endless sky of honey*, as Kate Bush termed it, but she had a feeling things might come together. Too many times, she'd come close to settling down but it had never been quite right. There was something natural in how she interacted with Tom, even though their lives had subsequently been turned outside in. She loved talking to him. He made her laugh. Out of adversity happiness comes; the paradox syndrome. And Christ, he loved Steely Dan. Any friends of Messer's Fagen and Becker were bound to be good soulmate material. The sex had been good too, even though he was nervous, the lad had potential. She laughed to herself. It was out of character for her to have a Mills and Boon moment. This was all new territory for her. She was more used to being in a classroom, worrying about levels of development and accountability, stuck on the middle-aged escalator bound for a care home. It had been a brave decision to break from conformity and no-one could have foreseen the events that unfolded in Prince Albert, yet now, faced with an open road, the bright shape of things to come was forming in her mind.

The terrain began to change; valley sides steepened, the undulations in the road dipped in a series of ever-increasing troughs. The sheer physicality of the task dried up conversation and they had to be careful to avoid potholes and loose rocks strewn across the track. A sheer drop to the right meant the pace slowed. The sweat beneath the helmet trickled down Tom's forehead, the saltiness irritating his eyes. He was at the upper limits of his capabilities. Oh to be seventeen again and in full rugby training but a protracted diet of lethargy and lager had taken its toll.

The track clung to the hillside as they veered sharp left. A cavernous valley appeared from nowhere, shaped like a Zulu shield, the lush vegetation near the river, in stark contrast to the arid dryness of the surrounding area. They paused for another photo opportunity. It reminded Tom, in a weird way, of the Eden project in Cornwall in the sense that it was so completely unexpected, hidden until you were practically inside it. There were no futuristic domes but he could make out a road with a string of old houses dotted along it and what looked like a camp site but they were hundreds of metres above it and the rollercoaster road snaked down to the settlement. He was thankful it was downhill, he didn't have the strength for any more climbing, his arse cheeks were already red raw. The valley couldn't be more than six hundred metres wide. He strained to see the end of it but there was no obvious road out of there. It looked like they'd ridden into a dead end, like a fly crawling into an empty bottle, shit. He kept his thoughts to himself. It was no use panicking Carla at this stage. They'd have to investigate. Faced with the dilemma near the top of the pass, they'd had no choice. Now the options seemed even more limited. He swallowed hard and collected his thoughts. They'd managed to extricate themselves from the bad guys, but it wasn't over yet. If the hoodlums tracked them down, God forbid, there was no way out.

Chapter 53

Steyn summoned his tag team helpers and the four of them sat around a table in Celestino's. Smit had cleaned himself up, but he would have needed a professional make over to disguise the bruises. The two young cops were surprised by his dishevelled appearance but knew better than to ask questions. They had been on the wrong side of his tongue on numerous occasions, often for the most trivial of things. Van Buren suppressed his desire to laugh, though it wasn't easy. The boss looked like he'd been on spin cycle in the station washing machine. Strydom waited for Steyn to speak, it was clear that he was in charge now.

"Carla and Tom got away from the drugs gang. They're on the way out of town on bikes. We need to find them fast."

"Why didn't they go to the police station?" Strydom was perplexed. Smit started to speak but Steyn waved the royal hand and interrupted.

"That's not important; the priority is to locate them before the thugs do. The answer to your question will come later. They left about an hour and a half ago. Cyclists do on average 15km/h so they won't be far away. I reckon they'll stay clear of the main tar road. You guys live here, what would you do?"

Strydom answered quickly, Smit was more intent on sliding his foot to cover the bent cop sign.

"The main road would be a no no. I would head down the gravel road to Leeu-Gamka or over the Swartberg pass towards Oudtshoorn. It would be pointless going towards the dam or Welterfreede because they're dead ends."

That makes sense. We should split up and check those roads out. Van Buren you come with me and Strydom you go with Captain Smit. We'll take the pass, you try Leeu-Gamka."

"As the senior officer, shouldn't I come with you Steyn?"

Smit wanted to stay close to the outsider to monitor his every move. That was the only way to stay ahead of the game.

"No, it doesn't make sense having two rookie cops working together. We need someone experienced in both cars."

***

Malherbe watched the three police cars outside Celestinos's with interest. He was sat in his car, parked a safe distance away. They'd wanted a guided tour around town; the criminal convoy had taken less than twenty minutes. He'd seen the increased police presence as they drove down the back street, there must have been developments. Carla might even be in the building. He jumped out and ambled over to Cloete's car, asking him to go and check it out. He was conscious he'd been wandering around the town for a couple of days, it was better if a stranger did the dirty work. As Cloete walked past the back gate four policemen emerged. He dropped his keys on the floor near them and tried to listen in. He paused for a few seconds and turned on his heels, walking away at a steady pace.

"I couldn't hear much, they were talking quietly but they mentioned bikes and said they hadn't gone far."

"Shit, there were a couple of bikes in the backyard a while ago. They must be trying to cycle out of here the dull bastards. They'll still be fairly close to town", said Malherbe.

"If you didn't fuck up in the first place, we wouldn't be on this wild goose chase."

"Look, Johnson was to blame, I've told you that. It's time to move on. I'm going to get Carla, that's my business, and in the process I'm going to deliver Radebe on a plate. That's what your boss wants isn't it? So cut out this blame bullshit and fucking work with me ok?"

Malherbe wanted to fill the guy's face in, the cocky bastard. If push came to shove during the end game, he wouldn't bat an eyelid if a stray bullet buried itself in Cloete's forehead. He might even pull the trigger himself.

"Radebe's got a plane here hasn't he? Call him and tell him to get his arse in the air. They should be easy enough to spot, it's not like they can hide in the suburbs. In the meantime, we'll have to split up and follow the cops, discretely, if you're capable of discretion of course."

His contempt was hardly disguised. Malherbe was about to respond when the tallish cop turned around. Fuck, he recognized him, it was Steyn, older and leaner but it was him. The man responsible for putting him behind bars; the endless beatings came back, the metal doors, the bare corridors, the sound of clinking keys and warden's feet, the untouchable sky through the bars. He shuddered. The bastard must have become involved when they found the body of Joseph in Jonkershoek and now he was here to tie up the loose ends, snooping and sniffing round Carla, piecing together the jigsaw till the picture was revealed. He was a hard-nosed fucker, ruthless and efficient.

"What's wrong?" Cloete could see he'd gone pale.

"Nothing. I'm just tired of all this shit. I'll call Radebe. Let's finish this once and for all."

Radebe was near the Bush pub when he got the call. They turned around immediately and headed for the airstrip, parked the stolen car behind a shed, out of sight of the main road.

"How much fuel have we got?" Radebe was usually glad of Gerber's silence but sometimes it was a fucking hindrance. He was fine with a simple question that just demanded a nod of the head but anything more complicated involved amateur sign language or a pencil and bloody paper. Gerber pointed to his watch and held up two fingers.

"Two hours?" The thumb went up.

"Ok, go out twenty kilometres and circle the area and we'll move in closer."

They took off towards Prince Albert road and banked to the right. Radebe picked up the binoculars from the back seat, next to the machine gun. The time for talking was done, if he saw Carla and the guy, he'd mow them down. They needed to be silenced forever and the whole sorry episode consigned to history. He touched the stick hanging around his neck and slid the gold ring around his finger. They dropped lower and he began to scan the terrain below.

***

"I'll take the fat cop and his cub, you take the tall one."

Malherbe wanted to stay as far away from Steyn as possible. That guy had a mind like a well-ordered filing cabinet, never forgot a face. If you lined up all the men he'd sent down they'd stretch to George but he'd probably remember every one of them; each success a mental trophy to polish. The irony was he would make a great bad guy, never missed a trick, but he'd never come over to the dark side. Oh no, it was the path to righteousness for him. Serve the state, clean up the country.

"Ok, keep in touch."

Cloete and his henchmen followed Steyn, past the dam on the hillside with the wooden cross hanging over the town and turned right onto the dirt.

"They're going over the pass baas, towards Oudtshoorn or Calitzdorp,"

Cloete nodded.

"Stay back and keep a safe distance."

Malherbe lit a cigarette and relaxed. It was good to be alone again. Laurel and Hardy seemed to be in no hurry to set off and he exhaled slowly. The pot was about to blow the lid off; Radebe, Steyn, Gleason's mob, Carla, all circling round the town like hungry vultures in search of a meal. If he pulled the strings correctly they'd all be helpless puppets in his hands. The fat guy eventually got behind the wheel and they were on the track to Leeu-Gamka, the drugs barn a burnt-out husk as they drove past, all that money gone up in smoke, the rolling hills rippled in the heat haze but the road was empty.

Chapter 54

Your parents are all you know but you don't really know them. You see them project themselves on the screen of the outside world, all laughter and smiles but the intimate grimness happens behind closed doors. They feed you, clothe you, give you what love they can but in the end you're on your own. It's you against the world.

That's how Jeff felt. He was back home after dark. Mum had been furious, screaming at him. She didn't listen to his worries about dad, said he was a waster and probably just on the piss like usual. She'd sent him to bed with no supper like the kid in Where the Wild Things Are. But no forest grew in his bedroom, no boat came, there were no monsters to dance with. The monsters were in his head and he had to keep them at bay. He understood, now, that he couldn't get to Africa to find dad. It had been a bloody stupid idea but he'd felt helpless. He'd even thought of running away; the King of ideas he was. But he'd seen the tramps on the streets with their polystyrene cups and dogs on strings, the beer cans hidden behind them, cardboard signs resting on knees. He couldn't survive on the streets, didn't belong in that world but the old man was on his way there. He knew dad had a drink problem, his scruffy flat was always littered with beer cans and empty wine bottles, but he could never talk to him about it. Those conversations belonged in the grown-up world and he was just a kid.

Half the kids in school didn't see their dads. A lot had never even seen them. In this fucked up world, all he ever wanted was a dad to look up to. He knew dad was a mess, a car crash but he was his car crash and people got out of wrecked vehicles and walked away unscathed, didn't they?

Jeff remembered a line from the Shawshank Redemption, it was one of his dad's favourite films and they'd watched it loads of times – something about choosing living over dying. In the late hours he realized he had to keep the faith, keep going. There was no other alternative. At the end of the day, you had to look after yourself. The happy family photograph on his bedside table may not be reality anymore but he owed it to himself to look outwards. It was, although he was unaware of it, the first tentative steps towards adulthood. The future was uncertain, but it was his future and he had a new found determination to make the best of it. Mum said he was over reacting, like some soap actor in EastEnders. Maybe she was right. He packed his school bag for the morning and switched off the light. As his dad always said, tomorrow is a new day. Sleep came quickly. The phone under his pillow didn't buzz.

Chapter 55

Every uphill has a downhill. Tom was glad of the golden rule of cycling; the prospect of climbing another set of steep slopes didn't bear thinking about. The road down into Die Hel was treacherous, picking a line through the loose rocks and stones was difficult and you had to negotiate the innumerable bends very slowly to avoid the prospect of hitting the deck, or worse still, plunging over the side. This was no Tour de France descent at breakneck speed. It was a crawl to safety. As they reached the valley floor, Tom was overcome by the experience, it may have just been fatigue but he felt like an ant crawling on a giant's palm. The valley sides loomed large, excluding the rest of the world. This was the land that time forgot.

The main group turned into a camp site, the tents had already been set up for them but there was no sign of a support vehicle. Carla continued on a couple of hundred metres and stopped at a picnic site, Tom trailed behind, his legs were cramping up. He lent his bike against a tree and sprawled on the floor, exhausted.

"Shit I'm knackered, I've got nothing left." His limbs were shaking, and he couldn't get up if he tried.

"You chill out a bit, I'm going to have a word with the leader of the cycle group, see if there is a way out at the end of the valley. Drink some water. I'll be back in a few minutes." She placed a bottle next to him, but he didn't move. He was asleep.

***

"Tom, wake up." He raised himself up on his elbows but it was an effort.

"What's the news?"

"Not good. There's no road out the other end, just a very steep footpath up the western cliffs, over the mountains to Ladismith. I asked if I could use one of their mobile phones but there's no reception down here in the depths. So, we're on our own, the only sensible way out is back the way we came."

"Straight back into trouble you mean. What if Malherbe's on his way here now? We're caught between the devil and the deep blue sea. I can't cycle back up there."

Tom gestured towards the spindly path etched into the rocks. He checked his watch.

"Anyway, by the time we get up there, it'll be sundown and it goes dark here real quick. We'll be fucked without any lights and there'll be no shelter, who knows what animals wander around at night? This isn't Wales where all we'd be likely to encounter is a hedgehog is it? This is bloody Africa."

Carla laughed.

"Jeez Tom, you're a doom merchant. There must be something we can do. Christ, I bet your rubber duck died when you were a kid."

"My dog did eat my guinea pig when I was five, if that's any consolation to you."

"Be serious for a minute, what the fuck are we gonna do?"

"Well, I think we should check out the path you mentioned, see if it's a viable option, then we should find somewhere to doss for the night, get up at dawn and make our move."

Carla nodded. "It makes sense, we've still got some food and water left, enough for the night anyway."

They followed the road, it was an eerie sort of place, the old houses perfectly preserved but empty, only the memories lingered. There were placards near some of the buildings, listing the original occupants and their professions. It reminded Tom of the Museum of Wales, St Fagans, but on a grander scale. The names: Marais, Swanepoel, Cordier, Mostart, conjured images of hard men, living off the land. A simple life governed by the seasons. No doubt there were conflicts, it was human nature, but they would have to be settled within the confines of a tight knit community. The road from the top of the pass was a relatively recent development and it would have been the death knell for the place. It pricked the bubble of isolation, opened eyes and ears to the outside world; the rancorous clamour of civilization. One by one they would leave, maybe just over the hills, but the spell was broken.

It looked like the properties were owned by the Parks Board now and you could come and stay in some of them but the heat of the summer had dissuaded visitors. It was a ghost town. They passed a building that was in the process of being renovated. The sign outside said it was the honeymoon suite. It didn't have a door so they walked in. The place was being rebuilt using traditional materials; the walls from unbaked mud bricks, the rafters hewn from indigenous olive trees, a rye straw thatched roof and a ceiling constructed from local reeds bound together with strips of bark from thorn trees.

"It must have been a simple life but a rewarding one, nothing but the bosom of the family to rely on. It's a different world Tom, a different world."

"Yeh, they would have to make their own entertainment, be self-sufficient, with just the valley to bear witness. It's hard to comprehend; the complete opposite to our pampered high-tech existence. We'd have struggled to survive, well, especially me. I'd have trouble banging a nail in the wall but it must have been good for the soul, plenty of thinking time."

"Not so good for you then Tom, you think too much, analyse every detail instead of living life. If you look back all the time you'll bump into the future."

He could have taken it as a criticism, it didn't take much to chip away the veneer of his fragile self, but she was right. He'd known it for a long time but the drink had masked his inadequacies, in a fog of depression admittedly. She'd helped him turn his head forward in the brief time he'd known her.

"You don't mince your words do you? But you do have a point."

They cycled on and crossed a river. It was hardly a raging torrent, reduced to isolated pools by the severity of the summer. There was a burning heat gripping the valley, little breeze, and Tom had a headache. He was sweating profusely again, like Ralph Richardson in the *Four Feathers*. There were dense riverine shrubs and an abundance of thorn and wild olive trees close to the river. You could hide an army in the thick reeds. They dismounted and pushed the bikes across, stepping carefully on the rocks, testing them first. The houses were thinning out as they neared the end of the road. A guest farm on the left, Boplaas, was closed for business, the car park empty. They paused under a

Poplar tree and viewed the ragged path, twisting and turning skywards through the mountain fynbos. It was littered with rocks and boulders and there were little offshoots heading in all directions.

"Christ that's hard-core, we can't carry the bikes up there and we've no idea how far it is to civilization. It would be stupid to try it now; we could be stranded up there in the night, minus a torch."

Tom wiped his brow, he was worried.

"Yeh, it'd be too risky, even though it's tempting. You were right earlier. It's the honeymoon suite for us tonight, up at dawn and over the hill to Freedom Ville."

Tom laughed. "It sounds like the title of a poem."

"It can be your next project when all this is behind us."

Carla got back on her bike and headed back towards the river. Tom was still sat on the wall. He shouted after her.

"Thanks for waiting, I'd carry you over the threshold but I'm too tired to pick you up."

She was sat crossed legged, laying out some food on the floor when he got back to the house. They could have done with a rug, like Gillian Welch performed on at Hammersmith, to add some intimacy to the bare surroundings. There wasn't much left to eat; a few bananas and flap jacks but it was enough to tide them over.

"Do you believe in fate?" Tom was stretching his legs; his calves were tight.

"Not the Thomas Hardy sort of fate when your past comes back to haunt you, if that's what you mean? I think you can have good or bad luck but it's more about the kind of choices you make." She replied.

"There speaks the teacher, the voice of reason, but I've got a theory."

"Come on then, backwoods cavalier, let's hear it." Carla was expecting some left field ramble.

"Most people believe in the power of nurture over nature and I agree, to some extent. A good, moral upbringing surely increases your chances of making well intentioned, informed decisions but it's a simplistic concept at best. Look at me, to the outside world, I lived behind middle class curtains, nicely clothed, well fed, well educated, spoilt, yet something wasn't right. In a way, I had too much love, I was smothered." He paused and took a small sip of water.

"A couple of years back I found out that my mum had had a traumatic childhood and she over compensated, did everything for me, stifled any independent streak within me. She never ever came to terms with what happened to her as a child; never got the counselling that she so obviously needed. She was a closed book, and a sad one at that. It's the unseen that drags you down. The failings of one generation handed down to the next."

Tom was holding back the tears, his voice breaking.

"Go on."

"Then, to top it all fate comes along in its fucking dark chariot and mows you down, kills a part of you."

Carla thought for a while, he was on the edge of an emotional precipice, but she wanted to make a point.

"The doors to recovery are never permanently closed Tom. These last few days you've begun to open up. Look we're in the middle of nowhere, we might not live to see another day if those bastards find us, just let it all out for fucks sake."

He stood up, propped himself in a corner and looked at her. Finally, the field of tethered balloons was to be cut free. It was time. No more hiding, no more bullshit, no more fucking navel gazing. The irony of it; a dark secret revealed in the depths of a hidden valley.

"This could take a while babe, bear with me."

She crossed her legs and sipped some water, not knowing what to expect

"I was fourteen. It was February 17th, 12.30 pm, it's carved in my bloody brain. We'd had lunch and streamed out into the playground. For some stupid reason that day, I didn't fancy playing football with my best mates. I wandered down to our form room. It was at the far perimeter of the school grounds down a gentle slope. On the left was a fence and the woods. I was on my own, throwing stones at the trees. A classmate, Stuart was his name, came over."

She could see how hard this was for him. He was gripping his hands tightly together.

"I remember it was a cold, bitter winter's day. I never usually hung around with him. He wasn't one of my close mates. Christ, how many times have I wished I'd played football that day?"

"Over the term the more adventurous amongst us had devised a game. Near our classroom wasn't patrolled by staff, so it was easy to hop over the fence. You know, it was the thrill of breaking the rules, taking a risk. The trees were thick and within seconds nobody could have spotted you. It was like a different planet over there, we thought of it as our uncharted world. The ground was a mixture of earth and coal dust, I think it was an old coal tip, there were mines nearby. It became our private theatre. We acted out Star Wars or pretended we were cops pursuing the baddies, hiding behind trees, covering each other. Someone would always have a watch and we'd be back in time for lessons when we'd checked the coast was clear."

251

He paused to sip some water.

"That day, me and Stuart jumped the fence, he was agile, the only kid who could do a back flip when the rest of us lumbered around the gym equipment. We chased each other through the trees. At the edge of the woods there was a clearing that abruptly ended with a thirty-foot drop to the river, flowing black with coal dust. It had taken us a few days to discover the river, initially we hadn't strayed too far, exploring more and more on each trip."

Tom paused and wiped his brow. It was a strain to vocalize all this shit that had been a constant interior monologue for so long. His inner defence mechanism was still trying to shut him down. She watched him, not wanting to interrupt. It seemed like it was an out of body experience for him, his eyes were glazed.

"Across the river was a pipe, it had a vertical metal grid at either end to prevent anybody crossing it. Within a couple of days, the bravest of us soon climbed around it. I eventually bowed to peer pressure and edged across; anything to avoid losing face. I did it just the once, that was enough for me. Stuart came with us a couple of times and ran across as if it was flat as a road bridge."

He paced the room without pausing for breath.

"It was a freezing day. I can see it now, the ice on the pipe. I told him not to do it but he looked at me, laughed. I knew he thought I was a wimp. In a flash he was off, running across it like a madman, screaming and hollering."

Tom stopped again, the memory too painful. Carla watched him silently, giving him time to compose himself. His face was strained and pale.

"Half way over he slipped and tried to grab the pipe but it was too big to hold. I screamed. He fell into the swollen water. I heard his head hit a rock just below the surface. That fucking sound will live with me forever. His head split open like a watermelon, a bloody spume spouting up. I.. I saw his body floating, arms and legs waving at the mercy of the water. I stood there, numb. Carla, I was bloody fourteen, that's all. I didn't know what to do. I couldn't think straight. I stumbled back through the trees, spewed my guts up, stopped before the fence became visible and slumped by a severed stump. And that's where I came up with a plan; a stupid, childish plan to supposedly protect myself. A fucking plan I've had to live with since that day."

He paused, ran his fingers through his greasy hair. She was just about to speak when he started to talk again.

"I was naïve but I was convinced he was dead. You won't bloody believe this. I just climbed the fence and went to registration as normal. Stuart didn't get his mark but that wasn't unusual, he had a history of absconding and nobody seemed too bothered. It was only that evening, when he didn't return home that his parents alerted the police. An old woman walking her dog found his body washed up on a muddy bank, a few miles downriver. The police came to school, asked us if we'd seen him that lunch time but I kept quiet. You see Carl, I thought if I admitted being with him they would have said I'd pushed him but I didn't, I know I didn't."

He sipped the water to ease his parched throat.

"The coroner recorded a verdict of accidental death and the matter was closed but not for me. I have had to live with it ever since. If I'd acted quickly could they have saved him?" I've replayed the film of that day every fucking day of my life. It changed me; a spark in me was extinguished. My parents attributed it to teenage blues but I knew different and I've never fully recovered."

Tom slumped to the floor exhausted. Carla cradled his head. She sat opposite him, trying to make sense of what he'd told her. She couldn't imagine being the keeper of such a dark secret for so long, watching it eat away at you, feeding off your insecurities. It was a life sentence but from the outside you appeared free. The emotional outpouring had drained him. He was pale and his eyes oddly lifeless. It was a few minutes before she spoke.

"Christ Tom how have you kept that bottled up for all these years?"

He replied in a quiet, measured tone, as if detached from himself.

"Through the power of fear and self-loathing; there's not been a day when I haven't questioned my actions, replayed what happened, cursed my weakness and stupidity."

"Tom you were just a kid, you made a spontaneous decision to protect yourself. He was probably dead anyway. You can't view what happened through adult eyes."

"Probably dead has never been enough, what if he was still alive, what if I could have saved him?"

"Look, this sounds grim but you saw the blood, you heard the crack when he hit his head on the rock. He must have been unconscious. He would have drowned. You didn't murder him and it wasn't your fault, you need to let go Tom, for your own sanity."

She spoke to him firmly but with a calm pragmatism. He knew she was right. For the first time in years he stopped thinking about himself, stopped over analysing the barrel load of problems that beset him and actually looked outwards. Somehow this woman, this comparative stranger, had unlocked him. True, he had released his feet from the concrete that encased him in London, escaped the torpor but it just seemed so natural talking to her. She was something to behold and he was bloody lucky to have met her.

"You're right babe, it's time to move on." He never ever thought he'd say that. He felt like it was someone else talking, a robot only programmed to talk sense.

They huddled together, neither feeling the need to speak.

***

Tom grabbed the water bottle and took another slurp.

"It's thirsty work baring your soul." He smiled.

"You should be a life coach. You could make a lot of money." She laughed.

"Most of it is common sense Tom; deep down you probably know it yourself. I'm sorry for involving you in all this shit. When we get out of this mess, I'll be there for you."

He was thankful his outpourings hadn't alienated her. She was one strong woman.

"It's not your fault and I'll be there for you too."

She kissed him and laid her head on his shoulder.

"By the way, what's your theory on fate? You didn't get to that."

He smiled. He felt weightless, free.

"No I didn't, did I? Got side tracked. I call it the snooker theory. We are all balls on the green baize; they're all scattered, hard and random. There's a trail of collisions, some roll to safety, others drop in the pockets of doom."

"But who rolls the balls?"

Tom was about to reply when they heard the drone of a plane above. They went outside and stood by the bikes, trying to catch a glimpse of it.

"There's no crop to dust." He said, smirking.

"Probably bringing in some supplies or it could be the flying doctor." She replied.

The plane banked and came full circle, dropping low over the valley. They waved like the kids in *The Railway Children.*

"Christ, it's flying low."

It was following the road, barely above the rooftops. The dust jumped around them. There was a metallic clunk as a bullet hit the gear sprocket on one of their bikes, ricocheting between them.

Blood and Dust

It was more than
The blood
The dust and his body
That flowed
Down the river.

My driftwood soul
was caught
in the current
of those
blackened waters.

I watched it
crash against
the rocks
and arch its back
in pain.

Chapter 56

The twists and turns up the valley mirrored the investigation. Steyn wasn't able to put his foot down. It was frustrating. Van Buren sat in the passenger seat, too nervous to open the conversation. It was down to Steyn to break the ice.

"What's it like working for Captain Smit?"

"Off the record?"

"Yup, what's said in the car stays in the car."

"He's a bit of an arse, barely talks to us. Nobody likes him. He keeps himself to himself, disappears for long stretches and comes back in a foul mood. I'm thinking of asking for a transfer, it's not what I signed up for."

"Is he close to any of the officers, any favourites?"

"Nope, he hates the lot of us."

"Noticed any changes in him lately?"

"If anything, he's become more distant. Seems like he detests the job, must be hanging on for retirement, why all the questions?"

"Just curious, he's tried his best to hamper my investigation from the start and I wondered if it was out of character, but it seems not."

"It's because you're an outsider, probably thinks you're a flash guy from the city, come to invade his kingdom."

"Do you see him around town when he's off duty?"

"Not much, he's a home bird, seen him playing cards in Celestino's once in a while, when I've stopped for a take away coffee."

"Is that so?" Steyn kept his eyes on the road, they were nearing the top of the pass and the road had been empty.

"Captain Steyn, can I ask you a question?"

"Fire away."

"What happened back there, who beat him up?"

Steyn hesitated but there was nothing to be lost by telling the truth.

"He says it was Tom and Carla, but I find that hard to believe. Why the hell would they attack him? I've got my suspicions about your boss but that's my problem. You just keep your eyes open; give me the benefit of your local knowledge. Where does this road lead?"

"Towards Oudtshoorn and Calitzdorp."

Van Buren raised his eyebrows, he had more questions but he'd been put in his place.

The phone buzzed and they pulled in at a view point close to Die Top. A family were having a picnic, overlooking the valley below. It was Botha and he was animated.

"Sorry for the delay Captain but I think we've got something. We've tracked down Radebe, couple of drug and violence convictions when he was a youngster, Cape Flats connections but listen to this; he's living in a penthouse flat overlooking the harbour. Rumour is, he's a big player. Clean record for years but he's extremely wealthy and apparently unemployed. That's not the best though. There were a lot of Malherbe's to sift through but one stands out, you know him baas, you know him."

"Go on."

"Remember that drug related attempted murder in Camps Bay a few years back, that rich Russian guy?"

Steyn recalled the case. It had been front page news.

"Yeh, we caught that blond guy, nasty bastard as I recall, so that's Malherbe I presume?"

"Yeh, he's been out of prison for a couple of years, he's a hit man baas, a pro. Been lying low but that doesn't mean he's been inactive. Lives fairly close to Radebe and they're both out of town. The Cape Town cops are on it.

"Interesting, dig deeper, see what you can come up with. Malherbe: tall, blonde, blue eyes, muscular, is that the guy?"

"That's him."

"Keep me posted, if there are any developments."

Steyn turned to Van Buren.

"The picture is slowly being coloured in."

They got out to stretch their legs and walked to the edge of the cliff. The air was still and it was roasting hot, not a day to be on a bike for hours on end. They wouldn't be able to go far in this heat. The steep gradients would surely take their toll. Steyn wandered over to the picnic brigade, eyed the sandwiches and plastic cups of wine with envy. He flashed his police ID.

"Been here long, seen any cyclists coming over top?"

He didn't waste time with pleasantries.

"Yes, a whole troupe of them came over a while back."

"How many do you reckon?"

"I'd say about twenty."

"Were they all together?"

"Eventually, two of them were a fair way behind but they were pedalling hard to catch them up. They took the turning into Die Hel."

"Die Hel?" Steyn had never heard of it.

"It's a remote valley, hidden away by the mountains. Rather them than me." He sipped his wine from the safety of his camping chair.

"How long ago was that?"

"A couple of hours at the most."

A small plane was turning in ever decreasing circles above. Van Buren was watching it. They got back in the car.

"Captain, that's either a rich tourist indulging himself up there or they're looking for something."

They watched it veer off along a valley.

"What's that way?" Steyn asked.

"Die Hel."

"That's where Carla and Tom have gone."

"The bloody idiots."

"Why do you say that?"

"Because it is a dead end."

Steyn blew out softly.

"You'd better ring Smit and tell him to get his fat arse up here. We are going to need back up."

"Ok baas, it's the last chance for communication, phones don't work in Die Hel."

Part of Steyn wanted to leave Smit in the lurch but he was better where he could see him. Van Buren made the call as Steyn turned off for Die Hel. The 37 km sign would prove to be deceptive. You couldn't go above twenty on the dirt track, if you wanted to preserve your dental work, that is.

***

Cloete parked just beneath the brow of the hill. They'd seen Steyn pull over and they waited until he moved on. They followed the dust cloud as he turned onto the side road. Malherbe headed for the pass, Radebe had called him. So, all the roads they'd been on, all the planes they'd been in. led to Die Hel; a valley rich in history with another chapter soon to be written.

Chapter 57

Their natural instinct was to run for cover. The sanctuary of the honeymoon house had morphed into Hitler's bunker. The bare walls lost their charm; a symbol of confinement, a sightless cave. The sound of the plane's engine signified the immediacy of its return. The doorway seemed to have grown bigger, and the windowless square above their heads was an open invitation. Tom looked at the floor. He imagined a hail of bullets bouncing off the deck like a well-aimed volley at Wimbledon but there would be no cheering from the champagne set. As the roar filled their ears, he closed his eyes. People in fear always wanted to hunker down and round up the wagons, centre themselves on some form of security blanket. He wasn't a religious man, but he prayed. The rhythmic thud of the machine gun rattled the air; the cowboy ting of bullets ricocheted around the room. The noise of the engine diminished and he opened his eyes. Carla was curled up in a ball in the corner.

"We can't stay here Carla, we'll have to make a run for it, head down to the river and hide in the bushes and reeds until night fall. They can't fly around forever."

He popped his head through the window frame and scanned the sky, he couldn't see the plane but he could still hear it. It was difficult to gauge which direction it was flying in. Carla was sobbing. The pressure of the last days had finally made her crack. She was glued to the floor, making no signs to move.

"Come on, we're not dead yet but we will be if we stay here."

He helped her to her feet and dragged her into the sunlight. The plane was on its way back again. It would have been suicide to belt down the middle of the road and there wasn't time to get far before the next attack. They scuttled across the road and hid in the small space between the old school buildings.

"It must be Radebe, he came to Prince Albert in a plane didn't he?"

Tom was too out of breath to reply, he nodded. Now they'd been spotted the noose was tightening again. There were only a certain number of times you could walk up the steps to the gallows and stand next to the hangman without the trap door opening. They were accustomed to the loop of the plane, though they couldn't see it. The sound of it thundered over the roof tops, the bird life scattering to the safety of the trees. A rush of bullets splintered the window frame and tore through the thatched roof. The bikes were still propped up outside but the tyres had been punctured in the barrage.

Behind where they were standing was a row of small trees leading to some sort of outhouse. It was flanked, on either side, by a small wall, less than a metre high. Tom pointed towards it and gestured to Carla. As the sound of the engine temporarily receded, they made their way towards it, hunched low. The old door, with its flaky paint and rusty hinges, creaked open. Inside was a load of garden furniture and a musty parasol, frayed and covered with mould. They closed the door and pulled out a couple of chairs.

"Jesus, what else can they throw at us, doodle-bugs?" Tom slumped down and scratched his head.

She'd picked up the bag when they'd left their previous residence and handed him a drink, there was no food left and just one water bottle. The gun was in the bottom of the rucksack, she gave it to Tom.

"Not much of a defence against a machine gun but it's better than nothing I suppose. I wonder how many bullets it carries?" He didn't want to fiddle with it in case he shot himself in the foot.

"It won't be like the movies, where the hero miraculously fires away for hours and steps over the bodies into the sunlight, that's for sure."

"We could do with a Hollywood ending Tom."

"As long as it's not *Butch Cassidy and the Sundance Kid*, or *Thelma and Louise*," he replied.

It would have been funny over cocktails but neither of them laughed. The back drop to their limited conversation was the repetitive wail of the engine, swooping down to kill them.

"How long can they keep this up?" Carla was feeling claustrophobic in the cramped surroundings.

"It depends how much fuel they've got. They'd like to land and find the bodies, our bodies but the road's too narrow and close to the houses. It's the only thing in our favour." He allowed himself the semblance of a smile.

Carla looked at him. "Didn't you see the landing strip the other side of the river?"

His ashen face turned a duller grey. He hadn't noticed anything apart from the majesty of the mountains and the cluster of houses, his mind dulled by the experiences of the last few hours. They listened intently. The endless loop of the plane had been broken. They heard it descend. It landed, not more than half a mile away, the engine cutting out abruptly.

"Shit, they're going to scour this place till they find us. We can't sit here waiting for them to open the door, we'll go nuts."

He was right but there was no obvious alternative staring them in the face.

" If we stay here we're sitting ducks, if we get out in the open we're sitting ducks, catch bloody 22", said Carla.

"They'll presume we'll be holed up in a building, let's do the unexpected."

Sitting still wasn't an option. The fear would gnaw away at that them, the constant wait for the sound of footsteps approaching the door, occupying their every thought. They needed there to be more than one exit strategy, to be able to run, albeit erratically, for their lives.

"Come on, let's head for the river, there's lush vegetation there, we can hide until it gets dark. At dawn we can take that craggy path out of here."

He was getting impatient; every second spent dithering brought Radebe and co closer. She nodded.

"The path's called The Ladder, I saw the sign."

Tom opened the door and peeked outside. It was all clear. He moved round the back, there was an open field, no more than sixty metres long, that gently sloped towards the trees and bushes that lined the banks of the river bed.

"Follow me and run like fuck." He was off before she had time to reply. She overtook him within the first twenty metres. Christ, she had a good turn of pace. She disappeared into the undergrowth and he was still only half way across the field. The brambles scratched his arm as he dived in the bushes, landing in an undignified heap.

"What kept you darling?"

"Bloody hell girl, you're like hot shit off a warm shovel. I had to stop to sing an old Prince song, do you remember '*the Ladder*'?"

"No *Purple Rain* is the limit of my knowledge."

"It's about climbing the steps in search of the answers, appropriate don't you think?" He was about to launch into a quiet version of it but thought the better of it. She tried to humour him with a belated smile but she wasn't in the mood to dissect the meaning of song lyrics. At least they had made it this far; scratched, hair dishevelled but limbs intact. They sat there silently, eyes trained on the field and the houses in the distance.

Chapter 58

The convoy, evenly spaced along the dirt track, conformed to the rhyming pattern of a Shakespearian sonnet: ABAB, or in their case, cop, criminal, cop criminal. They were all a good distance apart, all occupied by their own thoughts, each with their personal agenda. Steyn was first to overlook the valley, the cluster of houses taking him by surprise as he rounded the last bend. Van Buren had given him a potted history of the place during the bumpy ride. Those settlers must have been tough cookies. As they snaked down to the valley, an oasis in desolate surroundings, Steyn focused on the road. You had to go at a snail's pace to avoid the deep pot holes and the sheer drops that flanked them on alternate sides as they twisted and turned towards the first of the buildings. Van Buren scanned the settlement on the way down.

"Captain, there's the cyclists. Looks like they're on an organized trip, there's a load of tents set up and they're having a braai. Turn in here."

They parked up under the shade of a tree.

"Leave this to me Van Buren, keep your eyes peeled. The plane was heading this way, it may have landed somewhere in the valley. Watch the road too, Smit and Strydom shouldn't be far behind."

He gestured towards the road carved in the mountain.

"Hello, Captain Dirk Steyn, Stellenbosch police. Did two cyclists tag on to your group, we're looking for them."

A tall guy, must have been six foot five, stepped forward, pot belly straining the flimsy cycling top.

"Why, what have they done?" He laughed and the others joined in.

"Don't waste my time, they're in danger, have you seen them?" Steyn's tone wiped the smile off their sweaty faces.

"Yeh, a girl and a guy, they joined us on the way up the pass. She asked me if there was another way out of the valley. I told them about the footpath up the hill at the end of the valley, the ladder, and I think they went to check it out. Well, they went in that direction anyways."

"The ladder?"

"Yeh, that's what the locals call it, its helluva steep, leads over the mountains towards Ladismith. It's easy enough, if you're a goat." He nearly laughed again but thought the better of it when he saw the expression on Steyn's face.

"Captain, we've got company but it's not Smit", said Van Buren.

They saw the car at the very top of the mountain just about to begin the laborious descent.

"It'll take them some time to get down here, we'd better move quick." Steyn ran to the car.

"It's a pain in the arse without mobile phones. We're gonna have to live off our wits, this is going to get nasty, you up for it Van Buren?"

"They could just be tourists Captain." The young cop swallowed nervously.

"In an ideal world they would be but, uh ah. My money's on them being from the criminal fraternity, coming to claim their prize." Steyn was driving through the houses.

"Look out for any sign of them Van Buren, we need to find them first."

The place was like a deserted film set; the buildings locked and shuttered. They found the two bikes propped against a house that was in the process of being renovated. It would need more work now. The wall was riddled with bullet holes, the window frame splintered by the impact of the heavy artillery. Inside the walls were pock marked, clustered like a rash.

"Shit, they want them badly and they've got a machine gun. Judging by the angle of these bullet marks, they fired from high up, the plane." Steyn walked back outside and scanned three hundred and sixty degrees. There was nobody in sight and there was nothing more than a deathly hush blanketing the valley. Van Buren fingered the gun in his holster.

"What do we now baas?" He tried hard to control the tremor in his voice but Steyn knew he was scared.

"You check out the rondawels, I'll search the old buildings opposite. Keep your wits about you, don't fire at any lizards, each bullet needs to count so don't waste any, do you understand what I'm saying?" The poor kid had gone a whiter shade of pale.

"Ok baas, you won't leave me for long will you?" He sounded like a snotty child on his first day at big school.

"Pull yourself together man, I need your help, I'm not your bloody babysitter." Steyn managed to curtail his temper, he regretted not opting for Strydom, he seemed to be made of sterner stuff but it was too late now. They parted and arranged to meet in five minutes unless one of them shouted for assistance. At least they'd be able to hear each other call. They were hardly likely to be drowned out by the sound of traffic or the chatter of the crowds.

Van Buren scuttled off, Steyn felt like asking him to make sure he checked the corners in the rondewals but that would have been needlessly cruel and that wasn't him. Every cop had to start somewhere and he remembered his first few days in the force. A veteran had told him that everyone was scared but the trick was not to show it. They were all actors really, and you had to play your role with conviction. The kid would learn but it would be a baptism of fire.

Steyn read the sign in front of the building. It was the old school house. There were cobwebs on the door and, evidently, nobody had been in there for a good while. He slipped between the two buildings, down a thin alley. At the end of the path there was an outhouse. Its door was open. He slowly eased his gun from its holster and checked his pocket for the spare cartridges, not enough for an all-out war but it would have to do. Gently, he eased towards the building, careful to avoid loose stones and twigs that had fallen from the trees. He slid along the side of the wall, up close to the door and listened. No sound. He waited, to make sure. With a swift movement he was in, gun out in front. There was no-one there, it was full of ancient garden furniture but two of the chairs had been pulled out and placed next to each other. They weren't dusty either, like the rest of the stuff piled high up near the roof. Carla and Tom had been here, not long ago, it was too much of a coincidence not to be true. He exited and slipped behind the building. There was a field sloping towards the river. The dense vegetation flanking the water would provide good cover. If they had any sense they would have run there and hidden in the undergrowth. He followed the tree line in a wide arc, checking for any movement or a glimpse of clothing. He thought he saw some reeds moving but it was too far away to be certain. In any case, it could easily be an animal rummaging in the nature reserve foraging for food, he was hungry himself. Steyn turned; it was too dangerous to call out their names. The occupants of the plane could quite possibly be wandering about nearby. As he took his first step back to the road he heard the shot, the scream, the spray of machine gun fire, the final scream, the silence.

Chapter 59

Steyn froze, listened for the sound of footsteps but it was as quiet as an empty church, even the birds had fled. In the distance, he could hear car engines. Two of them were sliding down the hill like marbles in the marble run game his son had played when he was younger: rural rush hour, that made at least four cars in the valley, one of them should be Smit but, as for the other two? It could be more of the criminal brethren or unlucky tourists unwittingly entering a war zone.

He edged his way through the gap between the buildings and poked his eye around the corner. He saw the soles of police issue shoes twisted at an unnatural angle, trousers ripped and bloodied. He risked leaning slightly further. The kid had tried to be a bloody hero, tried to take out one of them with a single shot. Christ, they should have stayed together, he should have protected him. The tears welled and he wiped them with an angry hand. Death was a passenger, a constant companion that came with the job but it could never be desensitized, not if you had a heart, a sense of decency. He forced himself back into the now, reassumed the mantle of professionalism. The image of Van Buren; half the face blown off, mushed brains dripping on the dusty road, would haunt him but now wasn't the time for self- recrimination. He had to find Carla and Tom fast, before they were blown away, and get out of this place in one piece.

The cars were close now. It was time to retreat to a safe haven and watch the movements of the new arrivals. If he could team up with Strydom it would improve their chances of success. He walked back towards the outhouse, only small sections of the road were visible but there was no sign of anybody walking along it. The trees lay tantalizingly close, across the field. He ran for it, didn't look back and dived full length into the foliage. He expected to feel the firm ground beneath him but landed on something soft and warm.

"Fuckin' hell" Tom squawked, but Steyn covered his mouth with his hand and whispered, "sh, I'm on your side."

Tom was shaking. They'd fallen asleep, cuddled up in a ball. He thought a baboon or a bloody leopard had jumped on them. Carla sat up, befuddled.

"Steyn, Stellenbosch police, I presume you're Tom and Carla"

They nodded, too stunned to talk.

"I've been following up the Greg Joseph murder, keep quiet, Radebe and friends are on the prowl." He gestured towards the buildings.

"Did they land a plane here?" Carla nodded.

"Where's Smit? That guy pulled a gun on us when all we wanted was help. You're not working with him are you?" Tom was worried that it was a set up and all the cops in the world were as bent as a boomerang.

"No, he's fok all to do with me. I think he's something to do with the drug deal; taken cash and asked no questions." Steyn answered in hushed tones and waved his hands at them to do likewise.

"He thinks we worked for Joseph, accused us of trafficking drugs. The man's off his head. We're the innocent ones in all this shit. We're just bloody tourists. Help us." Carla was close to tears. Steyn nodded.

"I believe you. I'll get you out of this mess but it's not going to be easy. You have to listen to me. What I say goes ok? No sudden movements, no crack pot ideas. These guys are pros, they just slaughtered a young cop from Prince Albert, blew his brains out not half a mile away and you're next on the list. Didn't you hear the gun fire?"

"We slept through it." Carla was almost ashamed to say it.

"I find that hard to believe but I guess you guys are whacked. Here's the situation, Radebe is on the loose with a machine gun, Smit and Strydom have probably arrived and Malherbe and Johnson are likely to be here too."

"Christ, it's like a spaghetti western but Johnson won't be here. He cracked and walked into the sunset, that's how we escaped. It's the only roll of the dice that fell in our favour." Steyn was listening to Tom but keeping a close eye on the road. He could hear a car coming closer.

"We planned to hide here until dawn and take the mountain path towards Ladismith", said Carla.

"They'll try to cover that exit, there's only two ways out of the valley."

Steyn was trying to formulate a plan as he spoke. The fact that mobile phones were useless in the depths of the valley was a mixed blessing; it meant Radebe and Malherbe couldn't communicate if they were separated but the same applied to their own predicament. It would come down to a battle of wits, who could exploit the terrain best. Tom, in his pessimistic default mode, was thinking of a third exit: in the back of a hearse pulled by East End horses, sullen men in top hats, coffin bedecked with proteas.

"We can't take them on in a shootout; this hand gun's useless against machine guns. We've either got to draw them in, ambush them one at a time, or hook up with Strydom and drive out of here. Either way is problematic." It was an understatement.

Steyn rubbed his chin; one thing he knew was they had to stick together. He didn't want to have any more blood on his hands. The situation was even more complex because of the involvement of Smit. What would he do? If he was in it up to his neck, as now seemed certain, would he stop at nothing to protect himself? It came to something when one of your own turned out to be the most rotten apple in a stinking barrel.

"We've got a gun." Tom pulled it out of the bag.

"Do you know how to use it?"

"Well I've been paint-balling, if that's any use."

Steyn didn't know whether to laugh or cry. They had two hand guns, ok, but it was like having the two of diamonds and the two of hearts. The other players had all the aces. Tom and Carla were plucky, that was clear enough, but they were ordinary folk, amateurs. He'd be a fool to expect a dynamic response from them. He parted the reeds, watched the road like a hawk.

Chapter 60

It was like driving down a kid's marble run; the valley switching back on itself at acute angles. Smit had sat in silence the whole time, Strydom glanced at him; the dishevelled Captain looked very much the worse for wear. There were lots of things he wanted to ask him but he knew it was a futile exercise. Smit was licking his wounds and wouldn't take kindly to even the gentlest of probing from a subordinate. The man was an enigma; never gave anything away because he basically said nothing. Barked a few commands, reprimanded all and sundry, that was the standard fare. Nobody ever got close to him, or wanted to, for that matter. Strydom had noticed the evident tension between his boss and Stellenbosch's finest but had no idea what lay behind it. They were going to have to talk at some point. It was coming to the business end of the trip. Steyn was somewhere in the valley beneath them, they'd have to find him without the aid of a mobile phone; old time policing in the modern world.

***

Malherbe let the cop car get well ahead. It occasionally disappeared, like a small fishing boat lost between steep waves in stormy waters, but the tell-tale dust cloud pin pointed its location. The day was dragging on and his mood was darkening. The sight of Steyn had unnerved him and he was worried about Cloete. What if Gleason, sat in his luxury Joburg pad, overlooking the golf course, had told him that Radebe wasn't the only one that was expendable? There was no rule book in the underworld, only money talked sense. Nobody said what they meant or meant what they said. At the end of the day, you had to look after yourself. He glanced down at the bag, open on the passenger seat: the knife, the machete, the guns, the hammer and nails, the wrench, the drill. He'd used them countless times and his hands would be on them again before the day was out.

***

Cloete drove slowly past the houses. The car windows were down. Three pairs of eyes alert to any sign of movement. They rounded the bend and came to an abrupt halt.

"Look" Benson pointed to a pool of blood and brains, a trail of red leading from them to the open door of the house. The dust had been smoothed by someone dragging a body in there. Cloete slammed the gears in reverse and shot backwards, fifty metres, parked behind a shuttered building. They loaded up, fanned out and approached from three different angles, each darting from the cover of one building to the next.

***

Radebe watched with amusement. He was lying prone on the flat roof of an outhouse, slightly elevated from the road. His gun trained on each of them in turn. They didn't look like cops. When they came together at the door, he could mow them down without wasting too many bullets. He needed a few to dispose of Carla.

Chapter 61

All three of them heard it this time. The rapid fire made them jump. In a couple of seconds it was over. The valley reassumed its tranquil poise but the same couldn't be said of those hiding in the reeds. Tom's first reaction had been to run like a headless chicken and Steyn had to physically restrain him to prevent him from doing so. Carla felt faint. She covered her ears to block out the madness.

"Keep calm, stay still." Steyn's authoritative tone had the desired effect. They just looked at him, wide-eyed.

"Keep your eyes on the road, we may have to cross the river and head further downstream."

Steyn hoped it wasn't Strydom who was the latest to bite the dust but there was no way of knowing. It was too dangerous to check it out and he couldn't leave Tom and Carla on their own, he'd seen how scared they were. That made their reactions unpredictable and he had to keep them safe. There were no signs of movement on the road and they had to play the waiting game. Attempting to get to the ladder in broad daylight was worse than fool hardy, as was attempting to run to the car. If Radebe had any sense, he would have shot the tyres out anyway.

"Do you think Malherbe's here?" Carla shuddered at the prospect of ever having to come face to face with him again.

"Probably, Radebe would have called him to say he was going to land in Die Hel, I imagine mobiles work up high. I've got unfinished business with Malherbe, I banged him up for attempted murder years back but it appears the bastard's on the loose again."

"That fucker gives evil a bad name. God knows what he would have done to Carla if he got his way. You could see the excitement in his face when he inflicted pain; he's a very sick man."

Steyn didn't ask for details. It fitted the pattern. Van Gogh wasn't the only man to be deficient in the ear department. The Russian guy had been a gibbering wreck when they found him. He spared them the extra information; they'd had a guts full of Malherbe. It was pointless adding to their worries.

The sound of a car engine brought the conversation to an abrupt end. Steyn strained to make it out as it flashed by the buildings. It was brown, looked like a Jeep. Picking up pace, it disappeared out of sight, towards the ladder or, maybe it was bound for the plane?

***

Radebe stood up and dusted himself down. From his vantage point, he had a good view of the surrounding area, nothing was moving. He jumped to the ground and sprinted back to the road. Dragging bodies into the house was becoming a habit. The ants were crawling all over the dead cop, their feet getting caught in the treacle seeping from what was left of his face. The stench of dead meat made him gag. He was sweating by the time he'd towed the latest three in. He searched through their pockets, no police ID, they weren't cops. The wallets contained the usual credit cards and notes, family photographs never to be viewed with love again. He looked at the driver's licence in the first one; Frans Cloete, the face was familiar but he couldn't place it. There were cards from restaurants, all in Joburg. Joburg? Where had he seen him?

Radebe paused for a minute, checked the road but everything was still quiet. He checked the inside pocket of Cloete's jacket and pulled out an iPhone. The idiot didn't even have a pin number. He swiped to the contacts and scrolled down. Gleason, bloody Gleason. That's where he had seen him, in the hotel in Joburg, standing by the door, gun in hand. Something made him continue to scroll down and there it was- Malherbe. He pressed the name. It wasn't a dentist or a doctor, it was his man. The number didn't fucking lie; the double crossing, snivelling bastard. The red mist came down. He booted Cloete's face, felt the cheek bones crack but still he piled in. He was breathing hard now but the anger drove him on and on. When the head was reduced to a pulp he finally relented. His shirt was doused in sweat, pulse racing. It took a minute to calm down and think straight. He found the car keys in one of the other pockets. The car was parked behind one of the nearby houses. He sped towards the plane, time to collect the rest of the ammunition and the binoculars. There was work to be done.

***

Malherbe paused at the top of the mountain. He got out of the car and raised the binoculars. There was no point walking into a trap. His eyes were drawn to a group of cyclists spread across the camp site. They were having a braai, the smoke swirling up from the wood. He looked for the shapely form of Carla but it was difficult to make out faces. The cop car, with little and large in, was winding its way towards them. Fat arse got out and talked to some tall guy. There was a lot of arm waving and he pointed further down the valley. The car turned and vanished from sight behind the houses. He looked down the valley; it was seemingly devoid of people. There was another car on the move though. It was Cloete's brown Jeep, travelling at speed. Malherbe raised the binoculars slightly; he could just make out the shape of the plane's wings in the far distance. There was a spindly path behind it, trailing up the mountain in an erratic spiral. He jumped back in the car and reached over to the passenger seat, carefully placing the gun in his lap. Before beginning the final, slow descent into Die Hel, he glanced at his mobile phone one last time. His screen saver was a photograph of Carla, nipples clearly visible through the thin shirt. He smiled and shouted, loud and proud, "I'm coming for you honey."

Chapter 62

It was a surreal experience; lying in a field in a foreign land, your life hanging in the balance. The truth was, he was shit scared. The irony of it; it was only an hour ago that he'd come clean, purged his soul, but it could all be in vain. The cathartic confession reduced to a sad epitaph. This was real. There were men out there who wanted to kill him, kill the three of them.

Carla watched him. She could tell he'd gone for another trip around his psyche. She recognized that tangential-thinking look.

"Keep your wits about you man." She dragged him back to reality.

"Sorry, I was miles away."

"I wish we bloody were", she replied.

Steyn motioned to them to stop talking. There was another car approaching. It parked near the school buildings. He saw Smit, in his crumpled uniform, get out of the passenger seat. They could hear the doors slamming.

"The cavalry have arrived." Steyn watched them carefully.

"Come on, what are we waiting for?" Tom started to stand up,

"Sit down! Radebe or Malherbe could be holed up near them. Don't move until I fucking tell you." It was like looking after a toddler, Steyn sighed. Carla gave Tom a look that only a woman can.

***

Smit had seen the blood on the road, the trail of it splattered in the direction of the house. They could see the cloud of flies buzzing by the entrance.

"You check it out Strydom, I'll stand guard and keep an eye on the car." Smit's heart was pumping. If Tom and Carla's bodies were in there, he'd be in the clear. He needn't have worried. He had less than a minute left to live.

***

Malherbe turned the corner and slammed on the brakes. The police car was parked up and the fat cop was standing by it, smoking a cigarette, his last, but he didn't know it. The other cop was nowhere to be seen, probably doing a door to door. A pointless exercise, every house seemed to be shuttered and locked. The place had the feel of a rural college campus closed for the summer break. Malherbe pulled down his baseball cap and picked up the gun. It had been a while since he'd done a drive-thru murder, a while since he'd felt the tingle of anticipation.

***

Strydom stepped into the room. It was dark inside. The sun had dropped beneath the mountains and it took a second or two for his eyes to adjust to the gloom. He saw a tangle of arms and legs. Jesus Christ, there were bodies in there, piled up like rag dolls. The thud of a bullet made him jump. Something heavy hit the floor. He dived for cover, using all his strength to roll a body on top of him. Shit, it was Van

285

Buren, half his face blown off. The floor was wet and sticky, stained with blood. He lay still, waiting for the sound of footsteps but it was the noise of a car driving away that filled his ears.

***

All three of them heard the single shot. Tom and Carla ducked; Steyn watched a white car tear up the road. It looked like a Toyota bakkie. There was no sign of movement. The police car hadn't moved, he could just make out the open door.

"Stay here, I'm going to take a closer look. Keep an eye on me, if I wave my hands come as quick as possible." Steyn stood up behind a tree and stretched his legs.

"What if you don't come back?" Carla asked the question that had crossed Tom's mind too.

"Oh, I plan on coming back, been doing this same old shit for decades and I'm still here aren't I?"

He disappeared at pace, weaving across the field, before they could reply, reaching the safety of the alley in a matter of seconds. The road was silent, what little breeze there was had died down. Steyn edged closer to the edge of the wall, careful not to disturb any of the loose stones underfoot. He poked one eye around the corner; Smit was laying in the dust, staring at him with blank eyes, a bullet hole in the middle of his forehead, a permanent expression of shock on his face. There was no point checking his pulse. The truth died with him. A posthumous medal would be on its way. The press would have a field day. Such are the ebbs and flow of life: A reputation in tatters if he lived yet a hero when his body hit the cold, hard slab in the mortuary. All this raced through

Steyn's mind when he lent on the wall but his thoughts turned to Strydom, where the hell was he? There had only been one shot and Smit was the unfortunate recipient. Time wasn't on their side, Malherbe and Radebe, if it was indeed them in the cars, would be back to find Tom and Carla.

He stepped into the road, gun in hand and walked towards the open door of the house. A man emerged, stumbling, his clothes spattered in blood.

"Strydom have you got the car keys, we need to get out of here fast."

He fumbled in his pockets and threw them to him.

"Get in the car. I'll get Tom and Carla."

Steyn ran through the alley, waved his arms and shouted, "Quick, run!" He could hear a car, but it was a distance off.

Strydom was sat in the passenger seat, in a semi-trance. Carla and Tom bundled in the back and slammed the doors and they were off. Steyn put his foot to the floor and checked the rear-view mirror.

Chapter 63

The two cars nearly collided. Radebe swerved and crunched into a small wooden post. The radiator hissed, smoke billowing up above the buildings. He reached for the machine gun, jumped out and ran towards the Toyota bakkie, parked up on a bank at the other side of the road. Malherbe wound the window down and blew out a smoke ring.

"Ah baas, wondered where you'd got to."

Radebe had a good mind to blow the blond fuckers brains out. The bloody traitor deserved nothing less but he knew he needed him. There could be more cops and robbers on the way and he couldn't deal with it all on his own. Sooner or later his luck would run out. Anyway, the priority was Carla and that guy with her. He had to silence them.

He got in the car, chucking Malherbe's bag of tricks on the back seat.

"You seen Steyn or any of his cronies?"

"Only that local guy, the fat bastard but you don't have to worry about him no more."

"What about Carla?"

"She's here somewhere baas, can't be far away. This place is a dead end, we'll flush her out. Where's the body builder?"

"Back at the plane, waiting to fly us out of this shit hole. Drive past the buildings and keep your eyes peeled."

Radebe wound his window down and spat on the road. They drove a couple of hundred metres in silence, both scanning the houses and fields beyond them.

"You know anything about some Joburg guys? Just killed three of them back there." Radebe couldn't resist goading the dull bastard.

"Joburg guys, round here? No baas, all I know about is that wimp Johnson and the lovely Carla."

Malherbe kept a straight face and his eyes upon the road. He checked his back pocket with the free hand, felt the reassuring grip of the knife.

"Thing is Malherbe, I went through their pockets."

"And?"

"I found a phone; Gleason's number was on it."

"No way." He tightened his grip on the knife.

"How the fuck does Gleason know about Carla and the stick, answer me that?"

"Must be Johnson baas, explains why he legged it."

Radebe was about to reply when they heard the roar of an engine and saw a dust cloud up ahead. The conversation would have to wait

"Hit the gas brother, we've got them."

They exchanged a pair of false smiles, time for business.

Chapter 64

"We've got company Steyn." Tom peered out of the back window, the bakkie was drawing closer.

"Keep your head down unless you want to get it blown off."

Steyn screeched round the first bend of Die Slang, tyres squealing in protest. They could smell burning rubber in the back. They huddled down together, like two kids sharing a secret. The car was being thrown all over the road and they kept bumping heads. They heard the bullets hitting the rocks around them. The back windscreen shattered, showering them in fragments of glass. Tom closed his eyes and prayed for the second time that day. It was becoming a habit. Strydom lent out of the window and took a pot shot at the wheels of the pursuers. It was a lottery; the car was jumping around so much that it was impossible to keep a steady hand. Any success would be down to luck rather than skill. There was a brief window of opportunity when they snaked around each switch back bend. The cars were parallel for a split second and Strydom had the advantage of being elevated above the bakkie. He could only fire a couple of bullets but they missed and petered out in the mountain fynbos. On the straights the endless rattle of the machine gun peppered them. The wing mirror smashed and a fragment of glass cut Strydom's cheek, just missing his eye.

"Fucking hell Steyn, drive faster, they're closing on us."

Steyn accelerated but he was already driving on the edge of madness. This wasn't the N1 with the tar stretching out before them like some endless metre stick. Logic dictated they had no chance; a paltry hand gun against the rapid, staccato burst of a machine gun, there could only be one winner. If they blew out one of the tyres they would be over the edge, plunging down the rocky slope. The only thing in their favour was the rugged, undulating road and the fact that both vehicles were bouncing round like empty egg boxes in a hurricane. The advanced driving course that Steyn had been forced to attend, against his will, suddenly seemed to have been worthwhile. He slowed, almost imperceptibly before the bends and accelerated through them, picking the racing line. There was no time to avoid pot holes, you had to hold the wheel tight and hope for the best.

They reached the top, somehow still alive, and the road stretched out before them in a series of peaks and troughs. The bakkie briefly disappeared from sight only to reappear seconds later, like a fucking hangover that wouldn't go away. All the aloes, the fynbos, and the dry soil in between became one: A wild Jackson Pollack painting in shades of green and bunt umber.

"They're gaining on us Captain."

Strydom could see the face of an insane guy, blond hair ruffled by the breeze, sat in the Toyota. He was laughing. Steyn's heart sank. The bakkie was more powerful on the more open stretches. There was nowhere left to run. He pressed the accelerator flat to the floorboards, trying to squeeze out the last drops of power the engine possessed. Strydom lent out of the window and tried to steady his hand to take aim at the tyre. There were only a couple of bullets left. As he tightened his trigger finger, they hit a pot- hole, his arms were thrown up as he let loose. The Toyota's windscreen shattered. The bullet ripped through Radebe's throat, a hot gush of blood doused his white tailored shirt and the memory stick was ripped from his neck. Malherbe tried to push the body off him and hold onto the wheel at the same time but the bakkie took on a life of its own. It lurched to the right and smashed into a boulder, hidden beneath the small roadside trees. The back end of the car flew up like a huge wave and seemed to hang in the air forever before it came clattering back to earth. Smoke billowed from the mangled engine and mingled with the dust cloud that enveloped it.

The noise of the impact was deafening. Tom raised his wary eyes above the rear seats and surveyed the scene. As the dust cloud slowly dissipated, the wreckage came into focus. Someone was screaming from inside. He exchanged a frightened glance with Carla. Both of them were speechless.

Steyn pulled over, a hundred metres down the road and laid his head on the steering wheel, exhausted. Strydom wiped the blood from his cheek, he was shaking.

"Stay in the car." Steyn could see by the look on their faces that they had no intention of getting out.

He opened the door and motioned to Strydom. They walked towards the wreckage, guns in hand.

"Easy does it, these things have a habit of having a sting in the tail."

It was all new to Strydom but he took in what the Captain said. Steyn dropped to the floor and crawled the last few yards to the bakkie. The scream was intermittent now and weaker but he was taking no chances. At the last second, he sprang up and pointed his gun through what was left of the window. Radebe was a pulp, thrown half through the windscreen, neck twisted so he could see his own arse. It was

Malherbe who'd been wailing. His leg was smashed up bad, pinned to the rock by the look of it. He'd lost a lot of blood. Steyn checked his hands, no weapons, the machine gun had been thrown out of the window on impact and his other stuff was out of reach on what was left of the back seat. Malherbe turned his head and spoke quietly.

"Captain Steyn, we meet again."

"Same old blood and carnage; guys like you never learn Malherbe."

"Get me out man." His face was ashen and there was a trickle of blood at the corner of his mouth.

Steyn looked at his leg, only a specialist crew would be able to cut him out of the mess but by then it might be too late.

"No can do Malherbe, you're gonna have to wait for the medics to arrive."

Steyn placed the gun on Malherbe's temple.

"But my battery's died and I don't feel like ringing them anyway."

His finger tensed. Malherbe could see the rivulets of sweat on his face.

"Go ahead Steyn, if you've got enough balls."

"Easy Captain, don't do something you'll regret." Strydom came closer and put his hand on Steyn's shoulder.

"Taking orders from a teenager? There's me thinking you were the big man but you're just another spineless bastard."

"Don't push me. The world would be a better place without you."

"Captain; step back."

"Going to listen to the kid are you, you prick, go on, do it."

Malherbe tried to smile but it hurt too much. Steyn stepped back and gave the gun to Strydom. He was a better man than that. He stood on the right side of the line between good and evil. He was many things, flawed in many ways, but not an executioner.

"Ah, thought so, you're a weak fucker Steyn, like all the rest of you do-gooders."

Steyn turned and walked away. He didn't look back.

"Give me a cigarette man."

"The smokes provided where you're going." Steyn neared the car; saw Tom and Carla peering over the back seats like scared kids watching a horror film.

***

They drove slowly down the bumpy road. The light was fading fast. The petrol gauge was low and all they bloody needed was to run out of fuel in the middle of the wilderness. At the top of the pass the phones started buzzing. Strydom rang for back up and a fire crew set off from Calitzdorp; two police cars and an ambulance leading it out, sirens blazing even though the roads were empty.

It was only as they sunk down the valley towards Prince Albert that they began to talk.

"What happened to Van Buren?"

Strydom glanced in the back before replying, Tom and Carla were asleep.

"Jesus Captain, he was a mess, they blew half his face off. There were four bodies in there. One of them was kicked to a pulp. I had to hide under them when I heard Smit being shot. I don't think I can live with the memory."

"You have to son, it comes with the job, you'll learn to put it aside, lock it away. You're lucky you don't work in Joburg or the Cape Flats. It's commonplace there. Thank your lucky stars that you're in Prince Albert, things will get back to normal soon enough round here." Christ, he sounded like old father time.

Strydom knew he was talking sense but it didn't make it any easier to swallow. He shuddered. He needed to shower, burn his clothes and see his folks. He didn't want to spend the night on his own, reliving the horrors of the day.

"What about you Captain, will you be staying longer in Prince Albert?"

"No, my work is done here, I'll make sure Tom and Carla are tucked up safe and sound and I'll be back on the road again, tomorrow or the day after. I'll have to tie up a few loose ends first but it won't take long."

"Are you married Captain?"

It was an unexpected question and he hesitated before replying.

"Yes I am." He neglected to add in name only. He remembered Christel's text, the spectre of the marriage counsellor was looming. He'd try to slip back into his lame existence but the writing was on the wall.

"I'm getting married at the end of March, for a moment back there I didn't think I'd make it to the altar."

Steyn smiled. The kid was young, had the whole of his life ahead of him. It wasn't the time to discuss the pitfalls of matrimonial union.

He watched him nod off as they came out of the hills and approached the bright lights of Prince Albert. Sat behind the wheel, he mulled over the past few days. Things had to change. It wasn't just the relationship with Christel that was on the rocks, his love affair with the job had hit an all- time low. Doubtless there would be an inquisition. Sikosi would be keen to pack him off to a desk job, pushing files around a table in some back room without air conditioning. But, by Christ, he wouldn't give him the pleasure, enough was enough. Game over. He'd throw the badge on Sikosi's desk, make the fucker jump, and walk out a free man. Life as a PI, something he had scoffed at all these years, suddenly had a fresh allure. As they entered the main street he was overcome by a tiredness that seven nights sleep couldn't cure, it was a malaise of the mind, a suffocating burden that had finally worn him down. He looked at Tom and Carla in the back, all snuggled up, thought of Radebe dead, Malherbe pinned to a rock. It wasn't a bad way to bow out. And he wouldn't drag Smit's name through the mud, his wife was probably unaware of his crimes and he had no wish to associate her with her husband's guilt. Some things are best left unsaid.

Chapter 65

Gleason sat on the balcony of his Joburg apartment, overlooking the manicured lawns of the golf course. Two guys were teeing off on the eighteenth. The wide arc of the swing, the sound of club on impact, usually gave him a thrill; but not today. The fact that they were dressed like New York pimps ordinarily made him laugh but he was in a sombre mood. The habitual Cuban cigar was hanging from the corner of his mouth, but he was too pissed off to light it. He'd sent his wife off shopping with the gold card. She'd come back with another pair of designer shoes that she wouldn't wear and a shirt for him that wouldn't fit but at least she was gone. The bodyguards were hidden from view, a necessary, if expensive evil. He was on his own and fucking angry.

Trusting that slippery bastard Radebe had been a big mistake. He'd recognized the raw ambition in his face. It was something to be wary of but he'd ignored it. The money had gotten the better of him. The prospect of yet more cash flowing in had clouded his judgement. He'd regretted the deal as soon as *Denzel* bloody *Washington* had left the room. He already had enough cash to buy his own yacht but it was never enough. To stay at the top you had to move with the times, get richer faster. It was a runaway train and now it had derailed. Malherbe had crawled out of the woodwork. He was not to be trusted either but at least he had fulfilled a purpose: the obligatory man on the inside. He could choose his moment, dispose of Radebe, and Malherbe to boot, rake in the cash himself. But no, it had gone tits up. Some nobody in Prince Albert had done the dirty on Radebe, stolen some memory stick, full of incriminating information no doubt. To top it all, two bloody tourists get hold of the stick and escape from Malherbe and his cronies. If it was a film script it would be rejected with the red stamp marked unfeasible. So what does sensible Mr Gleason do? Sends down a trusty lieutenant to sort the bloody mess out, kill Radebe and Malherbe, kill the bloody tourists, kill anybody who had anything to do with the stupid, side line project. He wanted out. He wanted closure.

Gleason flexed his fat fingers and reached for the phone again. He dialled Cloete but it went straight to fucking answer phone for the bloody twentieth time. He closed his eyes and lent his head back, what the hell was going on? At 12.23 his patience snapped. He hadn't used Viljoen since the business with the diamonds but he gave him a call. The instructions were brief but he had faith in him. He was a loose cannon but, by God, he got results; by mid- afternoon the private plane was on its way to George.

Gleason poured himself a klippies and coke and dropped in four ice cubes. It was a bit early to start drinking but he gulped it in one and reached for the bottle.

Chapter 66

The Beginning

Tom was sat on the stoep, milky coffee in hand, watching the town go to work. It was 8 am. Carla was still fast asleep. The masses were immersed in excitable chatter, laughing and joking. It was a brand-new day. The sky had grown overnight; the deep blue blanket stretching tight above. He felt at peace with himself. Pen and paper to hand, he did what he had always done, wrote a poem. He remembered Brian Eno's definition of art as 'everything you don't have to do'; in other words, anything that didn't involve the mundane, the day to day slog of clocking in on grey days, earning the bucks to feed from hand to mouth. Creativity was beyond that, a wild sea where you could sail your boat to any waters. For Tom, writing was something he had to do. It didn't matter if it was shite, it was his shite. He wasn't after accolades, it was about self-expression, understanding himself and making sense of the world he lived in; a private confession box.

In a perverse way, the last few days had been oddly liberating. He'd seen evil, seen weakness, seen life as that wobbly tight rope walk across the canyon and he'd got to the other side. All the baggage, the self-obsessed garbage he'd carried around with him, had been tossed aside. He felt light. He felt free. It was onwards and upwards now, no looking back. The mistakes he had made in the past, the life sentence he had imposed on himself, were buried. He had Carla to thank for that, she'd managed to winkle him out of his shell. He remembered his old school motto- 'Ni dychwel ddoe'- yesterday never returns. He should have taken that message to heart all those years back and ever bloody since.

Tom thought about his mum, God rest her fractured soul. Scattering her ashes on that lonely hilltop overlooking the sea had had a profound effect on him. A door had closed that day but he realized now that there were new ones to open. He closed his eyes. It was then that the idea for a poem came to him.

When the Tide Comes In

When the tide goes out
we are stranded in the rock pools
with the driftwood
and the upturned crab,
waving at the seagulls.

When the tide comes in
We will be washed,
smooth as pebbles
strewn on the beach.
Drenched by the twisted fingers
of the ocean spray.

But it is only when we climb
Our own mountains,
Far from the ocean waves,
That we see how
The valleys interlock
And the roads converge.

As he finished, he smiled. It would be the last of his dashboard confessionals, time to turn outwards, to be more observational, tap into the vein of humour than ran through him. He closed the book and crept back inside. There was more to life than getting drunk and hiding from yourself.

Carla was still away with the fairies. His mobile phone was fully charged. He sent a message to Jeff, told him he'd been somewhere remote where there was no reception. The reply from his son was instantaneous- a row of smiling emoji's and a throbbing heart. Christ, the kids of today, can't even string a sentence together. He laughed. If only he had known the pain the kid had gone through.

Tom looked at himself in the bathroom mirror. He was as thin as a betting shop pencil, tanned but gaunt. He had some fattening up to do and the hunger pangs had kicked in. He cooked up some bacon and eggs and put the toast in. Carla was propped up in bed when he carried in her breakfast on a tray, complete with a fresh orange juice. He had a tea towel folded on his arm and went all silver service.

"Breakfast is served ma'am."

"Wow, but where's the Sunday papers?"

"Sorry to inform you ma'am, but I'm afraid it's Tuesday." Carla laughed. The plates were empty in no time. He took them to the kitchen and returned.

"What shall we do today Tom?" She was still bleary eyed and sipping the remnants of the orange juice.

He dropped his shorts and jumped back into bed.

"All part of the service ma'am."

They had a leisurely shower together and were sat on the stoep, enjoying coffee and a rusk when Steyn arrived, he was frowning.

"What's up Captain, you don't look too happy?" said Tom.

"Sorry to spoil your party folks. It's my boss, he seems to be blaming me for the deaths of Van Buren and Smit, accused me of cavalier policing. Apparently I failed to exercise due care and diligence." He sounded bitter.

"But that's bollocks, I'll speak to him." Tom was gobsmacked.

"I'm afraid you will, he's on his way from Stellenbosch to investigate the matter further and he's requested that you stay in Prince Albert."

"It's outrageous. You were just doing your job, without you Malherbe would have found us." Carla paled, it would be a long time before she could erase that blond bastards face from her mind.

"I agree but I would do, wouldn't I? It's a long story and I don't really want to go into it. There's politics involved."

"Politics?"

"I won't bore you with the details, suffice to say, my face doesn't fit. I was going to walk away from the job but now I've got to fight my way out."

"We'll back you to the hilt Steyn. We won't let you take the rap for this, its complete shite." Carla nodded in agreement.

"Thanks, but Sikosi has a habit of only listening to what he wants to hear."

"What happened to Malherbe?" Carla wished he was dead. Steyn sat next to them and rubbed the three-day stubble on his chin.

"The bastard survived. He was barely alive when they cut him out but he's pulled through. They had to amputate his leg below the knee. He's under armed guard at the hospital, not that he's likely to hop to freedom any time soon."

Tom stifled a laugh; he could see the look of fear in Carla's eyes.

"What, in Prince Albert?" She didn't want to be anywhere near that man.

"Rest easy, he's in George."

"So, what now?" said Tom.

"We're confined to barracks until the judge and jury arrive." Steyn had that hang dog look.

"Surely it can't be as bad as that, the world's gone barking mad."

"Time will tell but it doesn't look good."

"What about your wife, won't she be expecting you back?" Carla had noticed the ring on his finger.

"Yeh, she's arranged for us to go to a meeting tonight but I'm not going to be able to make it now. I'll leave you guys in peace, here's my cell number, give me yours, don't go far."

He wanted to give them some time on their own. It was pointless dragging them down with him. They'd suffered enough. He could see they were loved up, the lucky bastards. He needed time on his own to get his ducks in a row, two could play the game, Sikosi wouldn't have an easy ride. If he was to leave the police force it would be on his own terms with his head held high. As he left, he remembered something.

"Oh, I need to get in the coffee shop. The bent cop sign could be useful. I intended to leave Smit to rest in peace but needs must." A thin smile brushed his lips.

"No problem, I've got to pick up some clothes there later."

In the shower, they'd decided to move in together for a couple of weeks. Neither of them wanted to be on their own. Steyn waved and they watched him shut the gate and turn towards the mountain, he cut rather a sad figure as he disappeared behind the cypress trees.

"Shit, poor bugger, flogged for doing a brilliant job, makes no fucking sense at all. He's a decent man Carla. We've got to help him."

"Yeh, but we're two foreigners and there are things that happen in this country that we don't understand."

Later, they went for a walk down the main road. It was busy; the cafés were full of tourists enjoying the heat and the cloudless skies. They passed the cinema; the Hitchcock season was still in full swing. Tonight, it was *Rear Window*, with Jimmy Stewart and Grace Kelly. They looked at each other and smiled. Carla went to buy the tickets. Tom stood outside basking in the afternoon sun. The ugly creases of his life seemed to have been ironed out and he felt the warm tinge of happiness flood through him. Carla returned and they embraced. They sauntered down the main road arm in arm, with, for that fleeting moment, not a care in the world.

At the other end of town a car was fast approaching. As he saw the first buildings come into focus Viljoen slowed down and slid his revolver into the inside pocket of his jacket. He parked up in a side street, lit a cigarette and rang Gleason. There was no answer. He smiled to himself, time was of no consequence, he got paid by results and he was already rich for a reason.

Printed in Poland
by Amazon Fulfillment
Poland Sp. z o.o., Wrocław

49749157R00186